The Grist Mill Bone
A Novel

B.B. Shamp

Copyright © 2018 B.B. Shamp

ISBN: 978-1-64438-428-2

All rights reserved. No part of this publication may be reproduced, stored in a retrieval system, or transmitted in any form or by any means, electronic, mechanical, recording or otherwise, without the prior written permission of the author.

Published by Tidewater Publishing in cooperation with BookLocker.com, Inc., St. Petersburg, Florida.
The Sotweed Legacy was previously published by The Delmarva Review online in Chesapeake Voices.

Printed on acid-free paper.

The characters and events in this book are fictitious. Any similarity to real persons, living or dead, is coincidental and not intended by the author.

BookLocker.com, Inc.
2018

First Edition

Acknowledgements

I am grateful to my editors and literary muses: B.K. Burroughs and Barbara Stephanic. Thanks to Suzi Peel for her professional review of *Third Haven,* the prequel to *The Grist Mill Bone.* I am indebted to the critical eyes of Rabbit's Gnaw- Gerald Sweeney (founder), Patrick Cavanagh, JD Cooper, and Bruce Hutchison. Clayton Scruggs- thanks for your inspiration, your truck, and your patience. To Rena Jackson- your energy and advice are boundless!

To my mother, Evelyn, you were an inspiration and will always be with me. To Katie- my love and admiration for your winsome spirit. The Abiding Dude is vegan now.

"When it is said, as in the Testament, 'If a man smite thee on the right cheek, turn to him the other also,' it is assassinating the dignity of forbearance, and sinking man into a spaniel."
— **Thomas Paine, The Age of Reason**

"Homelessness is a nationality now."
—**Margaret Atwood, Cat's Eye**

Foreword

Readers are lackadaisical about forewords and so for some this will go by the wayside. I continue to have faith in those who invest in a book rather than sitting for hours scanning social media on their phones. There's a reason to write a foreword for a novel: historical hubris. I grew up listening to my father's tales of Chesapeake Bay life and so for me it holds special significance, the genesis of our Nation and a blending of cultures. If you like history, read on!

In 2012 in Lewes, Delaware north of the Rehoboth Bay, 11 graves were found at the site of Avery's Rest, a settlement dating from the mid to late 1600s. An English sea captain, John Avery, owned a tobacco plantation of 800 acres that was discovered 30 years ago littered with "oyster shells, tobacco pipes and pieces of Colonial pottery in a plowed field." (Washington Post, "Slaves' remains offer details of 17th – century life in Del.," Michael E. Ruane, Wednesday, December 6, 2017). The subsequent discovery of the graves led to a partnership of the Smithsonian and the Archeological Society of Delaware that together investigated the graves' contents. Complete skeletons, they gave up their DNA revealing age if not identity. In a separate burial area, "the biological evidence also hints that two men and a child of African descent, … likely were not born in Africa but instead somewhere in the Mid-Atlantic." (Delaware News Journal, "Burial site may transform history," Maddy Lauria, Dec. 12, 2017). The remains give strong evidence of a hard life clearing land for tobacco and dying young in slavery. The site now joins the rich Chesapeake Bay history of St. Mary's in Maryland and Jamestown in Virginia, two of the earliest English settlements on the North American continent. The Delaware News Journal quotes Angela Winand, head of the Delaware Historical Society's Mitchell Center for African American Heritage, saying, "The stories of their sacrifices in life and death are truly written in bone for us to interpret, understand and honor."

The following pages also reference the legend of the Cannon gang, notorious for its basis in truth. Once the Federal Government outlawed the importation of slaves in 1808, the slave dependent economy took a downturn. Patty Cannon of Reliance, Maryland and other family members formed a kidnapping ring for the express purpose of entrapping free black youth and selling them south to Mississippi and Alabama. If they were found to be feeble and unsuitable for selling, she had no qualms about burning them in the fireplace or killing them and burying their remains on her farm. After years of planned kidnappings and murder, she and her gang finally came to their reckoning and arrest. She died awaiting trial in 1829 while in jail in Georgetown, Delaware.

The Delmarva Peninsula (the easternmost sections of Delaware, Maryland, and Virginia) is an arm of land bounded by the Atlantic Ocean to the east and the Chesapeake Bay to the west. It developed separately from the mainland economically, socially and linguistically. Tobacco farming gave way to oysters, then to canneries and packinghouses and eventually, chicken processing. African American labor was essential to the success of these industries except when there was an economic crisis and the white ruling class took them back. Today, land is the most valuable commodity on the shore due to its proximity to Atlantic beaches and the vast numbers of retirees looking to vacate the nearby big cities of the East Coast. It hasn't always been so idyllic.

From the 1880s to the 1930s, seven young black men were lynched or brutally beaten on the Eastern Shore. One of the most horrific stories was that of Matthew Williams. It is recounted in *The Grist Mill Bone*. Some victims go unnamed and unrecognized to this day. However, they are included in The Equal Justice Initiative's work in Montgomery Alabama to memorialize the more than 4,000 black and white victims of lynching nationwide. Although debated, the U.S. Congress never passed an anti-lynch law.

Locally in 1967, a devastating decision by a city fire chief laid waste to two city blocks of the black business community in Cambridge, Maryland, burning them to the ground while the fire department stood by watching. It began with the torching of the Pine Street Elementary School that was built in 1918 for the local African American community. The vibrancy of the black business enclave of Cambridge, Maryland that rivaled Harlem has never returned to its former glory. It remains economically depressed to this day but is struggling to heal those old wounds. (Levy, Peter B., The Great Uprising, New York: Cambridge University Press, 2018)

That's exactly what "Reflections on Pine," a civil rights remembrance movement currently honors on the lower shore in Maryland. Cambridge's first black female mayor is now in her third term. Victoria L. Jackson, with the help of local activists, Dion Banks and Kisha Petticolas are working to create a dialogue about this time of racial strife 50 years later.

    The mill at Old Mill Bridge Road was a cooperative endeavor on the northeast side of Dirickson Creek during the early part of 19th Century. It was operated by the Derrickson and Johnson families. It no longer exists. This tract is the last undeveloped land on the Dirickson Creek tributary also known in early records as Indian River Creek or Indian River Branch. It spills into the Assawoman (Assawamen- historic spelling) Bay. As the original creek name indicates, it is the home of the Nanticoke Indians (Tag Archives, Dirickson Creek- tributary of Little Assawoman Bay, Feb. 14, 2016, Chris Slavens, peninsularoots.com) and undoubtedly contains artifacts of that time. Its forest also is home to multiple bald eagles. At the time of this publication, it has been surveyed for development.

—B. B. Shamp

1 CLAIRE

I wondered who would die first. The will and testament of a retired rear admiral signed in his shaky hand had made room for a new client, a woman of no particular renown, ready to join her Milky Way. This requires patience. Nothing about my job quickens my pulse, or leaves me intrigued. I might as well be on some isolated archeological dig of a dark, ancient world, my knees bent and back hunched. I sift sand, brush off a treasure and realize it's petrified camel bone—worthless, except for the weight of what the camel bore. That's where my work begins: the search of someone's past to guarantee a future.

In real time, I'm a catchpenny attorney trying to engrave in stone the wishes of the dying. Or so I thought until I met Velma Owens just before noon on a crystal white summer day. I was prepared. Her priest told me she was a reader, an amateur photographer, and a former racist. That word 'former' gave me pause, but in the end, I took the job.

Nothing about my decision was cavalier. In a previous life, I worked on Capitol Hill for a lobbyist. There, clients eat you for breakfast, regurgitate you at lunch and serve your bones to their dogs for dinner. As a young attorney starting out, I discovered everyone had a price and mine was never the money. That's why I didn't fit in their world order; D.C. is all about money and who can prove their personal integrity. I had to get out before I lost mine.

A leisurely job in an adopted beach town in slower, lower Delaware answered my call on a whim and a promise. Four years into this life, I have no regrets. Don't get me wrong, there's a ditch to dig wherever you land. Here on the shore, we have an opioid epidemic, summer gridlock, and beach drunks, but it's mostly safe. I've found the year round residents are honest and true but you can't dig deeply without hitting water.

I pulled into guest parking at Fairhaven Assisted Living, flipped up the car visors and took a look around. French blue pansies bordered spring grass, freshly mown. A whiff of rankness caught me unawares and I remembered that smells grow sharper when you're pregnant. With the windows open I breathed, wasting time, enjoying the shore breeze as the wind tickled my hair. It blows like that here, great gusts of wind that carry sand and the sound of distant waves. Promises from unknown shores. I've always thought they were the kind of promises that brought peace and belonging.

A shout broke my musings.

"You better hurry. The bugs!"

Searching under the portico, my eyes adjusted to the

shadows and I saw a woman –really, she was a teenager clothed in medical whites—stopping for me on her way into the nursing home. She nodded in encouragement, her face an annoyed question mark, like… doesn't this lady get it? Her ponytail, full of product, spun in the quickening wind like a propeller. Beyond her shoulder, I could see the familiar tight cloud of insects unfurling from a band of trees. Their chatter grew louder the closer they came. A host of green winged behemoths landed on my windshield like little cargo helicopters, their bulbous eyes staring at me.

Impatient, the girl was trying to be helpful. "I can wait a second," she shouted.

I put the windows up, gathered my bag and bolted from the car, my feet crunching across the shells of molted cicada nymphs. The adults engaged in an opera, singing the chorus, "Phar-aoh, oh, phar-aoh,"

"Yep. I'm right after you," I answered. The insects rose in unison from the car's hood and formed a backup battalion.

She stopped a few feet away from the entrance when a dark whirlwind surrounded her like some Egyptian plague. Arms flailing the air, she blew out in tiny shoo-shoos.

Yesterday, at home, my son Sam had the same reaction until I explained we were in a 17-year eruption. Ever the young researcher, he flew to his computer. In an incredulous childlike voice I don't often hear anymore, he exclaimed it was the East Coast Brood II and they would smother the mid Atlantic wherever there were trees. April, and this is only the beginning of the pestilence to come on the Delmarva Peninsula.

Since last October, we've suffered enough named nor'easters to fill a seaman's pocket diary. The only thing that can put us out of our misery is another asteroid strike like the one that created this sinking spit of land on the Atlantic.

Some days I yearn to move back across the Chesapeake Bay Bridge to D.C., to something more familiar, but then I come to my senses. Kind of like what other transplants on the peninsula do when faced with the western tidal wave of summer tourists. 100 days of their pompous demands, then they disappear, and we're in God's country until the fall storms begin.

The aide worker danced and ducked this way and that, afraid of these dive-bombing aliens. I wasn't shocked at the girl's response. Parroting Sam's research in my head, I reminded myself that cicadas are worse at summer sunset, farther inland, and in deciduous forests or treed suburban areas. It wasn't summer or sunset. We were three miles from the coast and a pine forest was behind the nursing home. This was the beach's first recorded inundation and nothing was following the rules.

"You run ahead, I'll catch up," I yelled over the hum of insects, thinking she probably had to clock in for her eight bucks an hour.

Fairhaven was one of those four story monstrosities with an entrance tower, multiple peaked roofs and blank windows. It sat on the entire corner of the intersection like a giant sphinx in a desert sea. Their advertising claimed it was built on "high ground," but we're maybe five feet above sea level. Liars. It's all low ground in Sussex. Sinking really. New

The Grist Mill Bone

Orleans gets all the publicity because of the hurricanes, but we're going to be treading water too. Booker, my husband and a native, thinks I don't notice, but I do. These are antediluvian days. We're just waiting to become another campground of flood refugees.

Flickers of bugs hit my back and I hunched over as if that would help. Then I realized it was raindrops—fat ones splattering my face and arms with the weight of latex paint. I had thought cicadas and rain didn't mix. I ran under the portico and the girl looked back at me, her key card hovering over the scanner at the front door.

"You can't get in without a fob," she shouted over their din. "They'll make you wait until they check the visitors' log. You have an appointment?"

Her nametag was pinned neatly above her breast pocket. Tyneice Armstrong - Aide. "Yes, with Velma Owens. I'm her attorney. Claire Solomon."

Her eyes widened and I could only imagine why. It's amazing how much money this generation of elderly widows have accrued. Husbands pass on leaving their wives another lifetime ahead. The poorer ones scrimp and save, barely living, afraid that there won't be enough for old age. A diet of cat food is not appealing. But this lady, Velma Owens, had an unusual amount invested. More than she could have saved digging for loose change in the couch. Assisted living—expensive, and it seemed she had no family. Not even a distant relative.

Tyneice held the door and I approached a busy receptionist who was expecting me, "Ms. Solomon? Sign in here. Mrs. Owens is in room 207B. Take the elevator over there." She pointed. Clean, carpeted, antiseptic smelling. A railing ran down the wall to balance those who tottered. Bright lighting, tones of beige and blue everywhere; beach themed for all the old folks who never wore a bathing suit and never caught a glimpse of the waves.

At the polished metal door, I paused, my hand hovering over the button that read "2." It's been five years since the firebombing at my firm in D.C. and for a while I couldn't ride an elevator without choking up. Fortunately, there aren't a lot of high rises on the beach. I'm over that now but still have vestiges PTSD. Flashbacks, crippling anxiety, night sweats. Mostly, it comes on when I can't find Sam.

Once recently, in a weak moment after I discovered him exactly where I knew he'd be, ensconced before his computer, I yelled at him, "Why didn't you answer me?" I had panicked thinking he was too addicted to whatever role play game had captured his interest; that he was giving away his real identity, our personal life, our vacations, and especially our family.

"Mom, get a grip," he said, removing his headset. His blue eyes squinted and his cheeks hardened. I apologized of course. I still blame myself for the bombing back in those days. I was too close to the risk. Sleeping with it in fact. Even now, when I see fire I wonder if my hands shake because I want to run away in fear or because I'm searching for clues in the flames. Sam has his idiosyncrasies too. Mostly trust issues, but what teenager doesn't?

The elevator door opened on a small lobby before an

empty dining room that smelled like old soup. Nearby, a small table held an unfinished puzzle. I recognized it as Monet's "Japanese Footbridge" and immediately picked up three small pieces from the carpet. Nothing more annoying than not being able to complete the picture. Mrs. Owen's room was to the left, her door slightly open and the TV was blaring. Pulling my laptop from my briefcase, I knocked gently, then louder.

***

The Sotweed Legacy

Spitting snow stung Father Ingle's ample cheeks as he fumbled for his key to the church. He raised his eyes to the stained glass window of St. Aloysius and thought, not for the first time, that its inscription, 'Patron Saint of Youth' taunted him. His hip ached from the cold. "Give me strength to endure this night," he muttered as he laid his thick hand on the doorknob. He leaned his weight against the wood, whitened from so many years of salt spray and sun. The sacristy door gave way to a green and white tiled floor. Yellow light glowed from the church proper.

In a guarded voice, he called, "Hello? Mrs. Owens?" Cautious, even after his seven years on the peninsula, the priest remained suspicious of these riverside residents. Five years since the riots of '68, he remained reserved around them. He brushed the snow from his overcoat and raised his head to the sound of a radio playing. Doris Day's sweet voice caught him, *"Whatever Will Be, Will Be."* He nodded and smiled. A slight hint of bleach wafted over him and he knew Mrs. Owens was busy at work. With the exception of the gleaming floors, there was no other sign of the woman who single handedly ran the Ladies Altar Society.

The white plaster walls reflected the light from his desk lamp. He scanned the sacristy, evaluating its tidiness with the eye of a man who had fussed over details all his life. The vestment drawers were polished, the wardrobe doors locked and his chair tucked in place. She had come despite gale force winds that rose midday off the Chesapeake, whirling east up the Choptank River. He entered, his galoshes scuffing across the floor leaving snowy slobber behind him. He balanced the church mail, his worn leather loafers, and a new snow shovel in his arms. Dumping it all on his desk, the shovel clattered to the floor and he muttered a mild curse as he tossed his fedora on the pile.

Grunting, the priest bent down to grab the shovel but his overcoat bunched up around his neck. His girth, the coat, and his generous lunch constricted his breathing. Straightening, he propped the shovel against the wall. The clip, clip of a woman's sturdy heels reached him and he wiped the sweat from his bald head.

"Father, you early. The dustin' not done," warned Mrs. Owens. He grinned at her thinking after all this time, he had not grown accustomed to her unique speech. She stood in the doorway to the main church, a squat woman wrapped in a bibbed, white apron and a shapeless blue dress. Beckoning him with one eyebrow raised in a high, boney forehead, she held up an enormous piece of cake wrapped in waxed paper.

He frowned thinking he needed to get out of his galoshes. "Planning for obligations prevents inevitable disasters, Mrs. Owens," he said. "The snow is deepening. You should take off."

She snorted and said, "I done brought you something. Smith Island cake!"

His mouth watered. He grunted and sat down suddenly in his leather chair. "I hate to ask you," he said, his voice filled with resignation as he raised one wet boot, "but would you mind helping me get out of these before I track up your floor any further?"

"Well, that's a whole 'nother story, right there."

She placed the dessert on the pile of mail, bent down on one knee before him and tugged. The boot came off in a swish, baring a worn black sock. "Did you bring yer shoes? Weren't that smart of you to not wear 'em under the galoshes? But yer feet pert near ice." She slipped on his loafers that splayed like flat tires and proffered her hands as if he were her child. "Let's get you out of that there wet coat."

Father Ingle gripped her fingers, placed his feet squarely and rocked as she heaved him out of the chair. She giggled lightly and he wondered if this was what it was like to be an old married couple.

Mrs. Owens clipped-clipped toward the space heater.

He shrugged out of his overcoat and hung it on the rack. Reading her thoughts, he said, "No, no. I'll pull my chair over to it. A mouse ate through the heater cord and Calvert wrapped it in electrical tape."

"Calvert?" The thick line of her eyebrows met, her heavy

forehead layering in wrinkles.

And so it begins, he thought, wincing. Mrs. Owens despised Calvert more for his color than anything else.

"You had that derelict in here a-working? Father! If I tol' you once, I tol' you a thousand times to keep him outta here. He's a penny waiting for change and crazy to boot."

"Now, now, Mrs. Owens," said the priest as he rolled his chair to the heater. "He needed some money for breakfast and I gave him a couple bucks for honest work. I know nothing about electrical. Besides, he was an entomologist of sorts at one time. A scientist."

"Ento- what? You mean he's sly like a fox. He steals."

"Entomology, my dear. The study of bugs. And if I were homeless, I might be driven to steal as well. The Lord says, 'Blessed are the poor for theirs is the kingdom of heaven.' "

" 'The poor *in spirit*,' Father," replied Mrs. Owens, her hands on her hips. "Nothing spiritual about him 'less it's the spirit he throw down his gullet. He think he deserve everything we give him."

"Well, that might be so," said the priest as he held his toes to the warmth. "He is a little too dependent on us. I told him about a job at the fishing wharf. Cleaning up, mostly. Do you know that old coot wouldn't take it?"

"Not surprised. You cut that mangy hair, put clean clothes on him and it still weren't make no difference. No amount o' spit and polish help crazy."

"Blessed are the merciful, Mrs. Owens. Blessed are the merciful."

"Worthless human beings, Father," she said as she glared

at him. "Don't matter what generation it be, the cannery, the fishing' boats, or sotweed. We can't find no decent workers cheap 'round here."

"Sotweed?" He had heard locals complain about paying black watermen or cannery workers but he had never heard of sotweed.

Mrs. Owens clucked a few times as she stacked the mail. "Terbaccer. Cambridge were settled on terbaccer and ersters 300 year ago," she said.

"Tobacco and oysters. Yes, but that was when Maryland was a slave colony."

She removed the wax paper from the cake and miraculously pulled a fork from her apron, setting it on the desk as if to change the subject. "Never you mind. You eat yer cake while I go clean that altar and confessional booth."

***

The Cellar

The 16-penny nails scattered across the concrete floor spilling from a 10 gallon, wooden barrel. Like roaches scurrying from the light, they rolled under wooden shelving, behind the toolbox, under to the contractor's box and the workbench, and into the corner under the massive tank of home heating oil. The boy stood straight as a toy soldier in their midst, his head turned upward, his whole body on alert. Silence, and then he heard his father's low voice and footsteps clump across the wooden floor above his head. There was commiserating and the Saturday afternoon laughter of hardy men pushing to finish their chores so they could enjoy the rest of their day.

"You got the lighter fluid, Vickers? It'll take two cans." A gruff voice, it was unfamiliar to the boy.

"Just get the rest and be there 'bout mournful. Soon as the sun go down beside the Rexall," answered the boy's father.

"Did ya tell Velma we got it covered the way she want?"

"I'm running this wrecking crew. Our loties need to stay out of this."

"A shame we cain't lynch no more. Them days it were easier," came a raspy, older voice.

The boy sighed, expelling held breath, and grabbed the broom and dustpan. The hardware store's grit seeped down from the rough planking that served as a flooring above and ceiling below, caking his reddened his eyes. Wiping the crust from his wet lashes, he rolled the ball between his thumb and forefinger and flicked it into the air. He had grown so accustomed to his lot, his failing vision, and living in the cellar, but still, he longed for sunlight. At 13, he had the gift of superlative hearing—the first raindrops to hit leaves in the garden, the drone of bees outside, his father's whispered thoughts were all within his range. Often, he wished this gift on others so he could have peace, but at times he had to admit, it was a gift that saved.

Desperation clawed his stomach as his growing body pleaded for food...and his father, seeing his need, had begun to limit the bites he took in demand of perfection. Rubbing his eyes, the boy could make out the shiny nails that glittered in the florescent light like fireflies in the night air. Fireflies—

The Grist Mill Bone

they were a distant memory from childhood. He swept furiously, blindly eagle eyeing every square inch, determined to find each blessed nail.

In an hour, he had swept them up and into the barrel. Being cautious this time, he continued his original task, scooping the different sized nails from their crates—6, 8, and 12-penny, along with the framing and gutter nails, into the display case drawers. When finished stocking, he would tote the case up the wooden stairs after the store closed for the day. He would be allowed to eat then, but it seemed so far away.

He cocked his head to listen again and hearing voices at the cash register near the front of the store, he pulled a can of Spam from a hidey-hole in the stone foundation. He fingered the key from the bottom, wedged the pull-tab into its slot and unwound the lid from the can. Inside was the pinky-gray gelatin of congealed hog parts that made his mouth water in anticipation. He lit the propane torch, dumped the cube on the workbench and adjusted the flame. Spearing his only meal of the day with a galvanized gutter nail, he held it up to the flame, roasting it on all sides to a golden brown. Satisfied, he cut the flame and bit the meat, the grease burning his tongue. He panted as his mouth filled with saliva but determined, he wouldn't spit it out. Instead, he gripped the edge of the workbench and rolled his head on his shoulders, his eyes watering as he chewed when he caught a side eye of a figure on the stairs. His father.

*****

2 VELMA

"Yeah," called Velma Owens in answer to my knock, "Let's get this over with. My food's coming and I'm not missin' it."

Fairhaven staff was preparing for lunch in the dining room and I could hear the dishes clanking in a kitchen somewhere. I wondered why she wasn't eating with the other residents. Velma had a sweet, angelic voice that belied the roughness of her words. I pushed the door open to see a small woman in a wheelchair, her very large head wrapped in a blue, feathered turban. A window laced with shelves of African violets outlined her figure. So many soft pinks and purple petals framed her wrinkled muslin face that at first, I didn't notice the distorted shape of her chin, her forehead and brow. She had sunk into her wheelchair like a bolster of vibrant textiles, but on closer study I realized her face had the boney armor of a triceratops. My mind whirled with images; where had I seen this before? Then it came to me—here, in the flesh, was the Duchess of Alice in Wonderland. I composed myself and smiled, my cheeks puffed and mounded in false cheerfulness.

"Mrs. Owens, I'm Claire Solomon, your attorney. So nice to finally meet you." She ignored my hand and left it hanging in the air like a dog's limp tail.

"You don't fool me. People been looking at me for the last twenty years with disgust. All right. All right. I got more money than any of them, and probably you too, so it don't matter to me."

Ashamed of myself, I felt heat rise up my neck like an attorney on her maiden voyage. She was nearing 90 and I couldn't imagine what her life had been like. I started to apologize but she cut me off.

"Get the clicker and mute that TV so's I can hear you," she said, waving her crooked fingers in the air. "We need an understanding. I trust Father Caulfield. I don't trust any old lawyer. But you come on his recommendation, so I'm going with you."

Well, I figured I had best cooperate with her way of "understanding" or I'd be gone. I have run into many a person on the peninsula who feels a native distrust of all the newcomers. I don't know whether they are threatened by city ways and education or if they simply feel judged by outsiders, but it's another reason to hide my past. Besides, I'd need decades of embedded family lineage to advise rooted inhabitants about their money. Most of them had made it from farming or chickens and it hadn't come easy. Like all the rest, this lady was going to take some buttering up.

Talking heads appeared on the local news channel. Her

eyes returned to the television, and I followed the banner across the bottom of the screen. "HUMAN REMAINS FOUND IN WOODS..." SUVs marked with the state logo crowded the picture. I figured another drug related murder on the western side of the county—there were too many these days, spoiling idyllic beach life. Only recently the body of a homeless man had been found in Indian River Bay, a leg missing. Thankfully, my husband, Booker, is a retired Maryland State Detective, so I never worry—well at least not when he's around. It's not like this is anything approaching the crime in D.C. Momentarily, I was caught by the image on the TV as a camera ran a close up of a driveway that looked vaguely familiar. I dragged my attention from the screen and the announcer, shutting him up with a push of my finger on the remote.

Stepping between her and the television, I said, "Mrs. Owens, I hope to gain your confidence as we go through the process of writing your will and trust. I'll do the best job I can for you based on your wishes." I didn't know what else she had heard about me. That I had inherited wealth, that I didn't need to work, that there was a family murder in *my* past? Maybe my words were just an attempt to reassure myself.

She raised her massive head and with a salty look, said, "Well, it ain't going to be nobody else wishing. Sit down."

One gnarled finger pointed to a chair at a small wooden table. A plate of chocolate chip cookies, their crumbs scattered across some unopened mail littered the surface. I guess I passed the first test. She wheeled in opposite me with no assistance. Like her character, there was nothing weak about her arm strength.

***

The Sotweed Legacy

Father Ingle scooted his desk chair, groaning and squeaking over to the cake. With great reverence he slid the fork through the ten chocolate layers, muttering, "a legendary cake," and watched them fall like a tower near the plate's edge. Carefully, he pierced a gob loaded with icing and slid it slowly into his mouth. He leaned to one side, closed his eyes and savored its sweetness, thinking that for all the grief she gave, Mrs. Owens was a godsend. It was Saturday afternoon and he sighed, resigning himself to an evening of ministering the Sacrament of Reconciliation.

With his first bite he exhorted himself saying aloud, "I will redeem the sinful face to face, and heart to heart." The older he got the more frustrated he grew, doling out absolutions for the penitents who would sin again in the same ways. He'd heard it all: lost tempers, stolen trinkets, and marital betrayals. Jealousy, greed, and lust. And lies. Lots and lots of lying. It was the same everywhere.

He took another bite of solace and resolved to warn them of spreading unintended hurts. Rarely were things lively enough in Cambridge to hear a mortal sin worthy of confession. Not since the school burned down in the riots along with two blocks of black businesses in '67. He had almost succumbed to his fears at the time, ready to ask for a transfer but in the end, he heeded his calling to minister to the whole community. He preached for everyone to be calm and carry on, to love one another in Jesus' eyes, but Cambridge's struggling economy and the intransigence of some members of his community, both white and black, could not be swayed. Finishing the last of his cake, he rolled out three Our Father's and two Hail Mary's for his own sake.

Rising, he lumbered to the doorway of the main church looking for Mrs. Owens. Her bucket and mop stood outside the confessional. He could see her sturdy heels beneath the curtain. Glancing to the altar, he saw his chair sitting near the lectern. He had scheduled private confessions from five to six and face-to-face reconciliations between six and seven. This last half always ran overtime. Inevitably, older parishioners, some personal friends and church leaders, expected counseling, benediction, and a smile. He grimaced at the thought.

Father Ingle grabbed the railing and genuflected. His knee joint popped and crackled under his weight. Heaving up the steps to the high backed chair, he drew it across the red carpet to the platform's edge.

When he received the Bishop's advisement, courtesy of the Holy See, he had agonized over the idea of open confession. In practice, he found it impossible to remain aloof. He was old fashioned and it disturbed him that he could see the waver in their gaze and smell dinner on their breath. The sinning would continue, no matter the method of confession. It was up to him to give the sacrament dignity and a degree of privacy.

First, he had the confessants line up at a distance along

the wall after the first pew. Once summoned by a wave of his hand, a reverent Catholic would approach him as he sat in his chair on the top step. From this vantage point he could look down upon their bowed heads as they told their sins. He could grant absolution and move the line along with precision. After a few weeks of this, he decided if the Holy See could change a sacrament, so could he.

On a January Sunday, he announced that once a month he would hold Drive-Thru-Confession. "Yes," he uttered at the end of Mass before a smattering of elderly Catholics. "You can drive through for your hamburgers. Why not forgiveness?" Father Ingle explained that he would sit in his truck in the church parking lot for the last hour of confession and the devoted could pull up next to his open window to confess and be absolved. Drive-Thru-Confession proved a huge success and he intended to repeat it in February when parishioners groused about the cold church. The bishop didn't need to know, and besides, it would save turning on the heat during cold winter nights.

To save the parishioners' money, he kept the lights low, had canceled the mowing contract last summer and, before Christmas, did away with the maintenance contract on the old oil furnace. It was risky and immediately, old Mrs. Hicks, who noticed everything, started a petition for a lights-on policy during confession. Then, the parish council admonished him for pitting their safety against his frugality. Affronted, he responded that a simple request would do in the future. He lamented that his congregation seemed to have grown grumpier as its size declined. Hell, he thought, the whole town was shrinking since the canning factory closed leaving many destitute, especially black workers like Calvert.

Four years had passed since H. Rap Brown's call to arms echoed along Race Street. "If Cambridge doesn't come around, Cambridge got to be burned down." That night the all-white volunteer fire department refused to muster up as the black side of the town burned to the ground. Concessions were negotiated. Jim Crow faded. But three years later the courthouse was bombed and folks, both black and white, were fed up with strife. A cordial, if wary distance between the races became the rule of thumb in public. The youth of Cambridge fled for a better life and Father Ingle was left to preach his message of brotherly love to elderly merchants and longtime farmers who revered their patch of dirt and way of life.

He shifted his altar chair to the perfect angle and realized a single spotlight over the center railing was out. Waddling to the bank of light switches, he flipped on all the altar lights. He hated the blaze streaming from above as it revealed too much severity in everyone, especially the aged.

Turning around, his belly bumped into a large man bundled against the cold. "Aaahhhh! F-forgive me," Father Ingle stammered stepping back and realizing from the stink that it was Calvert.

"Father, you hearing confession tonight?"

"Yes, Calvert. What can I do for you?"

"There's a free dinner and bed at the VFW. I'm needing a ride. It's cold out."

"Well there's no time for me to take you now, Calvert.

People will be here in a few minutes. Can I take you over say, around 7:30?"

"Yeah. But, but, maybe could Mrs. Owens take me now?"

Over Calvert's shoulder, the priest saw Mrs. Owens standing with her arms firmly folded across her chest, a scowl contorting her face.

"Well, that won't work either, Calvert. Mrs. Owens has been working for some time today and she has to get home to her family now."

"Yes, sir."

But the man didn't budge. His flayed work boots seemed rooted to the floor. His grimy overalls and layers of outerwear appeared an immovable mountain to the priest. Father Ingle had seen respectable farmers come in from the field like this during growing season but Calvert was different; he bore signs of personal neglect. His hair stood on end, his eyes were rheumy and the skin around his mouth chalky and crusted. The priest knew not one of his parishioners would allow him in their car.

"Come back after seven and wait in the narthex. We'll go over after confession." Ingle didn't invite him to wait inside the church. He knew the library was closed and with the exception of the police department, there were no other public buildings open on a Saturday night. In the meantime, Calvert could go back to his barricade behind the Rexall Drugs where he kept his meager belongings out of the wind.

"Yes, Sir. And maybe you want to sit down and eat with me?" invited Calvert.

This was too much. A homemade lasagna sat in Father's

refrigerator, waiting. He planned to eat it and watch *All In The Family* at eight. He swallowed. The religious obligations, the demands of the parishioners on Saturday night, coupled with three Masses on Sunday morning, overwhelmed him.

"We'll see, Calvert. We'll see."

"Thank you, Father. I'm so hungry I could eat a bark beetle."

"What, a beetle? We don't want that, do we?" The pine trees around Cambridge were dying from invasive bark beetles but surely Calvert wasn't eating them?

Calvert dragged himself to the front door, a hulk of filth and despondency. It wasn't that Father was without mercy. It was that he had to protect what little energy he had to give of himself. The priest said good-bye to Mrs. Owens, praising her work and giving her thanks. He returned to the sacristy.

***

The Cellar

The boy held his chin and jaw, pushing upward as if trying to disconnect his skull from his neck. Rocking on his mattress in the dark, his labored breathing filled the air and he whimpered in tight little cries, wishing he had a mother. He remembered a soft hand, a warm cuddle in a woman's lap years ago when he was small. Sometimes, he thought it was just remnants of a dream, a broken fantasy he thrived upon, but when sunlight beamed low in the sky, shooting through the square of dirty glass in the basement window, he could see her face and knew she had been real.

The greasy meat had burned the roof of his mouth and tongue, forming blisters on his tender gums. This had not caused his uneven breathing. His father had hit him in the throat and the wad of meat shot across the room, landing on the cellar floor. As the boy coughed and retched, the old man strode over to the masticated meat and toed it with his boot. He bent down for a closer look and when he stood, he held out his palm with two 16-penny nails. "You not only disobey me and eat without my permission," he said, "but you throw away the products we sell! How do you expect me to support you if you take away my livelihood?" The old man turned to his son and with a smile of benevolence he grasped the boy's quivering shoulder. " 'Everyone to whom much was given, of him much will be required, and from him to whom they entrusted much, they will demand more. Luke, Chapter 12, verse 48.' "

The boy wavered, unsure of his father's intention. His shoulder felt small and weak under the man's gangly hand but nevertheless he had touched his son. This small gesture brought forth a well of hope and endurance in the boy. Slowly, his arms rose around his father's waist and as he rested his head against the old man's sunken chest, he sensed this was the love his father could give.

He felt a firm grip on either shoulder now as his father held him at arm's length and looked his son in the eye with a steely blue gaze that reached into his soul.

"Davis, you be a good boy now and if you finish counting all the screws in the barrels and put them in the display case, I will let you eat that pile of shit you spit on the floor tomorrow. Now go to bed and don't make a sound when the police go knocking on the door upstairs. They just doing their rounds, boy. We got some thieving jigaboos in this town and I lay my trust in you to know the difference. Why, we got to protect our livelihood ever' night when the lights go out."

*****

3 THE FATHERS

"I want to leave it all to the Catholic Church. Not Catholic Charities. St. Aloysius in Cambridge. And I'm telling you right now it's going to two people." Velma Owens paused and leaning over the table, stared at me intensely. I was digging in my briefcase. "I'm saying, let's get this over with, girl."

I had thought this wouldn't take long since there were no descendants. Could be dead wrong. Who were her beneficiaries? A non-profit within the Church as yet unnamed? She had some peculiar misconceptions. Or maybe I did.

I placed a release form and the investment summary that Father Caulfield provided on the table between us and sat back in the chair. The first step was to slow her down. The elderly often have preconceived ideas about their legacies and snap out orders without considering the consequences.

Her blue eyes were hooded with distrust, her lips, a thin,

wrinkled line above a jutting chin. Her high forehead was only partially hidden by the elaborate turban. It looked to be made from heavy brocade. And the feather—was that peacock? I had to give it to her, she was a force all her own.

"Mrs. Owens, before we can discuss your situation I need you to sign a release."

She grabbed the pen from my hand, scribbled her signature at the bottom of the page and tossed both back to me.

"Thank you," I said. That was easy and I was encouraged. "Let's talk about your needs here before we start giving away your estate. Are you happy here at Fairhaven?"

She snorted and tucking her turban behind one fleshy ear, and said, "What's to be happy about? Ever' bone in my body aches and my heart is failing. Look at me. I pray ever' night I won't wake up in the morning."

"That must be awful. I'm sorry." Raising my voice, I said, "I hope there's something that brightens your day?"

"I get to make fun of the aide who come in here to wipe my ass. She bounce around me like a goat with hot hooves. Maybe one day she'll put me out of my misery and give me the wrong medicine. Dumb shit," she muttered under her breath as if I couldn't hear."

"You don't feel like you're getting good medical care?" I laid my pen on the table and looked at her, covering her cold hand in mine.

"I don't care, girl. I don't care. I just want it to be over."

I was struck by her sadness and decided to change the subject. "I hear you were an amateur photographer." There were Audubon prints framed on one wall above a grainy photo of a young man in combat gear but no other signs of her history. She had an affinity for growing African violets. Was there nothing else to keep her occupied? In our phone conversation, Father Caulfield said he remembered her picture albums full of parish events.

"That was a long time ago," she said. "There's a storage unit out on the highway with all that stuff. I 'spect those pictures covered in mold."

"I'd be happy to get them for you. It might be fun to go through them together." Loneliness poured through the halls of these nursing homes like vinegar on a wound. I had time to spare, time to make a friend of her.

Those tiny blue eyes fixed on me in disbelief. Or maybe affront.

"You being nice to me because you want something? You stay out of my belongings. I don't need to be reminded of the past."

Old Velma was a suspicious one! I've learned that dementia makes lions out of lambs. Usually the past was all my clients wanted to talk about: children, husbands, memories of their weddings long ago. But she had opened the door for me to ask a tough question.

"Father tells me you have no children and no other family."

Her massive chin rose in the air, "My husband Fred killed hisself thirty years ago after our son were run over by a drunk driver. I've outlived ever'body else."

That was it, I thought: a drunk driver. She had received a

court settlement for her son's death but it wasn't enough to keep her husband alive. Amazing what could be one person's undoing, could be another's reason to persist. We had something in common, then. I admit I've hardened over the years. Booker, Sam and I have been through worse and we're resilient.

"It's none of my business how you came in to such a large sum but I'm curious. Was it from a settlement over the drunk driver?"

Deadpanning, she said, "You're right, it's not your business."

Not giving up, I tried again, "Let's say you've benefitted from some investments and close friendships with the priests from your days at St. Aloysius?"

"The priests from the diocese. I worked the altar society for years. I know'd folks who worship there and some of them real good people whose own children deserve the best. " She pushed the pen back and I wondered if she was being cagey. The stack of mail sitting between us slipped at her touch, fanning out across the table. A return address caught my eye. Howard University, the historic black college of D.C. had sent her an alumni newsletter. This lady was more complicated than I thought. Raindrops splattered hard against the window's glass, the sky a blackened sea. I wondered what Velma had to do with a black university.

"I want my money set up the way I say."

"I understand. If it's a named Catholic charity then your investment goes to them tax-free. I assume that's what you mean?"

The Grist Mill Bone

"Young lady, you know'd what it mean to assume. Make an ass out of you and me. I didn't say nothing about a charity."

Undaunted, I spoke with more emphasis. "Mrs. Owens, the funds you leave private individuals will be taxed at the *full rate*. You reside in Delaware where there's no inheritance tax, but St. Aloysius is in Maryland where there is both an inheritance tax and an estate tax."

"I don't know'd how to be any clearer with you. Are you trying to not listen? I don't want to pay no tax and the money is going to the priests of the parish for the families." She harrumphed and her shoulders stiffened as she gripped the arms of her wheelchair. "You make them a charity."

"Certainly," I wasn't going to argue with her. I kept my tone reasonable. "If they haven't taken a vow of poverty they can have personal items and their own money. I believe the diocese pays them a small salary. So your gift would be in addition to that. How much of your financial profile did you want to leave them? Your 401K?"

One veiny hand slammed the table. "I want to leave them everything."

"All 5.6 million?" I asked in disbelief.

"Now you hearin' me. All 5.6 million dollars to Father Caulfield and Father Ingle."

I was confused, ... or Velma was. "Who is Father Ingle?"

She frowned as if she was trying to grab something from the distant past.

"That other priest. Not Father Ingle, God rest his soul. The one who helped me with the child."

"Velma, are you talking about Father Chilcott?" I asked.

"Yes, yes. That's who I mean. All the money goes to them."

She knew how much she had in her account but 2.8 a piece? That made for some country club priests. Why would she leave all that money to two old men when it could do so much good for so many people? Instead she wanted it to benefit the priests and a few parish families? It could feed the hungry, house the homeless, provide work programs, even aid unwed mothers. You name it; the Catholic Church runs the charities. I was missing something.

"Bear with me," I said. "Do Father Caulfield and Father Chilcott run a special charity of their own?" I repeated myself because she just didn't understand, "I'm just asking so we can make this a tax-free event. We can set it up as a trust. As it is, if you leave it to two men of the cloth…well, Mrs. Owens, that doesn't count as a charity in Uncle Sam's eyes."

She glared at me again and I was relieved when we were interrupted by a cheery voice.

"Mrs. Owens. It's time for your meds."

A stunning black woman dressed in a gray suit strolled through the door. A stethoscope hung around her neck tapping against a nametag that read, Deanna Seward RN. Brokering no nonsense, she put one hand on the arm of the wheelchair and turned it toward her. She met the old woman's gaze saying, "You remember me? I'm Deanna. You have two pills in this paper cup. I'm going to watch you swallow them." She produced a glass of water out of nowhere and hovered over the old woman.

"Where's my little goat, Tyneice? I want Tyneice," said Mrs. Owens.

"Tyneice is busy. You know an aide can't administer your meds. You haven't been treating her very well so you get me for the moment. Lucky you." The nurse flashed me a big grin.

"I don't know what you're talking about. I've been treating her just fine."

Nurse Seward laughed and nodded as Velma downed her pills. Then, without another word, she disappeared. A hitch in Velma's wrinkled cheek betrayed her. She was trying hard to suppress a smile.

***

The Sotweed Legacy

Studying himself in the mirror over the vestment drawer, in the harsh glare Father Ingle saw a ghoulish specter of a fat man. *How can they love me? I am humbled*, he thought. In the minutes before the first confessional hour began, he practiced faces of kindness, concern and compassion but try as he might the thick folds of his skin did not cooperate. He attempted a gentle smile. Then, pulling his pressed linen surplice from its hangar he flung it over his cassock and buttoned it as he trudged to the church sanctuary.

People leaned against the wall outside the confessional booth. The priest moaned softly and patted his rumbling belly. These might be his faithful, but he was not their psychologist. If he hurried, he could end early. He felt a passing guilt over his promise to drive Calvert to the VFW and as a gift for deciding against it, he thought some clothes from the donation box would satisfy him.

He shut the confessional door, rested on the velvet cushion and for an hour he enjoyed anonymity listening to their whispers. Over and over, he raised his hand in the sign of the cross as he granted absolution. Promptly at six, he emerged and ascended the steps to his armchair.

Mrs. Hicks, the emaciated owner of the town diner advanced to the lower step, inspecting his girth. "Bless me Father for I have sinned. It has been two weeks since my last confession..." The wizened town barber came next to say he had born false witness, gossiping, and the priest wished he had hair worthy of a cut. A humble line of chicken farmers followed, their calloused hands folded in prayer. Mr. Dixon confessed to cheating a neighboring farmer by setting his prices lower than agreed. Mr. Raynard confessed to lying about the number of spring chicks delivered and not paying for the extras. Father Ingle breathed a sigh of relief glimpsing the last person in line when he realized it was Theodore Vickers.

He waved the busybody forward. Vickers ran the hardware store and complained bitterly to anyone who listened about how morals on the shore were deteriorating. He would hold forth at his register about misguided government, the licentious behavior of Hollywood, and local derelicts who refused to pull themselves up by their bootstraps. Mrs. Owens grumbled that whether you were testing your TV tubes or buying carpet tiles for the porch steps, Vickers had choice words about the Cambridge community but never the nerve to confront the offending party in person. Father Ingle coughed in his hand and checked his watch. 6:40.

Vickers seemed agitated. Puffed up with importance. He claimed, "*I* have sinned." A huge mustache hid his mouth and the priest thought that was not all he disguised.

"I stole from my neighbor, Father. Just today, this afternoon."

"How will you make amends for this sin, Theodore?" asked the priest.

"I cain't, Father."

"Surely, you can return the item," suggested the priest.

"No. It were a lot o' junk and I threw it out."

Father Ingle paused. "Well, you know what they say. What is one man's junk is another man's treasure. You could find some similar items to replace the ones you threw out."

"I burnt it all in my back yard. I stood by in this cold wind off the bay to keep the fire from dying out in the snow, and don't you know, some folks help me. They knew it needed doing."

"Sounds like you think this was a community service," said the priest.

"That'd be true. A neighbor said to me, 'Why look at that fire, how pretty it glows.' "

"Theodore, the beauty of the fire is no measure for the loss you laid at the doorstep of the other person."

Vickers frowned, "I knew you'd say that so I done put a check in the poor box out front. You may want to go git it 'fore you shut down tonight. I'm saying my Act of Contrition."

In all his years of hearing confessions, Father Ingle had never had anyone strip away his power with one statement. It was if the man thought he was already forgiven. In a state of shock, the priest ordered him to say three rosaries and contribute to the poor box every Sunday for a year. He absolved him of his sin, "In the Name of the Father, and of the Son, and of the Holy Ghost."

Vickers left without kneeling to say his penance. Admittedly, it would have taken too long and Father Ingle, shaking his head, rose to lock up his church and head home for dinner. First he went to the narthex to see if Calvert was anywhere to be found and seeing it was too early, the priest gathered a winter coat and stocking hat, some corduroy trousers and a flannel shirt and laid them outside under the church's portico. Snow swirled in the darkness and he shivered from the freezing temperature. The entrance steps were covered in a crunchy white mantle, dotted with hollowed footprints. The wide ribbon of the priest's silk stole caught the wind and wrapped around his face, blinding him. He dragged it down but not before another gust whipped his long linen surplice and black cassock, entangling his legs. He shuddered against the closed door and thought that the steps would have to be shoveled before Mass in the morning. In a flash of habitual privilege he assumed Calvert would do it.

Almost tripping, he yanked on the heavy front door and struggled inside. He huffed and puffed smoothing his vestments. From an inner pocket he produced the same key he used for the sacristy door. A stab of hunger hit him squarely in the gut but he stopped at the poor box to pocket its contents making sure to read Vickers' check. The priest scoffed at the amount and plodded back to the sacristy, grabbed the snow shovel and nearly jogged to the front doors where he propped the shovel next to Calvert clothes. He locked up and made a beeline to the bank of light switches.

Taking one last glance over the darkened church he was satisfied that all was in order. Inside the sacristy he began to remove his vestments. Reverently, he folded his stole with its gold satin crosses and placed it in the drawer. Guilt gnawed at him. He proceeded to unbutton his surplice but paused at heart level.

The priest approached the crucifix on the wall and looked down at the red velvet kneeler. It had been a long time since his knees touched the cushion. One hand gripped the edge of his desk and as he placed the other flat on the wall, he knelt. "Bless me Father for I have sinned. My heavenly Father, I confess I lack the mercy I need for my fellow man but I am human and cannot rise above in this moment. I will repent for my sin by paying Calvert for clearing the steps in the morning and take him to the diner for lunch tomorrow. I will even give him money for dinner. Please dear Lord above, forgive me in my moment of weakness for I am hungry and I suffer in your everlasting service." Ingle said an Act of Contrition promising to amend his life and raised his face to the cross. "I am your faithful servant."

***

The Cellar

Davis woke to muffled noises outside: laughter, horse whispering, and heavy footsteps on the stairs. He rolled onto the cement floor and looked above the shelving toward the window. Pitch black. He grabbed the metal clock from the upturned box next to his bed and clicked on his flashlight. 6:30. He had only slept for an hour and hunger gnawed at him. Curling up on his haunches, he sat up slowly in the darkness, tenderly touching his sore neck. His father had warned him. He leaned against the stone foundation and its cold crept into his woolen jacket. Was it the jigaboos? But he hadn't told him what to do if they came!

The boy pulled on his boots, careful to lace them so as not to trip on the stairs. The men's voices had quieted but he heard the distinct sound of the front door rattling. A cold sweat collared his neck. The boy crept up the stairs possum-like, crouching and white faced, his right hand and foot pacing the steps against his left. Listening, he heard the front door creak wide and a cluster of feet stamping. He pushed open the basement door and darted into a dark corner just as a match lit a hurricane lamp down the store's main aisle. He blinked and blinked, trying to clear the fog from his eyes.

From his vantage he could see fresh snow on the welcome mat and a cluster of wet Neoprene muck boots. He raised his eyes to the hardened faces of old men, their thin smiles wedged between sagging cheeks and jowls, they were huddled in the lamp glow over a box of trinkets. A gloved hand reached, drawing items out as they chuckled and swore—a string of colored Christmas lights, a hot plate, and a leather dopp kit that was promptly emptied on the counter. This produced guffaws as they read their mangled labels—toothpaste, deodorant, an empty bottle of mouthwash. They laughed some more as one opened what appeared to be a pocket sized photograph album.

"It be a sin that gamey stinkhard have three daughters. More black kittens having litters," said his father as he pointed at the plastic picture book. "Shoulda thrown 'em all in the fire to burn."

A flashlight flickered on, sweeping the inside of the box, its beam suddenly catching the edge of the metal shelf nearest the boy. He sucked air involuntarily and panicked as all sets of eight eyes came to rest on him, frozen in the corner.

"What're yer doin' here, boy? Should be at home in yer nice warm bed," said his father as he strode toward him. As he came closer the smile faded from his father's face and looming above the boy, he took on the spectral visage of a demon god, his eyes burning red, his breath rank with cigarettes. The boy couldn't breathe and he fell in a stupor on the floor appearing dead as a doornail…or a possum.

*****

4 TYNEICE

I was aware of a presence at the door and turned to look just as Mrs. Owens yelled, "Don't just stand there, you simpleton. If it's time for lunch, get your lazy ass in here and wheel me off."

Tyneice waffled into the room. She wouldn't make eye contact with her charge and only nodded to me briefly.

"Here's my little black goat." Then to me, Velma ordered, "We're done talking about money." She stared at me myopically. "I can't even remember your name when I'm so hungry."

I waited for Tyneice to respond to the insult. She winked at me instead, a secret bargain to ignore the venom. I wasn't buying it and, at that point, I didn't care if I never returned to Velma Owens and Fairhaven.

Leaning in close, I said, "Claire Solomon. Remember, I'm your attorney?" Were her insults a result of dementia, racism, or both? "Mrs. Owens, in order for us to continue working together, you're going to treat the people around us with respect, regardless of race. Now you apologize to Tyneice for calling her a name."

Velma gave me the stink eye and slowly bowed her head, not breaking her gaze. I glared back. I swear I could hear her jaw clicking. I had often encountered clients who loved giving orders to anyone who listened, but never someone so openly racist. She wasn't royalty and Tyneice wasn't her personal whipping girl. "Velma, I'm waiting."

She looked over at her aide and said with a slight sneer, "I respect you, Tyneice. Why, we got to have an understanding since you have to wipe my butt now and again. You work for me and I give you trinkets, right?"

"I don't take anything from you Ms. Owens," said Tyneice in her childlike voice. I guessed Velma was trying to change my focus. This wasn't an apology but perhaps it was the best I could get out of a hungry old woman.

"Tyneice, did Mrs. Owens miss lunch in the dining room?" I asked.

"Oh, no, Ms. Solomon. Mrs. Owens eats her lunch in the quiet room. She prefers it, don't you Mrs. Owens?"

Velma tilted her head at me, her heavy cheekbone deflecting my words. "Who want to eat with those old biddies?" she said. "They just a nasty bunch of ol' women. And not a man among them who isn't drooling in his plate."

"I see. Well then, Velma. Is it all right for me to call you Velma since *we* have an understanding?" There was a slight nod in response. "You will not bribe Tyneice with trinkets as you know that would jeopardize her job. Now, would you like to continue our conversation some other time?"

"Yes," she said, drawing it out into three syllables. "You call me Velma and I'll call you Solomon. Good name for a judge. Come tomorrow after that Good Morning America girl is done giving us the news and smiling. You watch her tomorrow before you come and see if you can't take a lesson on how to be friendly."

Friendly? I had never been accused of not being friendly. As I said my goodbyes, I debated telling her to find another attorney, but then, I had to laugh at the utter ridiculousness that followed. Velma dismissed me with a flick of her hand and threw a $10 dollar bill onto the table.

"Get me some peach schnapps at the liquor store before you come back," she said.

I rolled my eyes. "Are you drinking that straight or do you need a mixer?"

"I got vodka and orange juice, Solomon. Bring yourself a drink and we'll have a cocktail hour," she answered.

After breakfast? The old lady really had her clock messed up.

Shaking her head, a smile on her face, Tyneice pushed Queen Velma to her private dining room. Velma's hands gestured about and Tyneice bent to speak in her ear. I wished I could hear the conversation. As I waited at the elevator door, tapping my foot, Tyneice rounded the corner.

She looked like she might keep going but turned to me and said, in a low voice, "You know, I'm about full of fed up 'round here. I can handle Ms. Owens just fine without you speaking up for me."

Surprised, I said, "I'm sure you can. As a matter of fact, I said it for my benefit. It makes *me* uncomfortable to see people treated that way."

"Lady," she said, "you need to toughen up. Words around here roll right off my back in this place. It's when that old bird gives me a Christmas present wrapped all pretty like and what's inside but a black Tshirt that says, 'HO' on it. Not, 'HO HO HO.' Just, 'HO.' She knew what she was doing. She always knows."

Tyneice walked off, no waffle in her step at all. Little powerhouse.

My feelings aside, I reasoned I had come this far and it wouldn't be professional to back out of my commitment. Velma might be suffering from dementia or she could just be really angry about being trapped in a body that was failing her. I'd hate being a prisoner of my own body. Besides, there was something pitifully intriguing about the old woman and I wanted to dig further. Father Caulfield deserved a follow up call.

On my way by the reception desk, I stopped to speak to the charge nurse. Deanna Seward came out of a back office pushing a cart with amber prescription bottles lined up, each labeled with a name.

"I only have a minute, Ms. Solomon. I have to get these meds out to the rest of the patients after lunch."

"Sure. Let me leave you a release Ms. Owens signed so you can speak with me about her condition and needs." She scanned the form and placed it on the desk on top of a pile of papers.

"I'll have to file that later. Is there anything you need

immediately?"

"Can you tell me about her health?"

"A little dementia, heart disease, advanced Paget's disease. She's hard of hearing and refuses to wear her hearing aids but that's just about everybody around here. And of course, she's just plain ornery, but I guess you got that, right?" She threw me a token smile and I thought she must save those winning grins for her recalcitrant patients. After a brief second she nodded. "If there's nothing else?"

"Paget's? What is that?"

Her shoulder slumped and she feigned patience. "Velma has it in her skull and spine. It's an overgrowth of bone where you don't need it and an under growth where you do, like in your joints. Not curable."

"Painful, I guess?"

"Very. She's being treated."

"Her photography. Why doesn't she want it?"

"She says it needs to be burned, ... moldy or something. Is that it?"

Her patience was wearing thin. "Shame—yes, thanks. I'll be back."

The nurse looked at me quizzically. I thought she was in a hurry. Then, picking up Velma's release form, she asked, "Aren't you that McIntosh woman from the kidnapping in the news a few years back?"

"I'm Solomon. Claire Solomon."

"Sure, sure you are," she said and sped off wheeling her cart.

Complications. Nurse Seward, while not completely

necessary to working with Velma, could be of huge assistance. If she was just being nosey about me, I could be honest with her at some point. My past didn't matter to Velma's future. As I paused at Fairhaven's front door, I speculated that I could boot myself off this client if I so desired. Pembroke, my boss, was a native; I wasn't. He's overworked dealing with our immigration clients, but maybe he would trade me two of his for Velma. The old girl was not very forthcoming. I had just found myself bossing her around, something I never saw myself doing, even if she was a bigot.

I pushed open the heavy front door and peeked outside. The rain had stopped as quickly as it had come… the skies still brokering peace, bringing an ocean breeze. Cicada shells had washed up against the sidewalk like a bizarre frosting of snow in April.

As I settled into the driver's seat, I threw my briefcase on the passenger seat and picked up the report from my doctor's visit that muddled my thoughts for a completely different reason. In the other hand, I clutched Velma's legal file. I had marked the tab *Seagrams V.O* which, in my opinion, tastes like gasoline. My mother used to drink it along with her rotgut cheap bourbon. Light a match around Velma and her tongue would burn just like my mother's, only not from liquor.

Flipping on the windshield wipers, I nodded reflexively, thinking that digressing into the past is symptomatic of my pattern of coping with stress. I have the past figured out. It's me in present time that's the question. My past isn't dogging me, but I'm still given over to doubt about this life I lead. It's the either/or question. Be a mother, be a lawyer, do both and will it be halfway and mediocre? At least I haven't inherited my mother's penchant for booze, just my parents' blue-blooded DNA that has apparently screwed me, and possibly my progeny. I mean that literally of course, just as a good attorney would interpret the plain language of the law.

Conversely, in the laws of heredity, there's no plain language. The DNA of blood passed down through the generations confuses me. As I scanned the medical report one more time, two words jumped out —"homozygous" and "heterozygous." I hadn't known until this: an inherited anomaly for blood clots came from *both* my parents. I had always assumed it was just my mom who passed this particular message on to me, but my dad had too.

And now, I am forced to have a conversation with Booker about babies…our baby, and the chance that he or she will carry the gene. I sighed and struck my go-to yoga pose, a modified Thunderbolt, to reduce the tension in my back and shoulders, lengthening my spine and crossing my arms over my chest. Cupping my hands under my arms, I felt the roundedness of my breasts. Suddenly, my eyes welled up and a small sob escaped my lips. Sitting in my little Mini Cooper with so many big changes beckoning, left me feeling small, inadequate. And now, I felt jailed.

I needed to drop the ruse and just be honest with Booker, even if I didn't know how he would handle the news of a baby coming. He had been a bachelor for so long that when we married we joked around about parenting, never making a conscious decision to take it on. My old therapist warned me that a good marriage isn't built on secrets, but then, that didn't help my first husband and me. Monster that he was. I am rid of him, thank God, ... and all that pent up hate.

I wiped my face. I am trying to be transparent with Booker but bad habits die-hard. How much do you share and not lose the love of your life? It was my fault. Birth control pills make it so easy but I can't take them. Can't blow another blood clot. Relying on an IUD had worked for a long while until it fell out in my hand in the shower three months ago. I made an appointment with the doctor right away, but it wasn't soon enough, I guess. I should've told Booker, but the passions of the moment were too much and we tangled in bed. He'd been gone across the bridge, working for Tosh and I'd missed him so. Given the opportunity, I don't need any help making a bad decision. I always do things the hard way.

I tucked my pen behind my ear. Pembroke, my legal partner and mentor, taught me never to carry a folder with my client's name into a nursing home, thus, the *Seagrams V.O.* mnemonic. Prying eyes might discover Velma's sensitive financial information. I pushed the file into my laptop case and looked down at the report from my doctor's office, crumpled in my lap. Life and death with me in the middle.

I took a deep breath, flipped down the visor and eyed the mirror. No wonder Velma had been put off by me: my splotchy right eye. The good one was a mixed up blue-green with a dot of brown in the iris and if that isn't enough weirdness for people just meeting me, today I had woken to a blood clot in the other one. Blood thinners and stress. Here it was 1:00 and I'd spent the day trying to make sense of

Velma's complicated investments so the damn clot was still there. I slammed the visor up and muttered a curse. I was going to have to make some changes in my life but not before I finished with Mrs. Owens. When you take on a client, you don't leave them in the lurch.

My former life in D.C was flashy, lobbying my soul away. I left K Street four years ago to find enlightenment working immigration law on the peninsula but that proved to be a tsunami sized mistake. Too risky. I like job security, but want to run under the radar. Pembroke took me on with the agreement that I would pass the Delaware Bar adding corporate law to my legal caché and his income. I did, but that's too high profile for me. I might as well have stayed in Washington and sold my soul to the devil working for multinational corporations. He and I renegotiated and I'm happy that I moved on to something simple—elder law, and in the process, I left immigration to Pembroke. Now, if I were asked, I'd say my ultimate directive puts me nearer to a grave every day.

It's a zero sum game being an attorney to the dying. I'm not doing it for the money, my client's inheritors are rarely satisfied, and let's face it, there's not much in it for the client, except hopefully meeting St. Peter. No, I'd rather be a stay at home mom, but Tosh expectations for my professional success are still defining me even though my parents are dead and gone. It's a generational thing—achievement. My reward is knowing I did my best and didn't slack, but it's also my price. The problem is work satisfaction declines the closer I get to my clients' last days. As much as I try to remain impartial, the old folks always get to me and I shed some tears in private. Booker shakes his head at me.

I was wasting time sitting in Fairhaven's parking lot lost in reflection. Looking up I could see burgeoning dark clouds pushing east as patches of bright blue broke free. A sheen of wet covered everything and two seagulls walking the pavement laughed at some private joke. What was always so pressing that I needed to rush wherever I went? I was exhausted and ready for a nap, something I never do. It dawned on me that there would be another seven months of being tired—and eventually, I'd grow clumsy from baby weight.

The house would be quiet, enough for me to catnap while I waited for Sam to come home from school. Booker would get in late from D.C. We'd have a quiet evening, one full of good news and wine to toast the future. At least I hoped Booker would think it good news.

I remembered the doctor's serious eyes as he warned, "alcohol thins your blood." There'd be no wine tonight for our baby. Instead, I'd have sparkling water, something Velma ought to do. I wondered if I could squeeze in time to research Paget's disease. I made a bargain with myself: she would be my last client before the baby comes.

I actually enjoy interviewing the near dead and establishing their expressed intents. In the past, my clients have been practical about who gets what. Not Velma. This time, when Velma passes I'll pay my respects at the viewing. This time, there'll be none of the usual confrontations from the heirs. And this time, I won't envy the make up artist and the funeral dresser who, unlike me, get no complaints from the living or the dead. In the end, they have the luxury of creating mom's last stage appearance. Only this time, their job will be really tough. I mean, how do you soften a face like Velma's?

Then, I'll get to announce her last wishes. And I imagine, even a priest might be uncomfortable with her intentions.

Listen to yourself, I thought, starting up my car that sputtered and shook as I backed out. I gritted my teeth wondering how I would fit a baby in the back seat. I hate buying cars but I'd have to break down and get something more family oriented. Nothing showy. Not like I used to be.

Compared to my former life as the only heir to the Tosh fortune, writing wills and trusts here on the peninsula is safe and anonymous. No guns, no gangs, no unknown threats. Sam and I came here looking for privacy four years ago and we stayed for Booker. We've made a simple, but very rich life together. I may be privately disdainful of my job at times but the serendipity is meeting someone like Velma, someone so foreign to my being, to everything I know, and helping her plan her ending saga.

My phone buzzed with a text. I was delighted to see that Booker was home early from Washington. *"Old mill bridge closed. Use point park."* He wanted me to go through the trailer park to the farmhouse instead of using the main driveway. The Solomon property, some of it woods, some of it tenant farmed, was what remained of an old African American enclave that rested at the juncture of a broad creek and a shallow bay. Street side, it bordered a beach artery and a colonial two lane road that crossed the creek at the ruined grist mill.

Odessa, Booker's mother and my heart and soul, had spun many a yarn by her fireplace, keeping me enthralled with stories of her ancestors. More than a century had passed since families of freed slaves left for D.C., Baltimore, and Philadelphia, allowing the Solomon family to buy small tracts of farmland and return it to forest. In an attempt to feed those who stayed, Booker's great, great grandfather had taken over operation of a gristmill at the headwaters of the creek in the days before it had silted up to a trickle. His own father, Odessa's husband, had made a commitment to keep the land in Solomon hands in the face of unbridled beach development. Only three miles from the ocean, out of state developers coveted the family's prime property. Odessa was stalwart in answer to their incessant demands to sell. While she lives on a short rise on the property, Booker, Sam and I live creek side in the original 1890's farmhouse. I couldn't wait to see him. There was so much to say.

My man is always thinking of me, even my route home. I'll drive in through the back door and he'll be standing there waiting for me, a glass of pinot grigio in hand. I guess that will start the conversation.

***

The Sotweed Legacy

Father Ingle heard a noise outside the sacristy door and cocked his ear. Scrape, pause, scrape. It was Calvert. The derelict was clearing the back steps to the parking lot. Ingle checked his watch for the third time that night. It was seven forty. Opening the scarred wooden door, he found the black man holding the shovel in one hand and a metal can in the other.

"Calvert."

"Yes, sir. I cleaned your steps front and back and brought you some more kerosene for the heater. Old man Vickers put it on the church's tab."

"That's so kind of you, Calvert. Come in for a moment. I have something to tell you."

His massive body passed through the door and Ingle could feel the cold off his clothes. Calvert pulled the knit cap from his head revealing a thick mat of black hair. His eyes watered from the wind and he wiped his hand across his face and under his nose. He put the kerosene down next to the heater that still glowed with warmth.

Ingle didn't want him to get too comfortable and not heeding his better self, he blurted out, "Calvert, I'm not able to drive you to the VFW but I can give you money for a taxi. You see I have not eaten either and I still have to write my sermon for tomorrow. Thank you for clearing the steps. You got the cap I put out for you. Did you get the clothes?"

Calvert's eyes narrowed. He raised a bare fist to his temple and tapped it gently, then harder. His mouth opened and closed, opened and closed. "Bark beetles, bark beetles," he mumbled.

"What did you say? No, no. You misunderstand me, Calvert. I will give you money to get a cab," said the priest.

"I can't. I can't," the big man muttered. "You got to help me tonight, Father. It's cold and my legs 'bout to break off at the knee. So much walking. I can't do it any more."

"Well of course you can't. That's why I'll call you a cab right now to take you to the VFW."

"A cab? No cabbie goin' to let me get in his hack. Besides, even if they say yes to you, they'll dump me out by the river and I got to walk back into town. It's cold tonight," he said again.

"Well, you have to try, Calvert. You have to try. I simply do not have the time to take you to the VFW."

"I can't eat any more bark beetles," he wailed. "You got to help. I don't have any more reason to live. Someone stole my camp. My hut, my blankets, my cor-gate cardboard cleared out."

Father Ingle had spent his wisdom for the night, his benevolence had evaporated and whatever shred of godly thought left to him was swallowed in the acid of an empty stomach. "If you had taken the job at the wharf, you might have some money to pay for a room."

Calvert's bare hands rose up between them as if he could halt the priest's words midair. Ingle's eyes widened in surprise. It seemed that Calvert had been struck in his solar plexus. The priest watched as the big man stumbled backward and his boot heel knocked against the heater. It toppled, spilling the kerosene across the floor. Calvert bent to right the heater and in his confusion the back of his massive fist hit the tank of kerosene, which clattered on its side. The screw lid loosened and its clear liquid spilled in gulps. A pungent smell wafted toward the priest and he stretched his arms outward to his servant. The sleeves of his unbuttoned surplice fell from his shoulders making white wings as the kerosene burst into flame spreading across the floor. Father Ingle's vestments caught, engulfing his flailing body. He screamed. The priest heard Calvert boom, "Father, you're the fiery angel of heaven come to get me!"

"Calvert, save me! Save me!"

Calvert wrapped himself around the priest and they tumbled around the room like a lit matchstick falling across the green and white tiles in front of the sacristy door.

***

The Cambridge Fire Department on Charles Street rang a five alarm. When they arrived the shingled exterior of St. Aloysius burned blue in the night sky. Yellow flames licked the pitched roof. In a cruel twist of Mother Nature the snow dissipated leaving only the brisk wind to fuel the fire. It burned hot into the church hall before the water guns extinguished the flames at the base of the altar. Oddly, all the pews were saved as if they were ready for the congregants at Sunday morning Mass. Only there was no tabernacle, altar, or priest. The sacristy door stood unopened supported only by its sturdy frame.

As the humped moon reached its zenith, the clouds cleared in the night sky leaving a scattering of stars. The first fireman breached the door. Nearing exhaustion, he pushed hard against an unseen weight. The door inched open and collapsed upon the floor he saw the body of a large black man, his arms wrapped around a fallen priest as if shielding him from fate. He sounded the alarm to the EMS team, "I got them. The priest and the black bug eater."

A collective groan rose from the small group of town residents huddled in the freezing air. A short, squat woman stood next to the owner of the hardware store.

"Vickers, did you do this?" asked Mrs. Owens.

His mustache twitched in the moon light and he barked like a sea lion, "You wanted it much as me, dearie. They done it to themselves."

"You idiot. You shoulda saved Father Ingle. He was one of us."

***

The Cellar

Davis rubbed his eyes and looked at the calendar by his head. Sunday, the Lord's Day and the hardware store stayed closed. The boy did not recall how he had made his way back down the steps to sleep the night through, undisturbed. He stretched mightily, and feeling long, he planted his fists against the wall, twisted his spine and pulled up his toes, tightening his legs. He pushed out through his heels and promptly felt a charley horse in both calves. Yelping, he brought his knees up under his chin and laughed at his traitor muscles.

Today was *his* day—or at least it would be after he attended church with his father...his day to finish the assembly of his toy airplane... his day to eat spaghetti and meatballs with a huge glass of milk and half a loaf of white bread. It was his day to work on the secret framework that made his father proud. It was a day to *call his own* once he was done with church.

The sun was up in a bright, white light slicing in the window, but he could feel the damp cold of a fresh snow breathing through the cinderblocks walls. He sat up, remembering details of the night before. What had the town men done? What had his father done?

It wasn't for him to know but he wanted to ask. He grabbed his towel from a hook and scuffed to the foot of the steps. He took them two at a time, headed to the store's toilet at the top of the stairs. He bristled with anticipation. On Sunday, he was allowed to speak to the other parishioners. Being observant, he was aware that he was different. It wasn't just their clothes; it was the way they communicated so easily with each other, the laughter and easy smiles. It was that they showed an interest in him. He *loved* Sundays.

And usually, afterward, his father would explain through old Bible stories the present workaday sins of neighbors and man and wife sins. There were sins about stealing, cheating, eating and having babies. This last one always brought the greatest emotion from his father and the boy was in awe of his knowledge of the Lord and His intentions. Why, he figured there wasn't a priest alive who could interpret the Word of the Lord better than his father. Especially not the fat toad of a man who led the congregation.

The only annoyance was a woman at the church. She was short and square, her heavy forehead creased with wrinkles.

The Grist Mill Bone

Her eyes peered out from under her brow like some Injun's stare, following him wherever he stood. Sometimes, she came late and sat in the back row behind him and he felt her watching, judging him…and his father. He wanted to ask his father about her but instinctively knew that if he did, he could spoil his blessed Sunday. So he didn't ask. He watched.

*****

5 HOME

Booker Solomon walked through the new front door of his rickety, creek front farmhouse and congratulated himself on his recent handiwork: how quiet and smooth the door swept on its new hinges. He had come to enjoy these little renovation projects. Home for a long weekend, he intended to finish the job with a coat of geranium red paint.

He dumped his leather duffle at the foot of the stairs and checked the accumulated mail of the last three days. It was quiet inside, no sign of Claire or Sam, his stepson. Oddly, not even the dog, Compass, came to greet him.

Walking to a closet under the stairs in the dining room, he unlocked the door revealing a built-in safe. He turned the combination back and forth to swing open the heavy door, revealing a disassembled AR-15 and his sniper rifle. Removing his pistol from his shoulder holster, he deposited it in the safe, spun the lock and shut the closet door against the prying eyes of teenagers. Claire hated having guns in the house and had argued with him incessantly until one day she finally agreed that his system was foolproof. Booker jiggled the doorknob and decided it was his turn to relax. After his long commute across the Chesapeake Bay Bridge in torrential rain, he heeded the call of a cold beer and ambled into the kitchen.

Tossing the screw top in recycle, Booker paused at the window above the old porcelain sink, trying to suppress his annoyance. Breakfast and dinner dishes were piled up as if Claire and Sam had left in a hurry. Well, he thought, Rosa, hasn't shown up either. Just more evidence of how spoiled Sam was. He sighed and decided the evening would include a talk with his stepson.

He gazed out over the black waters of the creek. High winds had pushed the rain off shore leaving clouds that neared the color of stout. Rolling white caps and rippling sawgrass churned below. He took a long gulp and felt something grating on his last raw nerve. Watching the force of water tear a clump of wetland mussels from their roots, Booker rested his beer on the counter.

He tilted his head upward, hearing voices in Sam's bedroom... low, indistinct. Claire's car wasn't parked on the rear drive. Listening closer, he caught a deep baritone—Little John, Trixie's 17-year old foster kid from the trailer park was upstairs. Booker grew hot around the ears.

Stepping softly to the dining room he pulled open the buffet drawer. Empty. He stroked his chin whiskers and rubbed his hand over his baldhead. Two strikes: company in the house while no adult was home and his laptop had been swiped.

Something was always missing these days. Booker had realized halfway to D.C. that he should've taken the laptop with him or locked it in the safe. A month ago, he'd noticed a Swiss army knife gone. Then his favorite fishing lure and an old depth finder off the boat disappeared. At the time, he ignored these small crimes thinking—hell no—hadn't Sam learned better 'n that?

But soon Booker's distraction with his new job working for Tosh across the bridge had proved too seductive and the missing items skipped his mind. He questioned Sam but the kid played dumb. After dinner one night, he repeated, "That laptop is off limits. Fo' real, boy."

Booker pressed his lips together and swept his hand inside the drawer. If there was one thing he hated, it was coming in from work and having to investigate in his own home. Over the last four years he had been diligent in tending to the kid's goddamn needs and this was how he was repaid.

He padded up that staircase, avoiding the creaky spot on the loose stair tread. At the door to Sam's room he watched their faces lit from the computer screen—absorbed… unaware of him leaning on the doorjamb. "What're you guys studying so hard? Not homework."

His laptop shut with a snap. Sam's freckled face drained of blood and Booker relaxed, nonchalant against the frame.

"Uh, when did you get home?"

"Better question: when did *you* get home? I was looking for that. It's supposed to be in the buffet drawer." He could see the boy's mind racing as his steely eyes wavered ever so slightly.

"Oh, we had a half day at school. I have research to do on how family DNA is passed down through generations."

Booker took a step in, keeping things calm, friendly. The boys had straightened up and appeared to be hiding something behind them. Little John—nothing little about his gangly shoulders and soft midsection—scooted to the edge of the bed. His jeans rode up revealing dirty sweat socks. The curtains were open and the window was up. Raindrops had splashed on Sam's desk. The room was slimy with heat. Amazed, Booker wondered why they hadn't heard his truck tires on the oyster shells outside.

Man, he thought, they were in the zone. He flipped the light switch and Sam squinted every so slightly, adjusting to the change. "What's the matter with your computer? You trying to soak it?" Sitting on the kid's desk in front of the window, the blank monitor taunted Sam with his own lies. Booker strode over and slammed the window shut. He waited, looking at the boys.

"Booker," Sam said, "you got too many parental controls on it so I can't find out about telomeres."

"Uh-huh." He shot Sam the side eye. Still, he was always amazed at the agility of the kid's mind.

Sam scanned his stepfather's face and met his stare. The boy's shoulders slumped and he looked down at the closed laptop. At 13, he was old enough to barrel his way through an argument, even if he didn't make a lot of sense. But this time, Booker could see his agitation get the better of him as he scratched his head and tossed his hair out of his face.

Meantime, Little John was so threatened he moved off the bed and sidled against the wall toward the door. Booker blocked his way. Pretending he didn't notice, Little John put his hand out as if he could move Booker's hulk aside like some ninja white boy with a super power.

"Where you think you're going?" asked Booker.

"I...I gotta get home. Trixie wanted me to dig out the vegetable garden."

"In the rain? Now you're a farmer. Or just a gardener?"

John winced. Booker bent within inches of his face. Nothin' but a delinquent 17-year old hanging out with a middle school kid. Trixie screamed herself hoarse every time she asked him for help. But there was more to this. John's usual butt-swag was missing. Real gentle like, Booker grabbed the front of Little John's Tshirt. "All you're growing is light fingered, man. You keep your fins off my stuff, you hear? I'll be talking to Trixie."

Fat lot of good that would do, Booker thought. He ran his eyes over John's face; his patchy chin hair, his pockmarked cheeks, and a Neanderthal brow. The kid had Skittle breath but there was a trace of fear in his muddy eyes. Trixie was too busy with her younger foster kids to deal with him. It was no account anyway because Booker didn't have anything on him except the suspicion of a stolen fishing lure and an old GPS.

Maybe it was time to talk to Claire even though he knew she'd get all het up. It had been four years since her father's death and Sam's kidnapping but she lived in fear of the unknown every day of her life, giving up immigration law to write wills and testaments for those with one foot in the grave. No, this kind of news would only derail her. Booker decided to deal with Sam himself and talk to his wife later. "Go on home," he said to John. "And tell Trixie to expect a call from me." He gave the boy a shove out the door and turned around to see Sam stuffing something under his bed pillow.

"What you got there, Sam?"

"Nothing."

Booker threw one hand out and stepped over to the bed.

A deep crease developed between Sam's eyebrows and he responded, "Come on. Just don't ask this time, Booker. John left something and I'll give it back tomorrow. I won't even look at it. Promise."

"You mean you didn't get to see what it is? Well, that's no good. Let's have a look together."

"NO, NO, Booker! I mean, I don't want to. You're gonna tell Mom and then it'll be really bad. She'll freak out." Sam's eyes filled but stopped short of spilling.

Booker knew he had him and didn't feel an ounce of sympathy. The kid needed a strong hand, unlike his mother's. "I'll tell you what. I won't share it with your mom if you show me. You're going to get interrogated by one of us and wouldn't you rather it was me?"

Sam leaned over his pillow, one hand beneath it. He sighed. He squeezed his eyes shut. He clutched the laptop like it was a love letter.

God Almighty, thought Booker. It had been a long time since he had seen so much teenage drama. Maybe, he thought, I should take pity on the kid.

Resigned, Sam slapped a small, brown cardboard box into his stepfather's hand. *Zoya,* was printed in elaborate script across its lid in gold letters. Booker opened it and was surprised by a red plastic cylinder stamped with a tiny picture of a blonde haired, black eyed woman, her outlandishly long legs spread, revealing the secret every adolescent boy wanted to discover. He felt his forehead compress in a layer of worry wrinkles. He opened the tube revealing a soft, pink plastic vagina.

"John's using sex toys?" he shouted. What the hell was the matter with that kid? What red-blooded male needed a pocket pussy at 17? He thought back. At the same age, he was poring over his dad's magazines. Curiosity? Sure, but sex toys were expensive. John could never afford to purchase one.

Words tumbled out of Sam's mouth like marbles from a jar. "He said it's Lloyd's, you know—Trixie's boyfriend? John stole it from him and wanted me to look it up online. But we never got to a site. Honest. I don't even know how it works."

"It's rosey palm's expensive sister. That's how it works." Booker slammed the top on the box, and with his nose two inches from Sam's, yelled, "You aren't ever to use my laptop without my permission."

"Oh, god, oh god," moaned Sam as he threw himself face down on the bed, his arms splayed out. "Don't tell her. Don't. Please."

Booker decided to lay it on thick, grind the accusation into his stepson's memory forever, "You weren't going to use it were you?"

"No! I wouldn't. Not ever. I was just wondering… It was stupid. Please don't tell Mom."

"Well, that's good 'cause no family DNA will ever get passed down using one of these. Plus, if it really belongs to Lloyd, your dick could fall off."

Sam sobbed. "Gross, Booker. That's gross. Don't say anymore."

"Okay. I won't say anything to your mom but listen here," he grinned. "Rosa didn't come today and you left dishes in the sink. Compass is nowhere to be found. I'll give you two seconds to get your lazy butt downstairs and take care of your responsibilities before this gets any worse."

He picked up his laptop and turned to leave Sam in his misery. At the door, Booker paused, putting a hand on the kid's dresser where Claire had left a small shrine to his childhood. A teddy bear sat slumped beneath a soccer lamp. He grabbed the stuffed animal and tossed it onto the bed next to his stepson. "Here, cry in your beer. Oh, sorry. I meant bear."

***

Sotweed

"Young man, what you think you're doing here? I told you to stay home." Stern-faced, Theodore Vickers dragged Davis into the shadows of a giant holly tree outside the town's Baptist Church. He threw his cigarette on the sidewalk and ground it out with his heel. The funeral for Calvert

Gordon was about to begin with mourners and sightseers, both black and white, crawling all over the church's concrete steps. Sometimes it took death to bring people together, thought Theodore.

The Baptist Church was hosting the funeral, even though Calvert's estranged wife and four daughters were practicing Catholics. Theodore had attended Father Ingle's funeral the day before at the Methodist Church and hadn't seen near the turnout as today. Aggravated with the community response, and the way national TV had turned Calvert into a martyr for trying to save the priest, the ensuing call for harmony and forgiveness had rode hard on Theodore. He had come to see this sideshow for himself. Sure enough, folks were dressed in their Sunday finest, ladies with matching handbags and shoes, men in their best fedoras and wool overcoats and everybody rushing to get the best seat in the house.

Theodore had caught a glimpse of his old friend, Buddy Carter, a reporter from *The Dorchester Banner*. He watched as the newsman approached a teen who tried to mix with the mob entering the church. His brown overalls and red buffalo plaid hunting jacket stood out against the better dressed and caught Theodore's eye. He cursed under his breath realizing it was his son. Charging down the steps just as the reporter singled the kid out, Theodore jerked his kid away as Buddy licked the nub of his pencil and asked the boy's name. He was scribbling "Davis" on a notepad when Theodore grabbed it from him and tore off the top sheet of paper.

"Buddy. Long time no see. You interviewing minors now? What's the matter—you afraid the upstanding citizens of Cambridge not gonna give you the straight scoop?"

"Ted. How're you doing? This your son?"

"Uh-huh. And I'm afraid he's off limits. My boy's got a stutter and it might take you a long time to squeeze anything outta him. You don't want to miss the goings on inside."

Buddy Carter thanked his old friend warily and continued up the steps.

Theodore dragged his son down the remaining steps and around a corner of the church. "Chill a little, Pa," the boy whined. "Ever'body's here. I wanna see this looney tune get buried."

"Ain't none yer business. Get home or I promise you'll see the tanned side of my belt later."

"Shit," said his son brazenly. "I know'd damn good and well why you here. You just trying to cover your tracks."

Theodore was surprised and angered by this challenge from his only child and looked around to see if anyone had heard. But no one paid them any mind, so Theodore shoved his son against the cold brick behind a large holly tree, gripping him just below his Adam's apple. "You don't know nothin' and no one's gonna believe you, no how. You keep your mouth shut. Why, half the neighborhood help us burn that wino's camp so you say anything and you gonna incriminate us all. Why you think they all showing up today? It ain't 'cause they suddenly got love o' their fellow man. It's guilt." He squeezed his fingers a little harder. "Now get on home." Theodore waited until he saw fear change to resignation in the boy's eyes and he slowly loosened his grip.

Davis rubbed his throat and crumpled, coughing. His

father sniggered as he kicked his son in his kidney, hissing in his ear, "Get outta here, girl, afore I have to ask you in public why you wet your pants."

The boy winced and over his shoulder stole a glance at his father, croaking out, "Yes, sir. I'll be in the backroom finishing up that stocking job." He stumbled briefly, his hands cupping his wetness, then sped toward his father's broken down hardware store, all the while wiping spittle from his mouth.

"Good choice," called Theodore. "I'll see yer at dinner." With that, the old man removed his felt hat and entered the church. It was crowded inside and in the darkness he made out a black face above a white shirt collar. A hand extended a program in the dead man's honor. Theodore ignored it and took a position in the last row, remarking to himself that the heathen Baptists had no kneelers and no pews, just chairs. They couldn't help themselves, he reasoned, for they weren't God's chosen people.

A diocesan priest in black vestments stood next to the Baptist preacher at the altar that was really just a simple table, not marble like the one at St. Aloysius. The cross was a huge oak piece, sanded and shellacked, and bare of Christ's figure. *Another strike against them,* thought Theodore. *How can the masses worship without a reminder of the Savior's suffering? More whitewashing of pain and meaning. Why, everyday the sinner needed to be reminded of their sin.* It wasn't that he took Christ's message to love thy neighbor as thyself so to heart, but there was a right way and a wrong way to do things. He muttered something to himself about a circus when he heard the priest introduce Calvert Gordon's wife and daughters to the assembled.

The little girls made their way in stair step formation down the center aisle clustered around their mother. They wore matching blue velvet dresses with Peter Pan collars as if they weren't hurting for money. The wife had on a wool coat and a flapper hat like one Theodore's grandmother used to wear. *These black toads recycle hats,* he thought, *'cause they sure seemed like they each own a haberdashery. Trying to look like the Queen of England.* He could tell the good Catholic women because they all wore a lace mantilla to cover their hair. The ones who came unprepared had bobby pinned in a Kleenex. No, Calvert's wife couldn't have been a devoted Christian woman and here was God and the world, ready to give her recognition.

He was about ready to leave when Velma took the seat next to him.

"Why'd you come today? Thought you hated Calvert," she asked.

"Like you two were best friends? Get over yourself, Velma. Don't play high and mighty with me."

"The police are investigating. They interviewed me yesterday. I said I didn't know nothing about his stuff getting burned. I was at the church all afternoon."

"I heard. Nobody's gonna talk. It don't matter anyway. Burning his belongings don't correlate with the church burning."

"I don't know, Theodore. They said they found a half-used can of kerosene behind the Rexall look just the same as the one in the church fire. You 'bout the only one who sells kerosene in town."

"In town. They sell it at the center outta town. Nobody burned down that church and the priest in it."

"You'll see. They asked me if you and Father were friends."

Velma's boney forehead creased up giving Theodore a vague uneasy feeling. Her eyes were beady and bloodshot, like she'd been crying. He didn't like her breath. Smelled like onion—how he remembered his wife. They had all been friends at one time. Too good of friends and it led to trouble. He didn't believe in friendship and had cultivated associates who followed his lead. His mind scattered and stopped at a certain thought: the check he had written the church the day of the fire. He wondered if it was still in the poor box.

"I'm leaving," he whispered. On the altar, the priest said, "I confess to Almighty God and to you, my brothers and sisters that I have greatly sinned in my thoughts and in my words..." Abruptly Theodore stood and squeezed in front of Velma, pausing to place a heavy hand on her shoulder. "You knew what we were up to that day. Be smart." He bolted through the front doors and down the steps.

At the yellow tape surrounding the rear sacristy entrance to St. Aloysius, Theodore caught his breath, his chest heaving from his flight down Race Street. Nearby, a light gust of wind played with the dried leaves of a pin oak, as if someone was crumpling paper in his ear. Theodore had to get that check out of the poor box at the front door. It would be easy to get inside since the entire back of the church was a hollowed, charred shell. He folded his considerable length in half and sidestepped under the police tape, ignoring the Do Not Enter signs. Climbing over the piles of rubble and detritus, he grabbed the frame of the door and swung himself up and over the foundation. Crouching so no one would see, Theodore scurried toward the pews and down the center aisle. The sun shone brightly through the beveled glass windows, fracturing the light against Theodore's cheek. He was sweating profusely and his vision was disjointed.

Reaching the narthex, he found the metal poor box bolted to the floor in the perfect spot for kindly contributors to toss their change and bills into its generous slot. He stared at its brass markings, its square corners and molded lid that was screwed into the base. A saint's name was raised in gold lettering on its ornate surface. It was as secure as a bank vault.

Theodore owned a hardware store, full of every kind of tool imaginable and in his hurry, had not anticipated the need for one of them. He grasped the sides of the box and pulled, hoping to yank it off its metal base. He grunted and bent at the knees and pulled from his center to no avail. He gripped the box and try as he might, he attempted to wield it back and forth. A desperate yelp escaped his lips and in frustration, he slipped his index finger into the slot. Paper. He felt the edge of a piece of paper, taunting him, ready to slip back out of the poor box in a reverse donation. "Please, God," he uttered. "Please."

Theodore slipped his middle finger into the slot easily to the first joint and stopped. His heart was beating wildly and he felt cold, yet sweat rolled down his grizzled cheek and dripped onto the poor box. He trembled in desperation and felt the urge to take a shit and squeezed his buttocks quickly. An ache crept up his left arm and he began to drool. A loud *ahwhaaa, ahwhaaa, ahwhaaa* swirled in his ears and in a last attempt to seize his check, Theodore shoved his fingers into the slot violently, knowing the skin would be ripped to shreds as he pulled them out. But he never had the chance.

A crushing pain enveloped his chest and Theodore stumbled forward, slumping across the poor box with his hand wedged underneath his body, his fingertips lodged in the slot.

The police were summoned for the second time to St. Aloysius in the space of one week, this time on the call of the same neighbors who had noticed the fire that had killed the good Father Ingle and his homeless savior, Calvert Gordon. In the glaring light of a stark winter sun reaching its apex of the day, they spied someone surreptitiously climbing about the ruins of the sacristy door and disappearing inside. When the beat officers arrived at the interior narthex doors they stopped in surprise at the slice of white light cast from the leaded glass window above the double front doors. It fell across the figure of a dead Theodore Vickers, draped over church's poor box engraved with the words, "Saint Labre, Patron Saint of the Homeless."

***

The Cellar

Days had gone by since the boy had seen his father or had any food. The first night, he had raided the candy bars at the register upstairs and found half a dried up bologna sandwich in his father's cubbyhole office. Last night, he had ventured out and searched the shoe store's trash bin next door. That had proved successful and he sat on his mattress thinking he should clean up the mess before his father showed up.

Davis rubbed his curly mass of hair. He was worried. His father had never left him or the hardware store for so many days. He had started counting too late, but he estimated that the sun had set four times. He wondered if there had been trouble from the night the church burned. He wondered if the jigaboos had killed his dad. He looked at the clock. It was eight, and yellow sunlight streamed in his square of basement window. He decided if his father didn't come by the end of the workday, he would go out into the world. He would find his way.

He heard the front door swing wide and the heavy clump-clump of boots overhead. Voices, none he knew, spoke quietly. They were searching.

"We've already been to the house, Father Chilcott. No evidence a kid ever lived there. Bunch of Vickers' tools and some writings—some racist rambling—but no kid. Velma Owens notified us. Said there was a teenager."

"You drove out there and got nothing? I'm sure you have more to do investigating the church than dealing with rumors about Vickers. I never saw the kid, but we heard from a number of parishioners that Theodore had a child. I just hope he didn't run away. Some folk say he was a little strange, not very good socially."

"Uh-huh. We got that too over at the station. Sounds like people are concerned and right they should be. It's colder than a witch's tit outside." There was a pause, then, "Sorry, Father. Why, the kid didn't even get to see his father be put in the ground."

In the ground? Davis jumped up and began cleaning up his trash, stuffing it all under the workbench. Was his father gone? He panicked and flapped his arms and hearing, "Ghya, ghya," slip from his mouth over and over, he knew he would be heard above but couldn't do anything to stop himself. There were footsteps on the stairs. He saw trousers, and a hand on the bannister. A black clad figure bent below the ceiling and a man's kindly face looked at him, surprised.

"Hello, there. I'm Father Chilcott. I knew your dad. I think I've met you before. Is your name Davis?"

"Ghya, ghya," said Davis as he backed into a corner by his mattress.

"It's okay. This is Officer Trumbull. We've come to help you, Davis."

They continued to the bottom of the steps and stood staring at him from a distance. Davis sat down abruptly, his legs crossed and he rocked muttering, "Ghya, ghya, ghya."

"Son, we're going to take you someplace warm and get you some food. Would you like to come with us? I promise we won't hurt you," said the priest.

Davis didn't remember him. He rolled his eyes and

The Grist Mill Bone

groaned, but as he spit on the floor, he was able to gain control. He crawled to his knees and reached out. "My—my father wants me. I have to finish the framework. He has special bones he's saved. I have to finish it."

The priest and the police officer looked at one another like they held a secret but nodded to him again. "Of course, you do. And we'll make sure that you get to finish it. Your dad will be so proud," said Trumbull. "In the meantime, though, why don't you come with us and get a hot bowl of soup and a nice warm shower. It's so cold down here."

"It make me closer to God in heaven. Am I going to see him?"

"Who, son? Who do you want to see? God?" asked the priest.

Davis stood up and walked over to him and police officer. He studied them closely and liking what he saw—there were no quick movements, only smiles and nods—he decided he could tell them. "Yes, I want to see God. He lives with my father. Will you take me?"

The priest looked at the officer who winked, saying, "Theodore? Sure, your dad has a direct line to God. Least that's what he always told us at the station. You come on up the steps now and we'll find them both. God and your dad and you can have some soup with them."

So on the morning of the fifth day, Davis followed the two men, one in a police uniform and the other in a black cassock, out into the light of day. He rubbed his eyes and squinted. There were cars parked everywhere along the street, something he never saw on a Sunday and people bustled about, bundled in winter coats. They spoke to the men who accompanied him but frowned slightly at the sight of him. He wondered if he looked that different and realized he didn't have on his Sunday best. As he stepped into the back of the patrol car, he looked at his hand that rested on the seat. He had fingers that were long like the rest of his body with dirty nails bitten down to the quick. They were working fingers, creative, maybe even artistic. A cold breeze ruffled his long hair from the open door and he looked up at the priest. Would he be allowed to assemble his frameworks in the light of day? He felt assured. This was change and it was good.

"Watch your head, Davis. Lift your boot inside the car and we'll take good care of you," said the priest, "We know someone, a nice lady, who wants to meet you."

*****

6 CLAIRE

If it was an accident on Old Mill Bridge, it didn't look like it. Police cars littered the intersection like a child's accidental spill of Tonka trucks while two uniformed state officers directed everyone away. I rubbernecked the best I could. A SWAT vehicle blocked the entrance to the road. Gripping the steering wheel, I slowed to a crawl as memories of Sam's kidnapping flooded back. There had been a rash of home invasions lately in addition to those grisly murders, even in broad daylight. My chest tightened and my mind wrapped around that horrible thought. Odessa, the grande dame of the community, had grown frail over the last four years. Although widely known in the community as living independently on her own, most folks knew that Booker and I lived on the property a stone's throw away. But that wouldn't matter to an addict bent on thievery.

A siren blipped and I watched a stern policemen mouth, *Move on*, and I snapped back to the road and getting home. I passed down the main road and turned into the trailer park.

One after another, the single and doublewide mobiles stared back at me blankly as if to yawn at my arrival. It was nearing three-thirty and after all that rain the neighborhood was quiet. Retirees were either napping on their canal side decks or leaving to nosh on free food at beach bar happy hours. Even the foster kids at Trixie's were inside, probably watching cartoons.

My tires crunched across the oyster shells signaling home. Behind the house I could see the afternoon sun flicker golden red on Compass' long, bushy coat. A circle of turkey buzzards flew overhead. My golden retriever was nosing around in the marsh grass at the edge of the creek, probably rooting out a dead field mouse.

I let loose a string of curses. Up to his haunches in muck, I figured Sam had forgotten and left him out. He's supposed to walk the dog on a leash when he gets home from school but the computer has become his constant distraction. Apparently combating monsters in the underworld of Dark Souls, some enigmatic role play game, is far more attractive than taking care of Compass who's known to roam and get into trouble. If someone asked, I'd say that dog is part swine the way he throws his food all over the floor inside and rolls in the mud outside.

When I hollered for him, Compass' big blocky head rose on alert but the rest of him didn't move. He's a stubborn animal. He looked me straight in the eye as if to taunt, then simply fell on his back and wiggled, coating himself in stinky mud, his paws pushing upward in the air.

I stepped from the car, leaving my purse, briefcase, and

jacket, then paused on second thought to fold my skirt on top of the pile in the driver's seat. I stepped out of my heels and tiptoed through the mud in a crepe blouse and underwear, looking around in embarrassment at the Gronski's house trailer an acre away. Our closest neighbors, they were busybodies, always reporting whatever they saw on our private property down their street till the story came to loyal Trixie who sliced and diced it like a Ginsu warrior. No one was outside but that didn't mean Mr. Gronski wasn't standing at the window with his binoculars. "Bird watching," he always says, like the black man and the white woman are new kinds of plumage together.

The downpour had been so heavy that I was up to my shins in stinky muck the nearer I came to water's edge. A trickle of sweat ran down my cheek and I wondered how the punishing humidity could return so quickly. The rank odor of a dead animal, probably a deer, filled my nostrils and I yelled bloody murder, grabbing Compass by the collar. It wasn't the first time he felt compelled to roll in rancid smells. He looked up at me wild-eyed but I think he was secretly snickering.

"Bad dog, Compass! Get in the house, now!" He scampered off, a blackened golden, his tail tucked low to the ground. As I turned to follow, I noticed a muddy black trash bag, half inflated from the wind, bobbing at the edge of the grasses. I hate plastic floating in the creek as much as the guns everyone buys around here. My feet squished-squished through the grasses as I squinted in the sunlight, shielding my eyes from the glare. I put my hand to my nose. Drawing near, I realized it wasn't trash. The smell of rotting flesh overcame me and I began to gag.

I screamed, my hand clamped over my mouth, but trying to gulp fresh air. "Oh, my God."

I heard the screen door slam. "Claire. What is it?" shouted Booker from the house.

"It's—it's a body. Booker, come quick! Someone's floating out here in the creek."

He ran and grabbed me from behind swinging me around. "Don't look at it!"

"Stop, stop." I yelled, pushing his hands away and turned to run for my car. "I'm calling the police." But Booker was punching numbers before I made it more than a few steps through the mud. It sucked at me and my sense of justice, of righting wrongs, and I grew frustrated thinking that I should be in charge. But my body, or the muck, was my enemy.

"Yeah, this is Booker Solomon. 714 Old Mill Bridge Road. The state police are at the entrance to my property right now. Send them up the driveway past the main house to the old farmhouse by the creek, ... we found a body in the water."

Shaking, I gathered my clothes from the car and dressed, deciding not to put on my shoes over muddy feet. I wasn't going to allow myself to become the 'little woman.' Not that Booker would treat me like that. It was an old haunt of mine, leftover from growing up with a father who defined my life. Gulping air, I composed myself and watched as Booker walked up from the creek. He stood next to me and looked me over.

"You okay?" he asked.

"Of course I am. I've seen worse," I answered wondering if I really had. I was desperate to be in charge, to feel a sense of control, at least of myself. It wasn't but a few minutes before a dark blue, unmarked SUV broke through the stand of beech trees and careered toward the farmhouse. It came to an abrupt stop as a man in street clothes burst from the truck with the confidence of a seasoned investigator. He introduced himself, "Detective Showell from the Georgetown barracks." He took in the floating body and promptly called in backup.

Holding the phone away from his ear, he asked, "Mr. Solomon, there's another matter near your driveway on Old Mill Bridge that's going to need your attention. The head of forensics is on site and she's coming this way."

"You're going to have an audience from the trailer park," Booker said, nodding to our neighbors. "They're a curious bunch."

The police made quick work of it. A small woman wearing a white Tyvek snowsuit and booties picked her way over to us in the wet grass. She pushed her white hood off her wispy brown hair. Beads of sweat had formed on her upper lip and her hair was soaked. Looking at us myopically through horn-rimmed glasses, it appeared that she was struggling to focus. She ran her bulging eyes over Booker's face and finally settled on his chin whiskers.

"Mr. Solomon? Nice to meet you. I'm Natalie Messick, Delaware State forensics. Can you tell me what happened?"

"I can," I interjected. "There's not much to say except our dog found it. I was chasing him out of the mud when I saw the body. Booker called it in and the rest, you already know."

She nodded and struck up a conversation with Booker. Detective Showell had walked into the high reeds to get a closer look at the body. A rescue squad and four state police cars filled up the back drive by the porch. I scanned the scene, suddenly aware that I was one piece of the bigger picture: just a small town attorney with a big time degree thinking I mattered amidst this havoc, my bare legs evidence I was unprepared. Compass waited at the screen door, anxious and wiggling for attention. Only the dog needed me. I opened the creaky porch door and as I sat down on the glider, he climbed up beside me, mud and all. We rocked together for comfort.

The back up team poled the body onto land. I couldn't watch them fish for it, yet my eyes were drawn to the grisly scene. From a distance, I could tell it was bloated and gray, the skin spongy and that of a black man. I wondered if he was homeless. As they dumped it into a body bag and lifted it onto a gurney, I caught a glimpse of its mangled form. They zipped the bag and the forensics team pushed, but the gurney stuck in the waterlogged grass. The bag rolled, almost falling off when a young trooper took charge and lifting the front of the stretcher, he dragged it behind him. The white suits strapped the body bag, reverently conscious of their task. My stomach lurched unable to take it any longer and I pushed open the porch door to throw up in the azaleas. I thought I was stronger but maybe I wasn't. Maybe, I thought, the baby was talking to me.

"Claire, I got this covered. Go inside to the air conditioning," said Booker. I hadn't seen him lurking so close, watching me.

Booker was right. It was a matter of details, of the professionals doing their job. I nodded to him and smiled weakly. As a crowd from the trailer park had collected on the driveway, a trooper walked the property line, his arms spread, warning them to stand back.

Leaving my muddy dog on the porch, I was resigned to escape when I overheard Detective Showell say, "Mr. Solomon, I'm going to finish up here on the creek. Would you mind heading over to your entrance on Old Mill Bridge to meet with the other team? Messick wants to show you that that site."

***

ODESSA

Booker left Claire sleepy eyed in bed and ready for a before-dinner-nap. He wished he could rid himself of the dead man in his head. Things turned up in the creek after a storm all the time, but never a body. After Hurricane Sandy dumped five days of rain, he had fished out 2X4's, plastic storage sheds, tiki torches and even a couch that floated by when the skies cleared. But this afternoon had left him shaken. Not that he had never seen a dead body before, or even a headless one, but that it was floating so close to home. He wished he could crawl in with Claire.

After his three days away, she appeared tired and out of sorts lying curled up in the bed. She smiled up at him, her hair spread across the pillow.

"What's with the bleed in your eye, Woman?" he asked.

"It's nothing. Stayed up too late reading. You better get to your mom's."

He kissed her, turned the window air conditioner on high to shake the humidity from the room and hoped its thrum would mask the house noise. The farmhouse was 120 years old and the upstairs was tight; three rooms, one shared bathroom. Claire was a light sleeper and for some reason he could never figure out, she dug her heels in about staying in the farmhouse. He shut the bedroom door and went downstairs to the porch.

Compass was covered in dried mud, and Booker gave him a stern look, saying, "Dog, you make some kinda trouble and you don't even know it. Come on, we're going for a ride." Together, they walked away from the backyard commotion around to his truck at the front door.

The dog bounced into the bed of the pickup and Booker slammed the lift gate shut. He thanked his ever-loving God that Sam hadn't been at the house and wondered where the kid had gone.

His Ma's house was minutes away up the shared drive through the stand of beech trees, a fact that had sometimes driven him crazy. He knew what would greet him. Her afternoons and evenings were consumed by talk television and game shows. Daily, his mom sat in her family room, the stars' best fan spouting game show answers.

Her proximity was not his worry today: it was the police—their proximity, their nosiness. And if they had disrupted her routine, there would be hell to pay.

He parked below the back deck of his mother's home.

The Grist Mill Bone

Compass barked and Booker uttered a single command as he walked up the hillside. The dog bounded to his side and standing perfectly still they looked out over the water. Every blade of grass in front of the creek was Solomon property, all 183 acres stretching in a triangle to Old Mill Bridge.

He would miss waking to this, miss the smell of a sea breeze, the quacking mallards and raucous seagulls. Mostly, he would miss his family heritage. He turned to climb the stairs to the low-slung glass and wood contemporary. Behind it was the roofline of the two and half story barn, a cathedral to veterinary care, where Booker's dad, the only large animal vet in Sussex County, had conducted business. This had been their last project together, built in their spare time, a new home for the Solomon family some twenty-five years ago when he was young and wet behind the ears.

These acres had seen it all: his return from the Middle East as an Army Ranger, his construction career, his sport fishing, and finally it had provided cover while he worked the Maryland shore as a detective. Compass looked up at him, a prescient gaze as if the dog knew change was imminent. Booker pushed the sliding glass door open. The television was on but he heard voices in the hall.

"Ma, what you having for dinner?"

Booker blinked as his eyes adjusted to Odessa's inner sanctum. He heard a male voice at the front door and could smell spicy greens simmering nearby on the stove. He swallowed thinking they were the perfect accompaniment to chicken and onions. He bet she had made his favorite dinner for his return from Washington.

"Who's here?" he asked with growing suspicion. Showell had promised that Messick would be at the investigative site waiting for his arrival, not inside his mother's house.

"Excuse my son, officer. Sometimes he forgets his manners. Booker, come here. It's the state police."

Two figures stood outlined by the afternoon sun in the open door. Overshadowed by the dark hulk of a uniformed officer in blue, campaign hat in hand, stood his Ma bent and bird-like. Booker took the hall in three steps.

"Mr. Solomon. I'm Officer Beavens with the Delaware State Police, Georgetown."

The trooper stuck out his hand and Booker looked but didn't extend his. The kid looked him up and down, his lip curling slightly, inspecting the black man as if he smelled dirt. Under Booker's stare, the boy's eyes fell to his hat, shielding his expression. Did he realize he had exposed too much? *Beavens,* thought Booker. *This one's a complete unknown.*

"If you don't want to come, I can always ask Mrs. Solomon, here," said Beavens. "I'm sure you'd be of assistance, wouldn't you, Mrs. Solomon?"

"You can leave my mother out of this, Officer Beavens," said Booker and his ma patted his forearm.

In his time working undercover for Maryland, Booker made it a practice to get the names of area cops working the Delaware side of the state line so he could commit them to memory. He had to balance the scales, knowing when he needed local help or more often, when he wanted them to butt out. And while the Solomon name had earned a guarded respect as landowners, Delaware state police never recognized him when he was disguised in dreads, hoodies and tats. Retired for four years, Booker could feel his game coming on. This boy looked like a new recruit, fresh off the college football field. *The younger the cop*, he thought, *the greater their risk of error.*

"Did you call in the FBI?" he asked.

"This is a local matter," answered the trooper.

"Huh. Seems like you'd want the Feds in with this string of murders."

"We have no evidence about a murder, but it is on your property. They're just bones." said Beavens.

"Uh-huh. Just left Showel with a much bigger problem over on the creek."

"Yes, I heard. We need you to come to the area we've cordoned off."

It wasn't a question this time. Get in a cop car with some pushy wannabe trooper? He didn't think so. "Well I don't know, Officer Beavens. You sure? Our property is a triangle next to a tract that belongs to the electric company. Could be on the utility's property."

"We have the plat. It's your property. We haven't determined if it's an actual crime that was committed on the spot but it appears those are human bones by your driveway entrance."

"You're leading this investigation?

"No. We got a detective from the day shift and Messick from the forensic unit just showed back up."

Booker took his keys from his pocket and put his arm

around his mother. "Ma, I'll be right back. You go on and watch your show."

He followed the squad car ticking off the possibilities. Could they have mistaken a deer leg? Was it a dog's cache? Had someone set him up? He had put some sketchy criminals away in Maryland during his time and had held a nagging worry over the years that one would come back to haunt him.

Hell, thought Booker, he had a nagging feeling about the attitudes of *officers* on both sides of the state line. But he had never made an enemy in the Delaware major crimes unit, … except, one name came to mind—Lowery.

He wondered if this young punk, Beavens, knew his history as Maryland undercover, but he suspected the boy thought he had some country nigger on his hands that he could push around. Irritated at how his day had gone, he decided things couldn't get much worse. The officer was young but he deserved respect until he didn't. The kid hit his brake lights, parking behind a line of police SUVs along the edge of road and Booker pulled in behind him. They got out, slamming their doors in unison.

A portly man dressed in an ill-fitting black suit greeted him by name. "If it isn't Wonderboy Solomon."

Booker smiled at his own bad luck. "Detective Lowery. You haven't hit retirement yet?" he asked, sticking his hands in his pockets before they gave him away. "I thought after the last case on the creek brought you so much fame you would've given this up for full-time fishing."

The man's gut protruded over his belt and his hair was combed in threads over his reddened scalp, but it was the same Lowery who had worked Sam's kidnapping, just older and possibly more cynical from the look on his face.

"Your black ass and my paycheck, Solomon. At least you can assist on this one instead of obstructing justice like you did the last time."

"My honor to help the men in blue," said Booker.

"You lying piece of shit," said Lowery.

A shout came from a cluster of forensics in white jumpsuits. "We're ready, Detective. Can you come over here?"

Lowery grabbed Booker's bicep. "You still working for Maryland State, boy?"

Booker squinted at him. He could take exception to being called "boy" and hold the proceedings up or ignore the old bastard. "I left four years ago."

Lowery snickered and nodded. "So you getting your cushy government contracts as the only black builder on the shore. Huh. I thought all that funny money dried up in the recession."

"You know as much about government contracts as you do being a detective," said Booker.

"What're you hiding? You're not going to O.J this. Detective work too risky now you got that prize heifer?"

Booker leaned back on his heels, his hands deep in his pockets. "You know Lowery, I am sorry I let you get away with a sloppy investigation last time. Altogether, you give a bad name to police and even worse to humanity."

"Why, Mr. Solomon, so formal," said the detective, shaking his head. "I see your girlfriend's improved your language." He strolled off to his group of workers who parted like the Red Sea.

Booker followed. A hankering grew for a catch-him-with-his-pants down moment. He could bide his time, knowing Lowery was stupid enough to walk right into it. It might take a week or a month. His chance would come.

Booker noticed fresh dirt piled on the edge of a shallow circle about a foot deep and four feet wide. A man stood aside holding a large camera while a woman standing near the hole held an EDM on a tripod, measuring the slope and distance to a whitened bone numbered with a slip of paper. Nearby, other bones were outlined in the loamy soil and marked by successive numbers. It was a more scientific scene than the body found in the creek.

As the assistant flashed the camera, Messick deftly pulled the bones from the earth in her gloved hands and dropped them into brown paper bags. When Booker took a closer look, he judged they were a tibia, a partial foot, and the long shank of a femur. An arm and hand had not been brushed free of dirt and marked. They were definitely human.

"Who found them? You know where the rest of the body is?" asked Booker.

"We don't," said Lowery. "We got a phone call from a lunchtime runner, some guy from Atlantic Physical Therapy near the corner. Saw a dog running along the road with what looked like a long bone in his mouth."

Messick broke in, walking over from the grave, "We never found the dog. The tibia has bite marks consistent with canine teeth. The ground was disturbed like it had been

The Grist Mill Bone

digging around here."

"They look kinda bleached out," said Booker.

"They're old, really old," she responded. "Yellowing around the joints. And they haven't been here long because this is a fresh, partial grave. The bones are in museum-like condition but there's some co-mingling. We have two femurs of different lengths."

Lowery rolled his eyes and Booker got ready for one of the man's idiotic pronouncements.

"You can't make assumptions without the lab work, Messick," said Lowery. "You gotta date those bones. Hell, this could be an Indian burial site. Are you saying there's more than one victim?"

"Yes. These bones were placed here recently for someone to find."

"Give me a break. How'd you know that?" said Lowery, snorting.

"Data, Detective, so stop with the grief," she snapped. "The earth is not compacted, but disturbed like it's been raked and patted lightly. There are no blowfly remains, no bacteria, no signs of desiccation. The bones are scrubbed clean like they've been part of a display. As a matter of fact, there are drill marks near each joint as if the bone was held in place by wiring in a skeleton. From the length of the femur the adult subject is probably male."

Lowery interrupted. "You got the sex? Go on. What's the race?"

Messick whipped around to face him, chin to chin. "There is no such thing as race in forensic science. We're all human.

You get down to bone and there's no way to detect the color of someone's skin. So, Detective Lowery, that's never a conclusive decision here on the shore where we have thousands of years of human data." Messick pushed her glasses up her nose. "Even a femur is not conclusive statistically. I would need the missing skull and pelvis to be more accurate so don't ask me for the impossible."

Booker thought Lowery wasn't listening because he looked away from Messick and yelled to her whole forensic team, "We need more information if we're making this a crime. This isn't some museum skeleton a professor threw out of his car."

"That's just exactly what it is. A skeleton preserved for viewing," replied Messick. "But the hand is what catches the eye. If I date the bones and we're really lucky, I may be able to match the DNA."

Lowery bellowed in laughter. "I told you," he said.

Booker was impressed but doubtful. Still, he thought the way Lowery bent, thrusting his chin in the woman's face was rude and he had to squash an urge to punch him in the throat.

"Now that sounds real scientific," said Lowery. "Even I know you need to match DNA on a cold case missing body."

Messick grabbed a soft paintbrush from her pocket and held it up between them. "Follow me, Lowery."

Booker and the detective dutifully trailed her back to the edge of the dig site. Messick knelt over the remaining bones and proceeded to brush away clumps of fresh dirt revealing a hand whose digits ended at its first joint. The camera flashed again. Messick stood and crooked her finger at Lowery and

Booker as she trotted over to a field table and grabbed the edge of a clear plastic tub. Reaching in, she pulled out a gray plastic suitcase. "Come here gentlemen. We found this gun case leaning up against the base of a tree before we discovered the bones."

Booker and Lowery huddled around the table. Setting it down, she flipped the key lock and raised the lid. "The cadets will search a wider area for scatter data since we may find other bones although anything more is just gravy, in my opinion. This was unlocked. Look here."

The open case was lined with thick gray foam. Nestled inside was a Browning pocket pistol that looked to Booker like a vintage Saturday night special. A line of neat copper bullets lay to its right. On the left, sat four others, obviously homemade, discolored and coated in what looked like grease.

Lowery reached to pick one up. "Never seen any bullet look like this." He opened his hand and it rolled into the center of his meaty palm.

"That's because it's not a bullet, Lowery," answered Messick. "It's a finger, a dried up digit cut from the hand of a black man."

Lowery dropped the finger into the case and rubbed his hand against his pant leg as if it had seared his skin.

"You really shouldn't touch the evidence, Detective," said Messick as she snapped the case shut.

Booker couldn't stop himself from laughing and shielded his mouth behind his hand. He backed up and wandered a few feet into the underbrush, chortling the whole way when he heard something rustle nearby. Too late, he caught a glimpse of a figure that ducked and ran further into the woods.

"Hey! You! Where you going? Come back here," shouted Booker as he took off after him. The hooded body sailed through the woods like a gazelle. Booker neared the clearing by the road's edge huffing and puffing. He cursed realizing he wasn't as nimble as he used to be. A dark sedan, shielded from view by the leaves, rolled into the bike lane. The figure yanked the rear door open and threw himself in the backseat. The car gained speed heading west toward farmland. Booker squinted into the setting sun as he tried to read the plate. Four cadets followed him, including Beavens. Booker turned and raising his upturned hands in the air as if he was praying, asked, "Did anybody catch that plate?"

He was met with stumbling and denial.

"The make of the car?"

An all out argument ensued. "Blue Mitsubishi."

"No, a blue Toyota."

"No," insisted another with confidence, "That was a Nissan. My sister has one just like it."

"What? You don't know any American makes?" Booker retorted and walked back to Messick. Lowery had left, he suspected overcome with embarrassment.

"Well, we all agreed it was a late model car with Delaware plates but that's all we got. Could've been a sightseer anyway. This business has been all over the afternoon news."

"Yeah, we'll let you know what else we find out, Mr. Solomon," said Messick, her mouth curled up on one side. "There are some good detectives in Delaware. But I'm sure

The Grist Mill Bone

you already knew that."

And in that instant, Booker decided to let it go. It wasn't his case to investigate. He had left that life in the dust and had better offers.

When he arrived home, the police had cleared the area, leaving yellow tape around the area at water's edge. The turkey buzzards had stopped circling above and soft waves rolled across the creek. The air smelled fresh, a hot and breezy afternoon. He thought the creek deserved a red sunset after the storm, one that would reflect in the water. It was time to wake Claire and see if Sam wanted to join them at his Ma's for dinner.

Hearing some clanking in the kitchen, Booker strolled down the hallway expecting to find Sam finally doing his chores. Surprised, he found Rosa at the sink making quick work of the dirty dishes. He hadn't seen her car. A wave of frustration rose inside as he realized that Sam had disobeyed him again. Booker greeted Rosa, asking where she left Bessie, her toddler.

Turning from the hot suds, her round face wet from perspiration, she dragged her arm across her forehead, declaring, "Mi amigo, Mr. Booker! I couldn't get here this morning to clean up so I come by after my DelAire shift. Good thing, you know? Miss Claire been tired this week and she need me. Mr. Sam upstairs. He just come in off his boat."

"Huh. I told Sam to clean up the kitchen a couple hours ago. I wonder where he went?" He glanced at his watch: 4:20. It had been over three hours since he had discovered Sam and

Little John holed up with the sex toy.

"He say he have to study for math test tomorrow. You have yellow tape in the yard. Lord, it's hot."

Out the kitchen window Booker saw Sam's Carolina skiff was tied to the dock at the bow but not at the stern. The boy knew better. The rule was that he had to ask permission before he took off in his boat. No, the skiff had been gone for a while or curious Sam would've made an appearance at the first sign of the police.

The recent spate of dead bodies had plagued the western side of the county, far from the beaches. As he looked out on the matted grasses he thought, when this makes national news, it'll affect the coming tourist season. And on second thought, having a body float onto Solomon property so close to the ocean was a moment of reckoning for him, if not the police. He had no choice but to take away the keys to Sam's boat.

There had been a couple local TV spots that had featured the killings, saying all of the victims were homeless black or Hispanic men, four of them altogether. Today's discovery made five. Some of the bodies were found mutilated and none had been identified, so there were no next of kin. If Sam refused to follow the rules, he was bucking to get grounded. Booker was just thankful that his Ma and Claire didn't keep up with the local news blow by blow. They would now.

Rosa squeezed between him and the dish rack to drain a frying pan. He wouldn't tell her what had happened either. The storm had carried the body in; the murder hadn't happened close by.

"Where's Bessie, Rosa?" he asked again. "They make her the boss at DelAire now?"

Rosa chortled and slapped Booker across the shoulder with a wet hand. "Mr. Booker. My Bessie she not feel good today with her allergy so I no take her to the daycare center. Pine tree pollen in her nose, make her all fussy. She stay at Lourdes' house with the other kids so she can have good food and good nap."

"Rosa, I wish you'd come to work for us instead of slaving away at the plant. You've been there what, like seven years now? Aren't you getting sick of the smell of dead chicken?"

"They pay me too good, Mr. Booker. We talk this before. You can't give me enough hours to match DelAire and they give me and Bessie our doctor cheap."

"Uh-huh. Are you going to be around tonight? Claire and I want to talk to you about that seriously this time."

"No, I pick Bessie up and we eat at home. I have late shift tomorrow so I come back in morning and do some laundry for you. I not be back tomorrow night."

"Rosa, Claire and I can get the laundry. You take such good care of us but you're killing yourself with your schedule. We want to make this right for you. Come in the morning and we'll talk some more."

Rosa smiled, her eyes shimmering with warmth as she nodded.

Opening the kitchen door, he whistled for Compass and the dog bounded into his arms. Booker scooped him up, throwing him over his shoulder like a couple of sacks of mulch.

"I got to give this dog a bath, Rosa. Thanks for coming by. See you tomorrow, okay?"

"You bet, Mr. Booker. I call if Bessie sick, but I want to work," she said as she swirled the dishtowel around a plate.

Booker thought he was good and tired of dealing with dirty pots and pans and dishes. In his next house, he'd have two dishwashers. And a beer tap.

***

TRIXIE

Little John turned his ball cap backward and opened the creaky shed door. The rain had subsided while the temperature zoomed into tropical range. Trixie had ordered him to ready the ground up for her annual tomato garden and since Booker's threat to call his foster mom, he decided he better bank some good will ahead of time.

He looked at the tangled weeds in last year's raised bed and thought one day, he'd have some Hispanic to hoe it for him. Even though the ground was soft this was gonna require four black plastic lawn bags. Trixie made homemade gravy, the kind old time Philly Italians cooked for days, throwing the kitchen sink into the sauce. She had ordered her garden dug deep and turned. John loved her gravy but he wasn't real motivated to dig a garden at the moment. He could still feel Booker's hand on his neck.

Sweat dripped into his eyes and he peered into the shed's darkness, a musty, dank jumble of rusted tools. A thin line of light streamed onto the floor where a hoe lay upturned. He scrunched his sour puss and entered, walking dead straight into a massive cobweb that wrapped around him. He cursed. Both hands came up, brushing his face over and over and he shook with anger that rose from his gut. Bile filled his mouth and he spat. Stamping his feet as if this would shake the sticky strands from his body, his toe caught the edge of the hoe bringing the handle upright, smacking him directly in the face.

Grunting and cursing, he clapped one hand on his forehead and charged out of the shed, to plunk himself down on a corroded aluminum beach chair that had outlived its usefulness. The legs folded and his butt hit the ground. John rolled to his side and lay defeated in the grass looking over the bulkhead into the brown water of the canal. The air steamed. The canal water stank like rotten eggs and blood dripped down into his eye. His white-hot anger narrowed into a scintilla of rage and turned on Booker.

He hated the son of a bitch. He hated that the man was rippled with muscle. He hated the black man's wide-open stare but mostly he hated that he couldn't stop cringing under it. He could still smell Booker's musky aftershave and feel his fingers gripping his jacket collar, drawing him so close that if John had spit he could have easily clouded the big man's eye.

He hated being called Trixie's gardener.

There was more to him than anyone knew.

He rolled on his back and threw his arms out to either side looking up at the roiling skies. There had been a time years ago that Booker had needed him. A time when he had information about Sam's kidnapping. Stupidly, he had offered it up with no promises in return. The Spic landscapers had been the link. In the aftermath, all the television cameras, the newspapers, the interviews of neighbors went on for weeks. Not one of them had come to John.

Trixie gabbed to this reporter and that newscaster. Even a Washington, D.C. anchor had come with his mess of hot lights and makeup crew to the community center, making the trailer park famous. He interviewed the detective, the one with the beer belly who had informed the FBI of Sam's whereabouts. In the end, Sam's picture was everywhere but John's was nowhere to be found.

He got up and dragged himself to the porch door. The blood had poured down his face and he smeared it across his cheek for effect. Conscious that his jeans were sagging in the back, he yanked them up to please his foster mother. He crossed the back porch and seeing her at the kitchen sink, he pinched his chin and pursed his lips. He opened the kitchen door slowly and tottered a little as if unsteady.

"What the hell did you get into now?" asked Trixie, her hands on her hips, her black eyes glaring.

"Nothing. It ain't me. Booker don't like me, that's all. He shoved me into the door jamb and told me to get outta his house."

Her face softened. "Well, you need to stay clear of him, John. C'mere and let me clean you up."

John stumbled over to his foster mother. She patted his shoulder and gently pushed him into a kitchen chair. She opened a cabinet searching for the Bactine. A slight smile grew on John's face as he said to her back in a pitiful voice, "Trix. I don't mind hoeing up the garden, but I need some money for a school trip to James Farm. My allowance is all gone. How 'bout you pay me this time for the garden?"

Trixie whirled on him, her mouth working but words failed her lips. "You…You playing me again Little John and so help me, I'll call your teacher and tell her for you clean toilets 'stead of the trip. You knew you were going. You shoulda saved your state allowance."

John sighed and leaned his head back as she dabbed at the wound. Teary eyed, he said. "It ain't enough. Just another ten this month." He looked at her soulfully. "Please?"

"Don't say ain't." She pushed him. "You're a lazy slob and you aren't pulling the wool over my eyes. Getting a man like Booker Solomon pissed off at you," she said shaking her head. Trixie blotted the blood harder and harder until he pushed her hand away. "You just go get a job if you want more money," she ordered. "Go down to the nursing home on the corner and ask if you can do maintenance." She flung the bloody paper towel in the trash. "Then maybe you'll learn the value of a dollar!"

John bolted from the chair to the sunlight, yelling and cursing some more. The screen door rippled as he pushed it open, tearing from a hinge at his passing. He shouted as if someone was listening, "Nobody wants to help me. I'm just here for you to punch on."

*****

7 CLAIRE

I woke to the distant caw of a seagull and stretching, rolled on my back. I ran my hands over my lower belly. It was small, but there was a little nugget. Smiling to myself, I crawled from bed.

I had rinsed the mud from my legs before my nap but I wanted a shower before dinner, thinking we would end up at Odessa's like we did every night when Booker returned from Washington. Suddenly, with a visceral shiver, I remembered the dead man and ran to the window to look out over the yard. Everyone was gone; the grasses were matted and rutted with tire tracks. How long had I slept? I glanced at the clock. Just after four. Grabbing my cotton robe, I padded to the bath and looking down the hall, I noticed Sam's bedroom door was shut tight. Maybe he was studying. Last quarter Geometry was kicking his butt.

Standing before the bathroom mirror, I pulled my hair up in a pony and studied my bleary eye, holding the Visine in the air. A couple more drops and maybe it would do the trick. I pulled the shower curtain aside and adjusted the water in the footed tub, climbing over the side. As I let the water beat on my neck and upper back, I heard Booker's steps.

"I was just gonna give this dirty dog a bath."

"You can't hose him off outside?" I asked.

"He stinks, Claire. You know he's gonna climb in bed with us tonight."

Damn. He was right. And then I thought, poor Booker. He's probably not had a minute to spare since I bailed on him to take a nap. All I could think of was Compass' dirty paws on the other side of the curtain. "Oh, Booker. He's going to get mud all over the floor."

"Fine for you to say, Woman. I'm the one standing here holding him."

Hopping out, I cut off the showerhead and held the curtain away so he could dump Compass in the water. The dog yipped with delight and lay down in the tub.

"That's a sight for sore eyes," he said glancing at my naked self. He leaned over for a kiss. "I've missed you."

"Me too," I mumbled in his lips.

He knelt, testing the temperature and began wetting down Compass' thick fur.

"Ma's fine," he said. "She's watching her game shows and has me on speed dial. They're cleaning up the investigation over there. Just some old bones somebody dumped by the driveway. I told her we'd be there by six for dinner." He smiled glancing up at me. "Let me catch up with you first."

Tenderly, he removed Compass' collar, muttering to him

about what a bad dog he was as he squeezed shampoo down his back. "Why don't you tell Sam to invite Josh over this weekend. I'll take the boys fishing."

Now, Booker has never ventured into teenage fishing trips so I took him to mean something had happened with our son. He used to take Sam everywhere. But recently, I had noticed there was a distance between them. Correction: there was a distance between Sam and the two of us.

"You might get Sam out of bed at dawn to go fishing but I'm not so sure about Josh. His mom says he stays up late playing video games."

"Josh is a hell of a lot better choice than Little John. John's too old to be hanging around a 13 year old and besides…" He mumbled something I couldn't hear.

"What'd you say?" I asked.

"I don't trust him in the house."

"You're being a hard ass. John's a good kid. He hasn't had anyone give him a leg up. We should be supportive." I toweled off in front of the sink.

"You're giving him a leg up into the same prison his father's in. And asking Sam to know where to draw the line. He idolizes him."

"That's ridiculous," I said, looking at his broad back and dark baldhead reflected in the mirror. The caretaker, the lover of animals, and a dad to our son, Booker had adopted Sam and given him the Solomon name. An artist's palette, our little family was an array of colors, not blended yet. Baby. It was time to tell him.

"Uh-huh. And that's why the two of them were up in

Sam's room when I got home. Checking out stuff on my laptop." He slapped my butt with a wet hand and it shocked me into understanding. I know what happens when you take your eyes off your child and I felt guilty for not getting home before school let out. But what harm could there be if he was in his room?

"Nobody's watching the store when we're both at work," he said turning to rise from the dog and kissing my shoulder this time. The mirror framed us perfectly. His chiseled face and deep-set eyes were full of concern. A little gray is showing in those chin whiskers but he doesn't show his age—42 and still playing Marvin Gaye like some old dude. We make a beautiful couple. Still, I left my bathrobe on, thinking this was a working bath and I didn't know if Sam would pop his head around the door. Not a lot of privacy in this old house. Which is probably a good thing when dealing with a secretive son.

"Stuff?" I asked. "Like teenage stuff? *Sports Illustrated* stuff or....sex?"

"Or. They were looking at OR, Woman."

Kneeling, he squeezed more shampoo on the dog's head and began hosing the mud out of his long fur. Mud is a condition of our existence on the creek.

"Booker. You'd tell me if there was something I needed to do?"

"Are you gonna listen?"

"Of course I will."

"We need to move over the bridge back to D.C."

"What? Are you crazy?" His head was down, his back to

me, his attention absorbed by the damn dog. I knew this position. Ignoring me, he wasn't going to argue. I needed to compose myself.

My yoga pants were piled in a corner. I snatched them up as I headed for our bedroom. Behind me, I heard Booker call Compass to shake-shake. I steadied myself on one foot and raised the other to point a toe in the pant leg when I heard a floorboard creak behind me too late. Booker slapped my butt again, throwing me off balance onto the unmade bed. He tumbled beside me, searching my eyes.

There was nothing to do but give up trying to shove my foot into the tights which is no doubt what he intended. I looked down at the white scars on my legs from the bombing four years ago at my lobbying office and realized I was trembling with anger. I don't like abrupt changes and he knows it.

"What're we going to do with your mom? Take her with us? And Sam's school?" Private high school, entrance exams taken, interviews done. "Odessa would miss her choir," I said, raising my voice, "and it's the wrong time to change schools when Sam's going into freshman year."

Now everyone knows that's the perfect time to make a change in a kid's life but I couldn't bring myself to say why I didn't want to return. He knew anyway. I got up and drew my robe around me tight, cinching the waist.

"See," he said. "I thought you were gonna listen. All you're doing is yelling."

Lowering my voice but with no less intensity, I turned on him, "Booker Solomon, if this is all about you climbing the ladder at Tosh, I've told you we are not making the company our life. I grew up playing its understudy and we are not doing that to Sam."

"I'm being practical," he said all jolly, his eyebrows sliding up his forehead like the body of knowledge behind them deserved some Einstein consideration. Propping my elbow on the dresser, I buried my hand in my hair and tried to match his expression. Underneath, I was seething, ready for his lecture.

"You can't hide him from it, Claire. Tosh is his to run someday. What are you going to do, stay here, live in this seedy farmhouse, and send him off to a third rate private school? He'll be a shining star for four more years and then you're going to throw him out there to an Ivy League and watch him fail? If you want him to be a success you have to groom him for it. Your daddy understood that and so did mine. You think I'd be where I am if it wasn't because he and Ma valued education more than fishing?"

"You are where you are in life because you have grit and you work hard. That's what I'm trying to teach Sam."

"Oh good. 'Cause you're the only parent doing the teaching?"

That pissed me off. "What?" I asked. "Don't put words in my mouth. You know damn well I didn't mean it that way." He was so calm. The eye of the hurricane.

"Your problem is that you think because you had it a certain way in a screwed up household that it's going to be that way for Sam. It's not. You're married to me. We need to make our own life together."

"You've never lived in D.C. You've never had bodyguards follow your every move on the street or had to carry a gun for your own protection..."

He looked square at me on that one.

"Sorry... It's the heat of the moment. I know you carried a gun every day. But you don't have to play detective anymore. They treated you like crap anyway. What we have now works for everyone. You work for Tosh and commute. If it's too much of a drag you can fly back and forth. I'll get a nanny for Sam. I can keep practicing elder law. It's safe and makes me feel valuable." None of it sounded convincing, especially the part about a nanny for Sam, so I gave it my last stab, "It's safer here than D.C." The finality of these words didn't quite ring true. I mean, there was the dead body.

"Don't you wonder why I'm spending more time over the bridge?" he asked as he leaned across the bed, his hand extended.

"What? Because you love it. Why are you changing the subject?"

"Because you never ask about my job or all your peeps at Tosh. You know, VanAnden quit. She got a job in New York working for some billionaire."

"Ha! The Ice Queen? Well, she'll be happy. I'm happy for her. We don't have enough billions to satisfy her needs. Money makes people evil. Besides, Washington is too tame for her style."

"My point is that I'm working more hours now and I'll be away from you and Sam."

"Well, they need to hire more people as senior project

managers so you can come home."

"I don't want to come home. I've got a great offer on the table from Tosh."

"Oh, that's it. What's so wonderful you want to leave the beach?" Somehow, my fists ended up resting on either hip and I realized this was never a move you use when arguing a case in the courtroom. Plus, I must have looked ridiculous wrapped in a bathrobe and my hair soaking wet. I bent to pick up my wet towel.

"The new FBI building. Tosh got the preliminary contract to build it and they need to find the best site: either northern Virginia or Maryland. You got to admit, I'm the right person for that job."

I *was* impressed. He *was* the right person but I threw the towel at him anyway and stared, my hands back on my hips. "But it's Tosh, right? You aren't going to work for the FBI, are you?"

"No. But they're still trying to recruit me." He pulled the towel off and said in the most rational way, "It's a natural next step. I can't have a wife, a kid and Ma blabbing to the world that I'm FBI. You guys stay here for a few months. I'll finish up the waterfront project with Tosh and see which one has the better offer. Besides, I don't want you to worry about getting all this done overnight."

I had waited for him to finish and reading the look in my eye, he shut up. It was time for me to lay it out—my turn. "It looks to me like you've made the decision already. Far be it from me to assume anything, but I'm going to reiterate. This is because you're climbing the ladder. Be honest. It may not be the Tosh ladder but it's a ladder."

"Oh, the princess has spoken. And I have to live my life for you and Sam? I'm not allowed any personal success? Let's be honest both ways. You found yourself a nice little niche practicing law in a stress free environment," he accused. "You're at the top of the food chain here. Why would you want to give that up?"

I sat down on the edge of the bed, my back to Booker. When he put it that way, I *was* being selfish. I have so much fear about returning to my old life that I just freeze thinking about it. We live like paupers by Washington standards. My circle of friends and family is miniscule here. I can control this life.

Returning to work for a lobbyist or practicing law when there's an office on every street corner is soul deadening. I'm highly credentialed but that's not really essential since I moved to the beach, since I married Booker, since I became... he's right. I'm the big fish in the little pond.

Yet, if we moved back, and I gave up law, I'd become what I swore I'd never do. It'd be days before I'd be pressured into running fundraisers, or dragged into organizing Washington galas: Kennedy Center Arts, the Washington Ballet, Wolf Trap. All that publicity and schmoozing. The handshaking, the payoffs. The thought made me want to retch.

It wouldn't matter how altruistic my endeavors were, the media would have something negative to say. They made a circus of our lives after the kidnapping, doing exposés on Sam and me, and Booker by extension. Our reappearance in

Washington social circles will rehash all those articles about the heiress and the black detective, like some sleazy British tabloid and we become a dinnertime trope.

You can't be a benefactor to the world. You have to pick and choose your passions. And my choices, immigrants and the elderly, would always be a rich woman's pastime in somebody's book. But maybe I needed to take stock.

We're safe here on our little creek.

Odessa's my mom as much as Booker's.

Sam's a star in school and soccer but that's an easy ring to hook.

There'll be no one around to keep an eye on him this summer.

Compass loves the boat, the water, and the *mud.*

I looked at my man lying against the pillows, one arm behind his head, waiting for me to come to a conclusion. *Booker's keeping secrets from me.*

And then it came to me. I was keeping a secret from him. You can't have an honest marriage if someone is hiding the truth, ... including me.

I crawled into the bed and wrapped myself around him, resting my head on his shoulder. "Oh, baby. I've had the best of everything all my life and now I have you. It's your turn. We should go." Reaching under his shirt, I stroked his bare chest, my fingertips whirling the wiry nubs of his hair.

"I have something to tell you," I said. "I went to the doctor just today, before I stopped to meet my new client at the nursing home. It's been a little over two months, you know." His fingers twined my hair and he tugged my head back till I looked at him. "You've been gone so much, I didn't have a chance to tell you and besides, I wanted to make sure." I could feel him hold his breath and I whispered, "We've made a baby."

I fell into his eyes, waiting. He blinked once, twice, his face a blank. For a moment, I thought this was how he studied the gigantic sea bass he caught last summer. A mixture of shock and admiration. Evaluating its lines, it's weight. But then, it seemed more than that, like he wasn't sure I was the same woman who had shared his bed for the last four years. He pulled me to him reflexively, and pushed me back to search my face. What else was there to say? Did he want me to say I was sorry? Did he want me to take it back? Or worse, was he worried this was going to ruin his plans?

"Woman! You makin' a baby?"

"Are you happy, Booker?"

"What you mean, happy? Shit. I'm happy as a puppy with three tails! This better not be no shuck n' jive. You serious?"

"Yes, I'm serious. I've got the printout down in the car. Ten weeks. We have ourselves a tadpole!"

He threw his arms around me and we rolled around on the bed. He kissed me, biting my lower lip, then whispered in my ear, "I love you, Woman." Suddenly he sat up against the headboard. Dragging me next to him like a ragdoll, he stuffed a pillow beneath my shoulders.

"Wait," he said. "You go and surprise me like this. I got questions that got to be answered. We weren't gonna get pregnant because of that hereditary thing with your blood. So what'd the doc say about that?"

"Oh, it's okay," I said, feigning nonchalance again. "You'll like this doctor. He's not a specialist but he knows how to prevent blood clots." Nervous, I brushed my damp hair away from my face. "He did the DNA test to find out who I inherited it from and it turns out both Mom and Dad had the marker. They know so much about Factor V now the dangers are really minimal."

"Okay, okay. But what do we have to do? What are the risks?"

"I stay on blood thinners but switch to a shot. I've got the filter so I won't blow another pulmonary embolism. Blood tests every two weeks to make sure it's the right amount of thin." I didn't want to tell him about the risks of miscarriage. I didn't want to jinx us.

"Shots? You have to do shots?" Suddenly, the worry in his face disappeared and he grinned. "Is this like those fancy hormone shots the Hollywood women do in the butt? Do I get to give them to you?"

"You know, you'd turn anything into foreplay if you could. No, not my butt; in my gut. And I can do it myself, thank you. It's a little tiny needle."

"Aww, man! I'm not getting anything out of this," he said, grinning more. His teeth sparkled against his dark skin. "No, I'm serious," he said pulling me over to rest his chin on my head. "Is the baby going to be okay?"

"It's a little higher risk but I'm under 35, I'm not fat and do plenty of yoga. It's all good."

I could feel him relax against his pillow. He laced his fingers in mine. "You're not fat, yet," he said pinching my waist. "So when am I going to be a dad?"

"October 24th."

He pulled my chin up to look in my eyes. "Well, you can tell Pembroke you're quitting. Tell him you have health reasons."

He sounded so serious, ... and presumptuous.

"We have money, Claire," he said. "Sam needs you and I need you. Hell, the baby needs you! Let's not mess this up."

All these orders! To be honest, I thought it was kind of cute but I was a little irritated. This was a new Booker. Big Daddy. I couldn't think how to respond as words kept tumbling out of his mouth.

"We'll ask Rosa to quit work at the chicken plant again. Ask her to come with us to D.C. You and Sam come look for a house while I work."

"Oh, Sam's really going to like that! Shlepping around all day with realtors."

"Why wouldn't he? We can buy any estate we want and take everyone: Mom, Rosa and her little girl. Sam would love picking out the right house."

"You want to take Rosa and her baby, too? Booker, you're rushing things. I have a brand new client at the nursing home. Plus, we have to explain this to Sam and your mom. Odessa's going to balk, Rosa won't want to be indebted to us and Sam—he doesn't want to take his eyes off Dark Souls for longer than an hour to have a conversation."

Booker gripped my shoulder. "That's what I'm saying. Our boy needs a kick in the pants. He's over-focused on video games and now he's figured out what porn is."

"Porn? Who said anything about porn?" I said, my voice rising. "Sam's been looking at porn?"

"Oh hell, I let that slip. I promised I wouldn't tell you, so you can't say anything to him, Claire. I got baby on my brain. Anyway, it's Little John's fault. They were up in Sam's room around one this afternoon with goof balls for eyes."

"One o'clock!" I shouted. "He had school. There wasn't a half day today or I would've been home."

"That's what I'm saying. If I catch that little bastard John over here one more time when we're not home I'm gonna light his ass up!"

I rolled back into the crook of his arm, reached over and dragged his brown hand onto my white belly. We would take care of this together. I would temper my man's hot head and he would prod me into reality. Sam was going to face the music—a sit down with his mom and dad.

There was a hard knot under the warmth of Booker's fingers and a slow smile grew on his face as a man who was a confirmed bachelor realized he had a future reading Dr. Seuss. His anger at Little John melted away and he kissed me long and tenderly.

*****

8 SAM

By age 13, Samuel McIntosh Solomon had buried one father and rescued the second from near death, but now he was toying with the idea that a third dad needed to sign up. Could his mom divorce Booker? He lay on his back in bed ruminating on his next step. Fingering a squishy ball, he tossed it higher and higher.

He could swipe Booker's beloved laptop and throw it in the creek. Or trash his holy fishing rods. Or he could just make it easy for both his parents and run away.

He threw the ball against the bedroom wall and caught it on the rebound, never raising his head off the pillow. In his experience, there was a honeymoon period with fathers, a time when they thought everything shared with a young son was an adventure or an opportunity for instruction. This smarmy bond wore off once the father set his son aside for what they really wanted: the almighty dollar. That's where he was on Booker's Ferris wheel. Stalled on the down side while Booker was ascending to greater heights. In the end, Sam

The Grist Mill Bone

concluded, a father's expectations of a son boiled down to obedience and loyalty, ... and to stay out of his dad's way.

He had locked his bedroom door when he heard the commotion in the bathroom. Relieved that it was the dog they were fussing over and not more embarrassing suck-face action or heated groping, he decided to slip down the stairs to clean up his kitchen mess when Little John called from Trixie's. There was no sense incurring Booker's wrath again. Even his mother's false sternness when she attempted to lay down the law filled him with contempt.

Sam threw the ball hard against the wall. If both his parents were scrubbing Compass, the dog must have been tromping in swamp mud and that would also be his fault. There were three strikes against him today: the sex toy, dirty dishes in the kitchen sink, and now Compass who was his to walk on a leash after school. He could just see Booker's eyes on him, hear his words, "Are you ready for the consequences, boy?"

They would be stiff; no video games for a month, or taking his skiff out on the water, maybe even forced attendance at the Baptist Youth Assembly with his grandmother. If he wasn't careful, they could turn up something else objectionable, like why he had allowed John in the house when they weren't there. Sam rolled off the bed and threw the ball onto the sheets. It landed next to the stuffed bear Booker had tossed at him. What had he said, the sarcasm dripping from his voice—*Cry in your bear?* Bears and balls. Children's toys. He opened his door to see if all was clear.

He laughed under his breath as he tiptoed toward their door at the head of the steps. He enjoyed creating an argument between them. At Sunday morning breakfast, his mom burned the toast lobbying *for* John (the poor boy) and Booker burned his hand on the bacon grease arguing *against* John (because he had the makings of a common criminal). His mother rolled her eyes and Booker slammed the frying pan down on the counter. In the end, they set a new rule: if one of them was home, John could visit. What a crock!

Pausing with his hand on the railing, he heard voices rise in their bedroom and stopped to listen at their door. He marveled that they hadn't figured out the window air conditioner masked all conversations. They could be so stupid. He heard his mother's voice, soft and sweet, then a pause as Booker's words hit him squarely in the gut. "Woman, you makin' a baby?"

Sam caught his breath, and froze before slumping down onto the cool wood floor. His heart beat triple time in his ears and he swallowed hard swiping his hair out of his eyes. He whispered, "Stop it. Stop it." The conversation that followed was intimate and joyous and *his* name wasn't mentioned once. It was all a bit confusing but Sam got the gist, enough to raise the hair along his arms.

They had not yet met Booker when his mom spent six weeks in a coma. On a cold February night in D.C., when he was a mere eight years old, his grandfather had taken him to the hospital and pointed to a chair in the visitors' lounge. "Sit there. Don't move till I come back." Intently, Sam watched as strangers spoke to the on-duty nurse at the window, how the double doors to ICU swung open silently almost magically and how people slipped in and out devastated as if they were the ones who were wounded. He played musical chairs till he sat closest to the gaping doors that let him dart through undetected.

He could still remember the mixed smell of cat piss and mouthwash. Striding down the hallway, trying to appear large and in charge, he heard his grandfather's deep voice and peeked around a curtain: a nurse adjusted a bag on a hook, blue boxes stood above the four corners of the bed, a rumpled figure swallowed in the sheets, a tube down her throat, her red hair spread like an octopus across the pillow. His mother's face was obscured by a mask that resembled the one Bane wore in *The Dark Knight Rises*. He could still hear the sound of the pumps on her legs.

And what he remembered from that night was one word: embolism. Was it a study of that African disease that had turned into an epidemic? Em-bola. Ebola-ism. He couldn't tell. He wasn't sure, but he knew he could find out.

As Sam sat crumpled in the upstairs hall, he heard Booker's concerned voice and felt that his had been usurped, silenced. Booker was always angry or flippant, making a joke out of things that should never be laughable. Sam scooted to the top step and remembering that moment in the hospital, he felt as sure of her belonging to him as he did of his own breath. She was his.

She survived. And everyone else in the family disappeared. The one vision that had kept him going in the ensuing chaos was that she needed him; that they had to start over with Sam at the helm. He had refused to dwell on these faded memories but he couldn't shake the sense that there was always going to be interference, a buzz of uncertainty.

He was just a kid when Booker saved them both years ago. But he thought of himself as the real hero, the one who had suffered the most, the one who had ended the chaos. His payback was that he had to share her with this tall black man who was different from any father he had ever met.

At night in the farmhouse living room they turned on a playlist and Booker taught Sam about singing the blues and dancing to Motown. Other nights, they all read aloud from *Sag Harbor* and *Rich Man Poor Man* and eventually *The Autobiography of Malcolm X* so they could discuss the finer points of meaningful literature. Sam listened and understood. He was being groomed. Every morning he got up, dressed in his private school khakis, polo shirt and blazer to catch the school bus with the kids who looked like him, joked like him, and aspired to the same colleges as him. At night, he returned home to a world that existed in two cultures. His friends thought Sam cool for having a black father but for others he was just different and avoidable. His curiosity about his new father grew until his pestering questions earned him a slap down.

"Boy, what about the word 'undercover' do you not understand?"

Sam gave up asking. And here he was four years later with nothing gained for all his trouble.

I have loved you, Sam thought as he leaned against the banister. *I wanted to learn about your secret fishing spots. I rode in your truck, and you showed me all the places you built on the beach, the Hispanic church, the county office building, the stupid courthouse. You had me shake hands with your friends—all those hunters and old geezers who have acres and acres of cornfields. Mom says I'm getting an education about real people but she doesn't like Tosh anymore. And you,* Sam thought, *you just want me to be like you.*

He wondered why they lived like poor people when he knew they had money.

Sam's former life had grown foggy in his mind. He still missed his grandfather, missed their stays at the family estate on the Chesapeake in Oxford, Maryland. When Booker married his mom, he brought Odessa with him and Sam had a real grandmother for the first time in his life. His mom waited on Odessa like a daughter.

Sometimes, after soccer practice when the weather was cool, the three of them would sit, watching the creek in the evening as the light changed on the water and they'd give names to the birds: Kahn, the Heron, Pavlova the Swan, Gertrude the laughing gull. Sam would giggle hysterically and they dubbed him Butthead Beavis. His mom sipped her white wine and Booker slugged back Heinekens. Sam was full of belonging. It would have been perfect except for his niggling thought that had grown into incapacitating flashes of fear—*she loves him more.*

Panic attacks surfaced at the littlest thing—upon seeing a needle at his spring sports physical, he had a fit of coughing and fainted. In late summer, he tried out for quarterback, thinking he could outrun just about anybody on the team until they threw him the ball, and as it spun through the air, straight at his face, his arms wouldn't leave his side. At the last second, he turned to run from that burning meteor of a football and it hit him square in the back, knocking him flat. That was the end of his football career. He withdrew more and more and found comfort on his computer in the animated world of Dark Souls where characters could appear and disappear at his whim.

His mom insisted on a therapist. Sam screamed at her that she was turning him into a girl and Booker laughed. His mother said, "Worse things could happen." Resigned, she plopped down in Booker's lap to kiss him. Sam stared at them... at her. He would not lose her again. Not to his stepfather. And now? Certainly not to Booker's baby.

The heat in the upstairs hall was unbearable. He didn't know how long he had been sitting outside their bedroom door but his legs felt cramped. He stretched them out and putting his hands to his face felt wetness. Had he been crying? He needed some air.

Not caring what they thought, what they demanded, what they would lay at his feet, he slipped downstairs just as he heard the window air conditioner chatter and hum. He threw open the porch's screen door and heard a car crunching across the oyster shells. Turning to see who it was—Rosa coming to fix dinner, he ran across the sloshy back yard to the broken down dock where his skiff was tied. Jumping in, he pulled the ropes from the pilings, started the engine and tore out across the broad creek.

The Grist Mill Bone

The warm air had cleared after the rain but an early evening mist settled above the warm water. When Sam looked back at the shore he could see the outline of the farmhouse's second story and roof. Where could he go? He ran a wide circle, slowed his skiff to a crawl and puttered the length of Trixie's canal, passing low-slung trailers where laundry dripped on clotheslines and little dogs yipped as he passed. He slipped his phone from his pocket and punched in the numbers. John answered.

"What're you doing?" he asked.

"Sitting on the bulkhead," said John. Then, "I told you he's an asshole."

"Yeah. I know."

"You want to get him back?"

"Depends."

"You just gonna sit and take it from him?"

"No. I'm coming down your canal. Wanna go for a ride in the boat?"

"Only if we can go to the stash."

"I don't know. You're gonna get caught, you know."

"I ain't never gonna get blamed. I got cover you don't know about."

Sam thought about this and wondered what the older boy meant. He liked the thrill of doing something subversive but he didn't think it was illegal or harmful. He and John were just playing at being badasses.

"Okay. I can see you now. Don't say anything as I come by. I don't want Trixie to hear us."

The mist cleared and he could see John's outline waving

from the bulkhead. He killed the motor and floated over with the help of a paddle. John hopped on the skiff and settled at the prow. Sam looked at him closely, at the jagged cut on his swollen forehead. "How'd you get that," he asked nodding at John.

"Trixie hit me. Booker called and told her about us."

"No shit," answered Sam in disbelief. John had it hard but he was tough. He could handle any adult, or at least get back at them if he needed. Deftly, Sam maneuvered the boat around and paddled it back toward the creek, only starting the engine when they were out of view of Trixie's trailer.

*****

9 BOOKER

He waved his hand to clear away the haze of no-seeums plastered over the screen door. Once inside a house, they stuck to fruit, ruined open bottles of wine and gagged him when he snored. If they were here at his mom's house then they would appear tonight at his farmhouse. Odessa had no patience for them and every year voiced her expectation that he spray the perimeter walls of her house. Sweaty work, it took days he no longer had. He simply hadn't prepared for bugs so early in the season. She would not be pleased but it was time to hire out.

Claire was in the kitchen pulling the steaming chicken from the oven. Her red hair fanned her shoulders blades and as she raised her face to him he saw her cheeks pinked from the warmth in the kitchen. Or maybe it was the sweetness she had inside. He took the casserole from her and put it on the counter. Wrapping her in his arms, he leaned his lips to her ear asked, "Where's Sam? You didn't tell him yet, did you?"

"He came in from the water all windblown and happy.

Said he has a Geometry exam tomorrow and he needs to study so I gave him some leftovers. He's going to brush Compass when we get home and feed him."

Booker leaned against the counter and smiled, guessing that maybe it had taken a little time for his discussion with his stepson to sink in. Maybe he didn't need to say anything to Trixie after all. "I wanted to give him the news when we told Mom, but we can do it later."

Odessa set the table for the three of them as Compass lay under it, his head sandwiched between his front paws. "Judas Priest!" she shouted at her son. "You going to eat my food, drink my wine and whisper in my kitchen like some sex starved teenagers? Come in here and kiss your old mother. I haven't seen you in a month of Sundays!"

Booker made his way around the counter and planted a big one on her cheek. "Ma, you'd have something to complain about if your bunions disappeared and God left you a winning lottery ticket."

"Well, I don't need to win the lottery. I got Jesus." She pushed him away and leaned against the table edge, getting back to her silverware. She smiled and muttered, "Grown man acting like a woman can't be without him."

Booker traded glances with Claire and rolled his eyes. His Ma knew they were both listening, that her litanies were expected and sometimes cherished, but often they grated.

"When you all come back for Sunday dinner, you make sure you bring Samuel. He's the one I want to see. Too busy for his old grandma." She looked over at Booker and said, "I guess you straightened those cops out?"

Booker smiled, "Naw, they're a pain in the ass but harmless. Nothing to worry yourself over, Ma."

Claire and Booker laid the table with food and took their seats. Odessa stood at the head reaching to hold their hands in prayer. She bowed her head. "Our Blessed Lord, you have released us from the bondage of sin and the life of eternal punishment it brings. You gave Your Son so that we would not have to give ours. We are helpless to redeem ourselves. God, grant us the grace to ask for your forgiveness, to make peace with our worldly desires and live in Your Glory forever."

Booker rolled his eyes at Claire again. *Somebody always needs to ask forgiveness around here,* he thought. He grabbed a serving spoon and scooped his Ma's chicken, some greens and hash browns on to his plate. Forking a mouthful, he glanced around realizing both women were sitting motionless, staring at him.

"You in a hurry, son?"

Claire looked back and forth between them. Booker caught her eye and pressed his lips together, shaking his head imperceptibly. His mom was drumming her fingers on the table. Time to deflect. "Mmm-hmm. Boy, are these greens good, Ma. Nobody makes 'em like you."

He could see Claire was impatient, wiggling around in her chair. She was never one to wait when there was a plan, especially if it was her plan. Time for the big reveal. Where to start?

Facing his mother, he suddenly wished he were anywhere else on earth. Moving her to D.C. would be time consuming—his time—and he'd never hear the end of it if he hired somebody to do the job. Overpowered by all the estrogen in the room, he grew quiet.

"Odessa, we have some news," Claire began. "Both good and bad, but we think you're going to be so happy you won't care about the second part."

His mom turned to Claire and patting the table, said, "Well, out with it. I like the bad news first so the good can soften it."

He watched Claire's eyebrows disappear under her bangs. "You want it, you got it," he said to her. "Don't back out now."

Her words came out naked and unadorned the way he imagined she would speak to a judge in a courtroom. "We're moving back to D.C. this summer, before school starts for Sam. Tosh has offered Booker the FBI contract to scout a new campus and we'd like you to come with us."

Odessa's fork clanked onto her plate and her hand rose to her chest. Booker had not seen her speechless in a long time—maybe the day that western shore pastor told the choir they needed new material. Odessa didn't take kindly to criticism of her choir arrangements. Booker hadn't been to the Baptist church in ages but he suspected she was stuck in the last century of praise music. Adjusting to change was not on her menu. Solemn, he watched his mother across the table, while he gulped down a few more bites of chicken.

Odessa started to speak. "M-move to…to…" She was so angry her spittle sprayed the table. She slapped a knobby hand across its surface jostling the collards. She glared at

Booker, then Claire. They sat idle for an eternity when Claire secreted a weak glance at Booker. He cast his gaze down as if still in prayer. Pushing his lips in and out he tried to ready his thoughts for his mother's inevitable tirade. Claire began to clear the dishes.

"I'm not done eating," he said.

Four years in the Solomon family and he couldn't count the number of times this very scene had played out before his wife. He had to admit that the only woman who had ever pushed him around was his mother. Being her only child left in the world, he folded to her wishes as if they were commandments. Claire encouraged him to stand up for himself and he would answer that she didn't understand. "No," she would always say, "you're the one who doesn't understand."

Booker shifted his weight in his chair, passed the bowl of greens to his mother and straightened his massive shoulders. He calculated his Ma's response and made a decision, saying, "Ma, I am forty-two years old and I've been taking care of you and all your bossy-ass desires by myself for the last 13 years. I—"

"Don't you dare call me—," Odessa broke in, hovering over the table, a wasp ready to sting.

"No, now you just shut up here," said Booker. "I'm gonna say what I got to say and you're goin' to listen and that's all there is to it."

He waited. When she stood up straight and folded her arms over her sagging breast he raised his eyes to hers, pushed back his chair and said, "I take care of this house, your yard, your grocery shopping and lately, I been doing your bills. I never ask for a thank you. I've done it 'cause you my Ma.

"I came back after my sister died and Dad got sick. I got work here at the beach when there wasn't any work to be found. I made a success of myself and earned the respect of most white folk around here separate from Dad's reputation. The FBI offered me a job after that business with Sam and I didn't take it at the time out of deference to you and Claire.

"But this is different and you can't just flick this off with a stick like it's mud on your shoe. This is a great opportunity that won't come again. And Claire says she'll go back to D.C. if that's what I want. It's what I want .., so you can either go with us, or you can stay here and we'll find someone to move in with you."

There was a long silence as his stinging words hung in the air. Odessa squinted at her grown son. She hunched over him and in a guttural voice said, "The curse of Ham will be upon you and Claire will be a barren fig tree. You'll see. Genesis 9. You two are selling yourselves out to The Man for guv'ment lucre. Noah said the black man suffers the curse of slavery for an eternity. You do this and you'll pay with your lives."

"Ma... you're acting like some crazy old bitty and nobody's going to listen to you any more. Martin Luther King, Jr. told us to forget that curse of Ham shit. You just calm yourself down over there by the fireplace while Claire and I do the dishes. If you want to talk some more before we leave, you got to act like an adult instead of some biblical horse trader."

Claire got up to find her purse. Booker carried the dishes into the kitchen. He scraped the plates and watched his wife swallow a handful of antacids. "Should you be eating them?" he asked.

She whispered back heatedly, "Don't you start telling me what I can and can not do. I'm not your mother!" Claire began loading the dishwasher as Booker put the leftovers in the fridge. *Damned either way,* he thought. *Can't boss one, can't pamper the other.* He wiped the counter down thinking he had never seen his Ma spout off like some fire and brimstone preacher. He needed to get her away from that church and all their talk about the coming apocalypse.

They hadn't even mentioned the baby yet. Odessa had to move with them. He couldn't leave his mother in this rambling house. She was too old. No telling what could happen any day that they were gone or busy.

Booker heard a cough behind him. Ma. How long had she been standing there?

Running her hand along the edge the counter, then a chair back, then the open air as if it would support her, she toddled to her rocker positioned by the fireplace. "I guess I got to be gettin' rid of everything since you kids moving me into an old folk's home," Odessa said stone-faced.

Claire grabbed the bowl of greens soaked in vinegar and threw them in the garbage disposal. Booker moved away from the faucet, leaving the water running. He stuck his face in an upper cabinet as if he was rearranging the dishes. Claire high-tailed to the buffet and put away the salt and pepper. Looking back and forth she whispered, "Oh, crap," and

Booker realized she was trapped between the two of them. He wondered if she would pick mediator or judge. He adjusted some dishes in the top cabinet.

"C'mon, Ma," he said, his back to them both. "Who said we're gonna move you anywhere. It's your decision, not ours."

"I 'spect you moving out with no thought as what's to happen with me if I stay?" she warbled.

Claire jumped in, her voice soft and pleading, the mediator he had predicted. "Of course we're thinking of you. We want you to be happy wherever you decide to live, but Booker and I would love it if you'd come with us."

"Well, I'm too old to make a move like that. I got too much stuff to sift through. I don't know how I could possibly pack all this." She had begun rocking and gripped her fingers around the wide mouth of an ugly brown jug by the hearth as if she could stopper the contents. A smile played about her face. Odessa relished a good argument and was a master at laying the bait.

"That's ridiculous, Ma. We'll hire people to pack you," said Booker from the safety of the cabinet.

Claire's eyes swept the room that was laden with all manner of tchotchkes, heirlooms and quilts. Was she thinking the same thing he was? She laid the final dish in the sink for him to wash and walked over to the head of the family. Here goes, he thought: the matriarch and the attorney.

Odessa locked her eyes on Claire and with sweet determination said, "You should have this."

'This,' was a 40-gallon face pot that stood two feet tall

The Grist Mill Bone

and nearly as wide. It had several thick handles, for surely it took more than one strong-armed man to raise it for pouring. On the broad side was the round face of a googly-eyed black man with a wide nose and broken white teeth shining against thick, dark lips. The potter had created curlicues of graying beard hair and a crescent moon mouth nestled across the bottom of the face. It was beyond ugly; it was hideous.

Booker's voice roared from the kitchen, "Ma, you're not pawning that thing off on me. I got some self-respect."

"Really, I couldn't Odessa. Booker told me it was made by a famous relative of yours."

"I won't live forever, Claire. You and Booker got to carry this on."

"Please don't talk like that. You're in good health and we'll always take care of you," said Claire. Booker banged some pots around in the kitchen. He could just imagine the mist in his wife's eyes.

"My 5X great grandfather, was a slave potter down in the Carolinas and when he was freed at the end of the war, he came here to Delaware where the land was so low nobody wanted it. No other folk were nearby 'ceptin' the last of the Nanticoke that hid in the cypress swamp. All together, they started a mill at the headwaters of the creek just west a' here and began cutting trees to create farmland. Well, people need vessels to store their grain safe from humidity, so Lucretius, my ancestor, started a pottery. He made medium sized liquor pots, and small spirit pots to put on graves so as to scare away the evil spirits and… and this here big grain pot. He was a poet, too. The bottom says, 'Pot take your buckwheat, feed your kin bittersweet.' "

"Well, I'm sure you can take it with you wherever you go," said Claire.

Thank God, thought Booker, looking over at her. His wife was bent over the pot, nodding at Odessa as if she were an unreasonable child.

Odessa scratched her nails against its surface, then stroked it, massaging the souls of all the Solomons who had carried the vessel over their shoulders. He shook his head at the mystery of his mother, who was alternately wedded to each and every family token or ready to throw it in the trash.

Booker knew it wasn't its ugliness that prevented Claire from wanting Odessa's gift. It wasn't its size or even his own obvious lack of interest in his heritage. It was that she was white and they were black. If she took it with her to put in their new D.C. home, or even at her family estate on the Tred Avon River, one of the original Maryland tobacco plantations, her elitist Washington friends at Tosh, Inc. would accuse her of cultural appropriation. It didn't matter that she owned the corporation. Her people could be cruel that way. And maybe this was why she didn't want to return. He could hear it now: *You married a black man just so you could stay relevant.*

Claire knelt down at Odessa's knee. She patted her hand and Odessa stole a wily gaze, her eyebrow upended, her chin rumpled as if she might cry. Booker wondered if Claire realized she was being played. Claire was no pushover. She had mentioned how Odessa's way of speaking became more homespun when she wanted something.

The Grist Mill Bone

"You know what riches do to folk. He's your husband. Why you lettin' him sell himself to the FBI to make a lot of money you don't need? You could stay here and make me some babies to take care of."

"Odessa, that's just what we've been wanting to tell you. We're going to have a baby in about seven months and we wondered if you could help us."

Booker peered under the kitchen cabinets and watched his Ma's chin fall open like the broken door of a rural mailbox.

"Well you waited long enough to tell me! Why didn't you start out with that? There would not have been an argument!" Her feet danced on the floor as if she was waltzing her rocker. "You two not getting any younger and God knows when He's gonna take me."

"Ma, stop with the death's door thing. You're going to outlive us all," said Booker.

Odessa grabbed the arms of her rocker and leaned forward looking back and forth between Claire and Booker. "You know, I've secretly been wanting to quit that old choir business and couldn't think of a way to be done with them and that new holier than thou preacher. Now, I got my excuse!" Her teeth about took over her face with a smile so big her lips couldn't stretch over them.

"There's no better excuse than a grandchild," said Claire.

"Samuel would love to have a little brother or sister. What'd he have to say?"

"We haven't told him yet," answered Claire.

"Well, Lord have mercy. He's more important than me. Booker, you got no business talking to me first. If Samuel wants to head back over the bridge to live, I'm going with you. And I'm not going into any old nursing home. And that is the end of it. Now, finish those dishes up and let's go over to the farmhouse to talk to Sam."

*****

10 SAM

Standing outlined in the light beaming from his open window, Sam realized they'd see him as they drove up. From a distance, he heard the crunch of tires on the driveway's oyster shells. Dusk had moved with the swiftness of a dragonfly into the night and he heard spring peepers chirping their refrain from wetland grasses behind the house. He turned off the soccer lamp on his dresser to sit in the dark and await their coming. His computer screen cast a ghostly white light and he glanced across the wood floor as the front hall light suddenly streamed under his bedroom door, glowing on the dull oak flooring. He heard Booker call from the foot of the steps and his mom and Odessa's voices, laughing their way into the living room. He suspected they were excited about a baby.

Sam lumbered down the stairs feeling like a death row inmate woken from his last sleep, wondering what his guards wanted him to say. He rubbed the bewilderment from his eyes at seeing Odessa visiting so late on a weeknight. She made him happy, unlike his parents who were always demanding or criticizing these days. As he entered the room, her radiance enveloped him and he slid in beside her on the couch, thinking he loved how she loved him.

"Samuel, aren't you just the picture of a good student," said his adopted grandmother, putting an arm around his shoulders. "You've been studying your Geometry so hard your eyes are bloodshot."

"I have a unit test tomorrow, Grams."

"Well, you'll clean up. You got a brain for math I never had. Now, if you want me to teach you how to sing, I can do that 'cause we got ourselves something to sing about!" She reached into the couch between them and pulled up a small teddy bear, its arms upended over his head. "What you have here, Sam? Did you bring a present for me or is it for somebody else?"

"You can have it if you want. I'm too old," he said.

"Ma, now wait a minute," said Booker as he fell into the armchair.

"Just say it, then," said Odessa.

"What?" asked Sam, playing along. "Why are you guys looking so creepy, smiling like that? I got to get back to studying."

Odessa chortled and Claire patted the cushion next to her but Sam didn't budge. Odessa hugged Sam and whispered, "Now listen to your mom. This is good stuff."

"Sam, we want you to be happy and I know it's been hard for you to adjust to living here at the beach. You've done a great job but we have an opportunity. How would you feel if

The Grist Mill Bone

we moved back to D.C. and you could go to school with your old friends?"

"What? Mom, this is kind of late to be talking about a school in D.C?" He wasn't going to make this easy for her. "I'm already scheduled for 9th grade here."

"Well, we could change that."

"Oh for God's sake, just tell him what's going on, will you?" asked Booker.

Claire stared at her husband. Odessa patted Sam's hand and Sam looked from one to the other.

"Sam, Booker has a job offer in D.C. We'll make this as easy as we can. I'll call St. Albans and see what they require to get you registered. I'm sure it won't be a problem. It's your grandfather's school."

"Now? What if I don't want to go back? What if I want to stay here?" he yelled. Then in a calmer voice, "I could live with Odessa."

At the mention of her name, Odessa fairly burst with the secret. Claire raised her hand in the air between them. Sam rolled his head backward against the couch and said with mock frustration, "You guys, what's going on?"

"Odessa's coming with us, Sam. You're going to have a baby brother or sister. In October," said Claire.

Sam followed the smiles from his mother, to Booker, to Odessa. He stood up, partially aware that he looked like a three year old, holding the teddy bear drooping in one hand. He didn't care. "Great. A baby. Like you've done such a good job with me, you think you'll be any better with the next one?"

He walked out of the room but turned as he neared the stairs and threw the bear into Booker's lap. "Here, you can pass this on."

He walked up the stairs and heard Odessa's voice behind him, "I'll go talk to him. You two stay here."

Odessa shut Sam's bedroom door behind them and sat next to him on the bed. "Sam, you got some nerve talking to your parents like that. You don't have to be happy about a new baby but Booker and your mom spoil you something daily."

Sam took a seat in his desk chair and swiveled it toward his Grams. His hair fell into his eyes and he combed it back with his fingers.

"They said after Dad died and they got married that this was a partnership, that we were a threesome. We would make decisions together. Well, I just got left out of that equation, didn't I?"

"You did. No question. It may look like your mom and Booker jumped into this idea wholeheartedly but I don't think they did. I think this baby is a surprise. Your mom doesn't want to leave her job here and me, well, you think this is going to be easy on me? *Everything*, everybody I know is *here*, all my life is *here*."

"Then why'd you agree? We could stay, you and me together. Booker and mom can come home on the weekends."

"Sam, I'm 71 years old. I can't raise a teenage boy."

"Yes you can. You're not old. Besides, I'll be a big help around the house. More help than you're getting from Booker."

Odessa blinked and swept her hand across the rumpled quilt. "Sam, Booker does a lot for me that you don't see. He's got a lot on his shoulders." She rested her elbows on her boney knees and clapped her hands together. "You know, my parents raised seven children on the farm right next to the Solomons. Booker's grandparents owned all this property next to ours and when my mom and dad got older, being the youngest, I ended up living with them. All my older brothers and sisters had moved away to make their fortunes. Booker's dad had near stopped farming too and went into veterinary. We all made a good living tending to the health of the farm animals 'round here. When we got married, Booker's daddy and I drove miles and miles around this county and everybody, black *and* white farmers, knew us. Booker and his dad built our big barn and we made enough for Booker to go to college to be an architect. Bet you didn't know that, did you?

"Well, he didn't get to finish 'cause his big sister messed up her life with some bad folk in Baltimore. And when she died, he joined the army. You know he was Special Forces, right? Well, he came home after his tour and when his daddy died, he stayed home and he's been here ever since. He built churches and fire halls and warehouses same time he did police work in Maryland, working his way up the ranks to be an undercover detective. And thank God he did. He saved your life if you don't remember?"

"How am I ever gonna forget? Mom reminds me everyday."

"Well, she should. And you need to be forever grateful.

My point is that it's Booker's turn. He's been taking care of people all his life. It's his turn to go somewhere now. And you need to act like the big brother you're gonna be soon. You're going to have some squealing little baby brother or sister who's gonna adore you for the rest of your life. Now that's a present that never stops giving, you know what I mean?"

Sam sighed and nodded. He was quiet, mulling over Odessa's words. "I'm not trying to give Booker a hard time. He's just so hard on me."

"Sam, he don't whip you with his belt, he don't curse at you, he don't embarrass you in front of your friends. When I was little, parents did that stuff all the time. You're a teenage boy and you need someone to ride your case, else you gonna think you're all is *the* all. He's the best father you'll ever know."

Sam paused to consider this and said, "I was being kinda selfish, huh?"

"Ya, think?"

"So am I gonna have to change diapers?"

"Probably."

"Okay. But I want you to show me how. No Mom. No Booker. They're like all up in my shit—oh, sorry, Grams—they're hyper around me all the time. Like I'm gonna do something wrong. It's so irritating. I just want them to leave me be.

"Honey, they did that once. Left you be. And you disappeared, you recall? So if you want them to trust you, you want to be in charge, you got to step up and show some responsibility."

Sam rolled his desk chair backward, and threw his arms up to lock his hands behind his head. "I have things I need to straighten out before I leave here, Grams. How soon do you think we're moving?"

"Oh, you got time to deal with your stuff, boy. You got plenty of time."

*****

11 CLAIRE

I was so hurt I couldn't feel any anger toward Sam. I'm his mom and I thought there would never be a day when he would look at me with such revulsion as if having a baby was an act of betrayal. Hadn't I raised him better than that? Apparently, he doesn't think so. It was a slam of us but worse, a shock to realize he doesn't think much of himself, like we're having a baby because we needed to replace the defective part.

Booker is out on the dock, checking the skiff, he said—to make sure that Sam tied it up correctly, but I bet he's looking for drugs or something that could give a reason for Sam's horrible words. I could see his torchlight flashing about in the darkness on the bulkhead. It's one of those pitch black nights where the only thing that can orient you out here in the country are sounds, like the spring peepers in the grasses by the water, or the cicadas in the trees. Or voices.

We often hear the voices from the trailer park at night with the windows open. Old Mr. Gronski talking in his gruff

The Grist Mill Bone

way to Loreen, his long suffering wife, about his know-nothing doctor, or Trixie yelling at the little kids to get their bikes out of the street 'cause it'd be a cold day in hell before she'd buy them another one. We can't hear Odessa. Her home is uphill and I suspect if we ever had words downwind, she'd catch them up there. She's never said. But Booker and I have never had a fight to speak of.

I'm so hurt, I can't yell at Sam either. I just want to cry.

I flicked on the bathroom light, washed my face, brushed my teeth and dragged the brush through my hair. My nightshirt hung on the back of the door and as I slipped it over my head, I thought it won't be long before there'll be a real bump under it's cotton drape.

I don't want to lose my figure. Other women say it's harder to get your shape back when you have a baby in your thirties. The weight fell away after Sam. I was so young, exhausted from twelve hours at work, nursing at night, pumping at the office during the day. A treadmill. This baby will be different. Sam's got to come around. We're a family.

I went in the hallway and found Compass curled up in front of his closed door. Always closed. I wanted to talk to him but he has that Geometry test tomorrow. His light's off and he's probably in that twilight sleep after Odessa's talk.

She's a godsend. One word she said to me that explained it all: "Teenagers!" She hugged me and left. I've banged around up here for twenty minutes but Sam's not buying it or he's exhausted from his outburst too. Maybe embarrassed. I'm rationalizing—trying to understand.

"Come here, boy," I called to Compass and we clattered

downstairs together, me padding down the hall in my bare feet to the kitchen and he, click, click, clicking along. I let him out for one last time before bed. It looked like Rosa cleaned the whole kitchen up, not Sam. Tidy. When Sam washes dishes they stay stacked in the drain, knives askew, ready to fall and take out a pound of flesh as they go. I don't fight it. Bigger battles. Like where he went in the boat this afternoon.

Tired – just exhausted from all this emotion. I can barely put my thoughts together. There's something I have to do.

The shot. My first one. I went to the fridge and looked at the package of boxes, each one with a tiny bottle of heparin, enough to last three months and then I special order more. I tore open the package of syringes and in my clumsiness, they spewed across the floor, plastic needles sealed up tight, scattered. I bent down to gather them and heard Booker's voice outside the door. Compass bounded inside and Booker after him.

"Woman, what're you doing up? I thought you were going to bed."

Then he saw what I had in my hands.

"Oh. You want some help?" he asked.

"I can do it."

"Ever done it before?"

"No, but the doctor explained."

"I'll do the first one and you watch. How about that?" he said.

"Are you an expert?"

"In everything. Army Ranger, remember? Sometimes,

you have to stick your buddy on the battlefield."

"Oh."

He took them from my hands and pulled me to the table, and opened one syringe package. He opened a box and set the bottle next to it. Turning the bottle upside down, he stuck the needle into the rubber cap and drew the plunger out, sucking the liquid into the syringe. He set the bottle on the table, squirted a little into the air and said, "Ready?"

"No bubbles?" I asked.

"No bubbles," he said.

"Good. 'Cause I don't want any bruises."

"Got it, Princess. Now shut your mouth and c'mere."

It really was a tiny little stick. I stepped forward and he pushed up my nightshirt, pinched an ounce of fat on the side of my belly and jabbed. I hardly felt it. He looked up at me. I rested my hands on his shoulders and kissed him. That started it all.

He swept the stuff across the kitchen table and lifted me on to it. We're so practiced it wasn't more than seconds before we were ready, expecting to tango as we always had except a baby was inhabiting the space between us. Cavorting like puppies was no longer a simple choice. The table was too hard, the kitchen light too harsh, and our clumsiness was naked to both our sight. This would take a practiced hand, one willing to slow down our impulsiveness and wrestle in the nest before falling asleep on one another. Our moment had passed and we dragged ourselves upstairs.

He wound around me in bed and I turned to whisper in his ear, "Did you find anything on the boat, Detective?"

"Nothing. Clean as a whistle, … 'cept for a spool of wire. Don't know where he got that. He's a good boy, Claire. He's just confused."

"I know. It'll be all right. I'm not worried."

Booker pulled me into him, his warm lips upon my neck and shoulder, his breath in my hair. His broad palm stroked my body, coming to rest on our baby. Pushing my arm over his head, he bent over my tummy, "You're hardly as big as a bobber and you're already sinkin' this fisherman. Little crappie."

"Is it a white crappie or a black crappie?" I asked.

"Speckled. Ours is speckled," he answered.

Undeterred, we started over, comfortable in our nest and what our future held.

***

Peach schnapps. It was a Tuesday, after bingo and before dinner. I hoped a little libation would open a door on the famously taciturn Velma Owens. I didn't want to draw the attention of the nursing aides so I ditched my noisy blender and brought pre-mashed frozen peaches and a shaker. Standing at Velma's little kitchen sink with her straining to see at my elbow, I wondered if I had been too rash. She had rolled her wheelchair in tight and was craning her neck to get into the spirit of the occasion—happy hour at Fairhaven.

"Get that rag and wipe up those peaches."

"Put the cap on the schnapps before you spill it."

"You're using too much orange juice. Fool. It'll make it too sweet."

"Next time bring some vodka. I'm almost out."

I was shaking her fuzzy navel over my right shoulder with all the panache of a professional bartender, but this last comment stopped me. Carefully, I poured her drink over ice in an old fashioned glass and garnished it with two maraschino cherries. I offered it to her with a flourish, cocktail napkin in one hand, fuzzy navel in the other. Then, I bent down to make eye contact. "Velma, the next time we have a drink together, we should do it over dinner at a restaurant."

Her eyelids fluttered but she wasn't discouraged. "I don't care about eating... unless it's cake," she said.

"Too bad. I brought some cheese and crackers. But I can take it home if you don't want any." I handed her my drink and not accepting any objections said, "Let's sit down and enjoy this."

I wheeled her over to the table by the window and unwrapped the plate of hors d'oeuvres. Velma studied the arrangement and looked up at me a bit astonished. Her maroon satin turban and brooch had slipped down her broad forehead and she pushed it back with gnarled fingers. Cupping her bulbous chin in her hand, she asked, "Is that bleu cheese? And caviar?"

"Yep. Jersey blue and English cheddar—Wyke Farm," I held up the wrapper. "Only the best."

"I haven't had good cheese in years," she said shaking her head. "Not since the Fathers and I shared drinks on Sunday afternoons."

She wheeled backwards unexpectedly and pushed across

the Persian rug to a small Chippendale buffet. I watched as she carefully extracted two dessert plates and laid them in her lap. She returned saying, "We must use the Limoges today."

"Of course." I said, my nose in the air to match her mood. I was curious. "Father Caulfield? Is that who you had a Sunday cocktail with?"

"Later. He came later." She paused looking at my drink, her eyebrows raised. "That's just plain orange juice. What? Are you drinking the angel's share?"

"No, no. Just watching my weight. I save my drinking for the weekend." Professionally, one never shares personal information with a client. Soon enough she'd notice my baby belly and I'd have to tell her, but today was not the right time. "You were saying about Father Caulfield?"

"No, it was Father George Chilcott took over after Father Ingle died in the fire. Father George and I shared many a good Scottish whisky and cheese," she replied smugly as she stole a deep gulp.

"I'm sure that was a lovely time. Your husband had passed before that I guess?"

Velma placed a crumble of bleu on a water cracker and dabbed some caviar on top. Reverently, she picked it up with both hands and brought it to her lips, inhaling its sharp earthiness before slipping it in her mouth. She leaned into her chair back and chewed, savoring the flavor, shutting her eyes as if I didn't exist. When she opened them, she said, "Fred died a long time ago. I raised my second son with Father Chilcott's help. You know after the fire, somebody needed to take care of that boy and Father George brought him to me."

"Your second son?" My heart flipped a few times. A fire? Did she have a beneficiary? Quietly I said, "I didn't know you had another son, Velma."

"Oh, he weren't my blood," she said, easy as pie. "I took him on as a teenager. He was 13 when his father keeled over from a heart attack and died and there weren't nobody else capable. Father George was a daddy to that boy but it was too late. You can't beat bad out of a stray dog that had to beg for its food."

"For heaven's sake! How long did he live with you?"

"Till he were 18 and then he left. He'd return off and on and I'd find him sleeping in my shed. I'd clean him up and feed him. Father George was the one who gave him money 'cause he said if I ever let that boy know how much I had, all he'd do was steal it from me. Besides, there were financial obligations I had to fulfill."

I was so tense my one hand had gone dead wrapped in the tail of my scarf. I let go and asked, "Is he still around? Do you ever see him?"

"No. He disappeared more 'an 20 year ago. All for the best. Father George and Father Caulfield advised me not to have any contact with him if he did turn up. Said he had got himself into some big trouble. The kind you go to jail for."

"What kind was that?"

"Don't know. Killing, I 'spect. He was always light fingered. And had a penchant for carving up dead animals. When he came back sometime in his early 30s I let him in the door, gave him a room and I found a dog's skull in his dresser, all pearly white except for numbers on each one of the bones. I told him not to come 'round no more."

"I guess so." I was devastated watching her be so matter of fact. I couldn't imagine how she had survived so much loss—a drunk driver kills her son, her husband commits suicide and an adopted son turns out to be a whacko. No wonder she found belonging in the Church. It was her family. I wanted to give her a hug but stopped myself. I had to remain professional. "Velma, that must have been so difficult. I mean, you're still calling him your son. What was his name?" I asked.

"Davis. Davis Vickers." She took another long swallow.

"But you never adopted him?"

"Good gracious, no! What do you think girl—that I'm feeble minded?"

Ahh, God almighty. I could feel the tension drain out of my shoulders. What an utter disaster had been avoided in those words—"Good gracious, *no!*" My mind flitted over the facts. He had lived with her every day for five years. There was no formal foster placement. But he had used her as a hotel through his twenties. She had told him to leave and had witnesses to that effect: priests even! If Vickers was alive he had to be in his fifties. If he wasn't living on the peninsula then perhaps he was in a halfway house or better yet, jail. Best of all—he was no relation to Velma.

But she had called him her second son.

Velma seemed to be having herself a clear day, one unhampered by dementia but I wasn't sure I could trust her account. I'd throw it out to Booker and see what he thought about putting a tracer on him. Father Caulfield might corroborate her story as well. But part of me wanted to let sleeping dogs lie. For all her demands, it seemed Velma could separate the vital from the irrelevant. Was her second son irrelevant?

"Of course you aren't feeble minded," I answered. "I'm just ever so glad that you had good advice from Father Chilcott and Father Caulfield over the years. They protected your interests. I can see why you want to leave them your assets."

Rosy splotches had appeared on Velma's cheeks. She was definitely more garrulous than I had ever seen her. In a challenge to facial symmetry, her one cheekbone protruded more than the other like a bee had stung her below the eye, but really it was the effect of late stage Paget's disease. She had flamboyantly placed an ornate Italian brooch on her turban above the softer cheek to balance her appearance. It was too heavy, however, for the satin wrap had begun to droop over her sunken eye. She remained unfazed and holding out her hand, clinked the ice in her empty glass to remind me of my bartending duties. I decided to water down the second one.

I walked to the sink and as she cleared her throat behind me, I heard her mutter, "They don't need my money."

I whipped around to find Velma dabbing her eyes. "Tears? What's this all about?"

"I'm not crying. My eyes are watering from all this pollen. I haven't ever seen the pine pollen so bad as this year."

I thought it probably wasn't the pollen at all but I

humored her. "It's all the rain we've had. It's better for you to stay inside if you have allergies. Everyone seems to be suffering."

"Well, that new maintenance man replaced my air conditioning filter today so it should get a little better. Look at those windowpanes, how yellow they are. Should be sending Tyneice to clean them!"

She was working herself into a snit and I thought it better to leave the rest of my questions for another day. A priest dying in a fire, a child left without a father. I could probably research these things on my own. We would sit and relax and talk about her African violets and who had influenced her very Velma sense of fashion. She was grumbling beneath her breath so I placated her, saying, "I'm sure Tyneice needs a day off now and then."

"No she doesn't. I don't like how they keep changing the staff around here. 'Specially when they send 'em into your private rooms. That maintenance man got a big bruise on his forehead and he smells like sotweed."

"Sotweed?" I asked. "Like you mean, um...that book, John Barse's, *The Sotweed Factor*. Tobacco, right?"

"Barth, girl. Get it right. John Barth. I grew up with him on Aurora Street. He didn't know nothing about sotweed. I had to tell him what it was. Then he looked up that damn poem and made his fame."

Velma was tired. Her poor little body slumped in a cocoon of maroon and pink gauze as if she were a Hindu shaman whose feminine energy was no longer eternal. I asked where she had found her brooch and her eyes brightened like silver dollars. She extolled her husband, Fred, and how he brought it back from his station in Italy after the war. When I admired her violets, she gave me scissors and told me to cut a leaf off each one to take home and propagate. Holding out a plastic bag for the cuttings, she told me to be patient—that it would take three months for the first sprout to show and five for clusters to separate in pots. In a shaky hand, she wrote out step by step directions over my protest that I could just look it up on the internet.

"Internet-shminternet," she retorted.

And then, my reward for the day came when she called me "Honey" and said I had better get going back to my family or I'd be late to fix dinner.

Fix dinner? I hadn't cooked in two weeks. Booker had vanished again, working at Tosh and Sam had a soccer game. He wouldn't be home till six or seven. The day had dawned with morning sickness and I called in to Pembroke. He answered the phone in his gruff voice but when he heard mine, faded and warbling, he had gone all soft on me, saying take as much time as I needed.

I went back to sleep barely aware of Sam rattling around in the kitchen. I wanted to get up and kiss him goodbye. I wanted to make sure he had money in his pocket for dinner. I wanted to wave as he got in the middle school van. But instead I rolled myself up in the comforter and buried my head in the pillow.

In the 13 years since my pregnancy with Sam, I have forgotten these details, forgotten how hard the first trimester is. It's all familiar now—the nausea, the bloat, the sore and swollen breasts. But I don't remember wanting to sleep all the time. I don't remember my legs feeling like lead. I trucked all over Georgetown University's campus pregnant and only slowed down when, on a dare, I climbed the Exorcist steps up from M Street. Heaven's Gate.

I was 22 and in law school. I could do anything back then. I thought, *I can be anything.* And that's what they sold us at Georgetown Law. We would be the future leaders of our Nation. I can't count the number in my class that earned internships with Supreme Court Justices. We all had jobs before we graduated. But I was the only one who started law school surprised by a pregnancy. I had choices. I could have not married Vance, not had Sam, or put him up for adoption. That was crazy. The pressure of family, tradition, and religion was insurmountable.

So no, I walked the stage on Healy Lawn second in my class, with a toddler in the audience. When everyone else went to The Tombs for one last drink together, Vance joined them and I took Metro home to Chevy Chase, changed a diaper, tucked Sam in his crib and fell into bed. I always do things the hard way. And now, I'm doing it again.

Velma was talking to me. Her soft tones pulled me away from my memories. "Girl? Are you hearing what I'm saying? There are some things I'd like to get out of that storage unit over in Cambridge. Matter of fact, I'd like to clear the whole thing out before I die so the scavengers can't have at it. I forget what all's in there."

She rubbed the side of her nose. I nodded and picked up my briefcase. I was no further in drafting her will and trust, but I had plenty of time. "I can help you with that, if you like, Velma. Do you want me to look into having it cleaned out?"

"I'll give you the keys and you go over and take a look. Come back and tell me what I need to do."

This seemed like a perfect waste of my time. I was getting ready to suggest she hire an auctioneer and just part with things before ancient memories cropped up when she said, "There are some items that need to go to the priests for safe keeping." As if the expression on my face was doubtful, her face grew a little stern and she added, "I want to look at things first. Then you can have it all sold."

She had read my mind. "Of course. Do you have the address?"

She reached under the pile of mail on her little breakfast table. "Here," she said, proffering a creased palm with a single key and wad of paper. "Take them and see. I'll expect your report on Monday."

It was Thursday. I guess I knew how I was spending my weekend. I didn't even argue. Taking the key and the address, I tucked them in a pocket of my briefcase and said my good-byes. Velma smiled expansively and shooed me away.

In the hallway, I had to step around a maintenance worker pulling two large HVAC filters from an enormous box that blocked my path.

"Sorry, lady," he said, dragging the box to the wall.

It was John...Little John, looking out of place wearing a uniform and certainly surprised at seeing me. Gray pants, black belt, gray collared shirt and his muddy eyes. I was so surprised I didn't say anything for a second. He was old enough to start work. I had just never thought of him as being employed anywhere but McDonalds for a first time job.

"John. I didn't know you work here. That's great." He had the vestiges of a scab and orange bruising on his forehead. I tried to pull my eyes away.

"Yeah," he said. "Anything to keep Trixie from throwing me out."

"Oh, John," I said. "Have you two been fighting again?"

"She's done with me. She's got the other kids to raise and I turn 18 in July. She won't get no more state money for me after that."

"Well, look. I'm sure we can figure something out. Isn't this great you have a job to help support yourself? I'm so proud of you!"

John looked at me like I had grown a cauliflower on my nose.

*****

12 THE GRIST MILL

Davis arched, looking up at the cloudless sky and rubbed the small of his back. Propped on a scythe, its blade gleaming in the bright sunlight, he decided that he was getting too old for this work. He gazed over the miles of tall grasses, their feathery plumes whisking about in a light breeze and he was angered that they choked the shoreline of his would-be creek. This was necessary work, part of the natural law to eradicate invasive species, making way for the organized planting of the indigenous ones. For the moment, the insects had left him in an uneasy peace, their constant singing drowned by a heavy overnight rain that spurred the slight ringing in his head to a crescendo.

He had spent the last four hours from early sunrise leaning and bending in a circular motion, taking a step forward, pulling the snaith, the scythe's long handle, back in a studied motion. He swept its blade in an arc across the invasive phragmites, cutting the roots low and depositing the windrow in a bank on his left. His massive forearms were weary and streaked with dirty sweat. Pausing, he breathed deeply, drawing in the sulphuric smell of creek mud that mixed with his own stink. A sound rose from his throat in repetition, "Ghya, ghya," and clearing the ball of mucous lodged deep, he spit. Drawing a faded bandana from his pocket, he wiped the back of his neck. In the punishing humidity his frayed shirt clung to his lean, wet body. He estimated that he had cut about hell's half acre of muddy wetlands that sucked at his boots with every step. It was time to stop before anyone noticed his bent figure hiding behind the tall grasses. He would come back at dusk if no kayakers appeared and lay a tight burn with gasoline on the roots.

Davis trudged up the short slope back to his new home, the ruins of the old grist mill. Against its frame, nothing but a one-story shell, a wooden water wheel, whitened by a hundred years of salty wind, sat stuck in sediment from the risen creek bed. The headwaters had narrowed to a trickle over the decades. Lush topsoil, enriched with chicken manure that generations of farmers spread across their planted seeds each spring, had spilled into the tidal waters. Sediment suffocated the native underwater grasses, killing all but the hardiest mollusks and building a thick stew of black mud. And…it was a perfect medium for the growth of invasive grasses like phragmites vulgaris, a "takeover plant" as Davis called it.

A lover of nature laid bare to its essential elements, he had watched the reeds' compacted rhizomes choke out habitat for the mallard ducks and nesting turtles, leaving only the voles and field mice. Even the black-faced swans, another interloper, had disappeared in the last month. He was

The Grist Mill Bone

determined to rid the area of the toxic reeds. He was determined to rid the world of everything that didn't belong.

He propped his beloved scythe against the grist mill's wall and stepped inside the darkened building. Its rock foundation had grown a thick cover of green moss, musky and dank, that automatically filled his sinuses. He pressed one side of his nose and blew out the other nostril then repeated on the other side, and drew his wrist across his nose.

In places, the roof was open to blue sky and beams of dusty light shot through to the bare plank floor. A wooden table, its white paint peeling, leaned against one solid wall, a rickety chair tucked under it. His stained mattress covered in worn ticking lay rumpled in a corner on the floor.

It was a monk's existence but he was comfortable, at home. Long ago, he had perfected this way of life in his father's cellar and some backyard shed. He couldn't remember where or when. As he ran his eyes across his dwelling, he decided that a few spare wooden shelves could be fashioned from broken siding. He didn't need much, just enough to store kitchen provisions. The storage closet of the mill kept his valuables safe—safe from prying eyes, especially young ones.

"Ghya, ghya," he grunted and spit against the rock foundation. That boy, John, was bothersome but after each of his visits, Davis had felt an inkling of satisfaction, of burgeoning importance. The last one, a younger boy had tagged along but hadn't spoken to him. Davis saw himself in the older one, the one with the heavy brow. He watched him scuff along as he had as a teen, head down, shoulders slumped and hands in his pockets. Those years were almost forgotten but glimpses had begun to haunt him since the boys' appearance. But he couldn't rely on his patchy memory.

There were watchtowers that marked his existence. Before he wandered about the peninsula, before he dug up his father's hoard, before he had learned to build a framework, and long before he had been jailed, he had once relished sorting hardware. Bolts and nails, screws and hooks, cables, screwdrivers, pliers, and wire—lots of wire for his cutters— all the items he needed for displays. When he wasn't driven to physical labor, when he wasn't trying to rid himself of his devils, he settled down to work on the bones.

His inner spirit warned him when it was time to stop obsessively running the back roads for miles and miles, or gathering trash to sort, or sweeping his scythe across the devil's reed. When he ran low on food, he walked to the door of his closest neighbor, a retired park ranger. The bearded man asked no questions and eyed him with rheumy sympathy. Davis' state check arrived once a month to the ranger's home and the man would cash it for him, buy some essentials at the store, and have the pittance that was left, a few dollars and cents, sealed shut in an envelope. Davis would thank him, try to control his compulsive, "Gyah, gyah!" and disappear into the woods.

This was his only outside contact other than the boy, John, and inevitably the interchange produced an undesirable response. Inside he would bubble and burn, he would hiccup and bite his nails ragged until he heard himself whisper over and over, "Ghya, ghya." Then he knew it was time to stop and prepare his ritual…his time to create another display.

He had only seen the other boy, the one that accompanied John, from a distance—the red haired boy that was much younger. But that was his target, the holy grail of vengeance, the way to rid his world of the black plague. Or was it the man in the uniform who was his real enemy? The one who called himself the solicitor general?

It had been years since he had stood trial for the death and dismemberment of another, a crime he didn't commit. But God had seen fit not to clear him and had visited the sins of the father on the child. Davis was sure it would be visited on the children's children to the third and fourth generation as the Bible said. He couldn't remember who the next child was but was sure that he had to stop it before it occurred. It was the plague he had to rid the world of—carried by mice, or was it their fleas? He needed to redeem himself, for his father had told him that God said at his birth, "Behold Davis, brought forth in iniquity, and in sin did your mother conceive you."

Davis hiccupped and poured brackish creek water over his head as he stood on the stone doorstep of the grist mill. Cooling his heat, he passed a hand over his face with the same dirty bandana and stared through the dense forest of pine, oak, and holly. The forest glittered with mid morning sun and at a distance he saw a doe lapping at the edge of a freshwater pond. A fawn gingerly emerged behind her, nosing her flank. Suddenly, a merle of red winged black birds fluttered upward startling them and they disappeared into the dense thicket.

For a second Davis relaxed and considered sleep. But, just as quickly, he reacted with alarm at the thought of this daytime laziness and he bolted down the beaten path, out to the writhing country road and into the distance, pounding the pavement until all thoughts disappeared.

*****

13 BOOKER

"I don't like the one with the naked lady fountain out front. It's gross," said Sam from the back seat. We should go with the house that has the indoor swimming pool."

"We can tear the naked lady out. Don't you want to be on the waterfront?" asked Booker. "We can have a jet ski and dock my boat right out back on the Potomac instead of at the marina." Booker sped up to pass a four-wheeler carrying auto parts to the beach. His old Ford truck groaned, but the engine responded. "I hate the idea of having to drive to a marina to go out on my boat."

"I don't like either of them," said Claire, shaking her head. She held one hand on her growing belly as they bumped along. "I don't want to live in Virginia. I think we should put a bid on the house on Mass Avenue, near Tosh and St. Albans. It's big enough. There are four bedrooms and an apartment over the garage for Rosa and Bessie. If we have girl, she can go to the Cathedral Girl's School and Sam will be right next door."

There was dead silence in the truck and then Booker exploded in laughter. "Claire, what you talking about? In four years, Sam will be off to college and the baby won't even be ready for preschool."

Claire raised her eyes from her belly and stared at the blur of cars they passed on the highway. Booker suspected she was hiding something when a large tear splashed onto her hand. He reached over and covered it with his. She turned, blinking hard.

"I knew when the words came out of my mouth that I wasn't making any sense." She shifted in the seat and bit her lower lip. "Sam." She whispered. "He's growing up too fast."

"I can't hear what you guys are saying," shouted Sam from the cab's back seat.

"Damn it, Booker," she said louder. "This old truck is so uncomfortable. And my Mini Cooper is no better."

In the thick of beach commuters, they crested the hill on Route 50 just after the town of Annapolis, hitting a wall of cars that slowed them to a crawl. It was Friday, late afternoon, and they had not anticipated the heavy traffic headed to the Chesapeake Bay Bridge. A broad billboard on the right advertised Springfest, the annual May craft and junkathon on the boardwalk in Ocean City. Claire sighed, and Booker realized too late that the trip would be stop and start all the way to the Delaware line. She rolled the window down and glanced at a parking lot of SUVs which sat on their right, the first landmark in a line of high-end dealerships that played gatekeepers to the wealth of the colonial capitol.

"U-turn," hollered Booker just as they came upon the service road that led back to the Mercedes dealership. "My woman needs a car then we're going to get her a car."

"Oh, Booker. I don't mean now. I was being facetious."

"Everyday you come home from work, you say your back is hurting. Let's fix that."

"I don't think the car is the only reason my back hurts," she said as one eyebrow disappeared under her bangs. In the late afternoon light, her eyes glowed as they welled with tears.

Jesus, she's emotional, thought Booker as he glanced back at Sam. The boy popped his seatbelt and squeezed his face in between them, looking back and forth.

"We can't go home without *something*," Sam said, the voice of reason. "This was supposed to be a house shopping trip but since we didn't get one, we should look at cars."

Booker caught his eye and winked. "Always the great negotiator."

"Well, let's do this fast or we're going to have to eat dinner in Annapolis. I can't go without food," said Claire.

Booker took the access road into the dealership and pulled over next to a row of sleek, newly off-loaded Mercedes, still band-aided with white wrap on their bumpers. He took out his phone and called in to Tosh. If he was buying his wife a car, he was paying cash, company cash. He needed Dean Campbell, the C.O.O. of the corporation.

"You're calling Dean?" Claire asked as he waited on hold.

"Uh-huh. We're not taking out a loan. Doing this right

from the get-go."

"Tell him to direct deposit the money in our beach account," she answered.

He nodded as Dean came on the line. Booker put him on speaker.

"Booker, I hear you two were in town looking for a house. Did you find one?"

"No, we can't agree on what we want," interrupted Claire. "How're you doing? I haven't seen you in a while. Missing me?"

"You bet. While I have the two of you on the phone we need to set up a meeting with the three of us and Ross to go over the security needs on a new house here in D.C. before you sign a contract."

Booker held the phone between them, his hand on the armrest. He glanced at Sam and saw him press his lips together. This was not the time to have a conversation about security in front of Sam. Too many memories.

"Dean, hey man," said Booker. "I'll call you back tomorrow with some possible dates. Right now, we need to get Claire a new car. The mini is not cutting it for the preggo."

Dean's staccato laughter cut across the distance. Claire punched Booker's shoulder and Sam rolled back into his seat, no longer interested.

"Finally going to shelve the mini," he said. "You've hung on to that thing a long time, Claire. I remember your dad shaking his head when you bought it. What are you shopping for?"

Booker responded, "We're at the Annapolis Mercedes dealership right now."

"Sure. Okay. I'll wire your home account and add in for a down payment on a house in case you find one. That way, if I'm busy, you know you have it. Ross is standing here and wants to remind you to order all the security features from the factory so we aren't adding after the fact."

"Hey Ross," said Claire. "I'm special ordering a German tank. You just have to widen the street parking on Connecticut Avenue."

They laughed and Booker shifted in his seat. Conversation like this came naturally to them. Security, paying for a car or a house in one fell swoop, and then joking about driving tanks in congested D.C. If that was what Claire wanted, he was pretty sure Dean and Ross would find a way to make it happen. He felt like he was running uphill in cement boots trying to keep up with them.

"Dean, Booker wants to buy a car and all I want is to get some dinner so we'll call back later when I'm not so hungry." She took the phone from his hand and ended the call. His woman had everything she wanted at her fingertips, except a meal.

Booker was dumbfounded watching the amount of snack food Claire ate. So, four hours later, after he laid the keys to his old Ford truck on the salesman's desk, after he signed the last piece of paperwork, after he had driven a hard bargain because in all his life, he had never purchased a new car—after all that—he wasn't surprised when he found Claire waiting in the lounge feeding her face.

Somewhere in the first hour, between wandering the lot and Claire's disinterest, the goal changed from buying her a car to buying *him* a car. And while he had driven some tricked out undercover SUVs in his time, he had never seen anything so beautiful as the Mercedes AMG G63. It occupied center stage inside the glassed walled dealership. Spotlights, a tilted platform and the mystery of no signage lured him in. Safety, security, elegance, concealment. His heart pumped, his eyes danced and as he passed his hand over the fender like a hungry teenager, he felt the secret of his own blue steel. Holding his ball cap strategically, he looked over the list of options the sales rep handed him and came to rest on the bottom line.

In the second hour, the prospect of writing such a huge amount had worn the sheen of excitement paper-thin and his rational self warned him that he was being a spendthrift. Or worse, he was gambling with his future paychecks for appearance's sake. He was no gangsta, no flash in the pan rapper. His hardness faded as he pondered that a move to D.C. meant reinvention. He didn't care what other people thought. He wanted to be nimble about his family's safety. But mostly, he just wanted to *arrive* and not be beholden to anyone.

A sweat had built inside the collar of his shirt in the third hour as he sat across the sales desk. Taking a break from negotiations, he strolled over to Claire for some reassurance. She was munching on French fries and sucking on a chocolate shake so hard her cheeks caved. Faced with his doubt, she looked at him blankly and said, "This is stupid.

There's a company plane you can use to fly back and forth until we find a house in D.C. You won't have to sit in traffic."

"Oh man, you just don't get it do you? What am I gonna do once I get there? Use the company limo to hunt building sites for the FBI? That's an image. What could go wrong? You're making me dependent on a pilot, a plane, the weather, and getting a limo through D.C. traffic? Be real, would you?"

"Let me tell you something. You can get a lot of work done if other people are carting your ass around."

"The optics aren't good, Claire. I don't want to look like I'm imitating some rich old white dude. That was your father. I'd just look like some kind of gangsta. I want us to get around in a safe vehicle with me at the wheel. You never give your security over to hired help."

She put down the shake and wiped her hands on a napkin, not meeting his gaze. "Whatever you want to do." The words echoed in his ears as he returned to the sale wondering how he had gotten here in the first place.

It had begun with a test drive around the block through a shady Annapolis neighborhood. With Claire and Sam in the back and the salesman navigating, the conversation pumped him up. Breaking through the canopy of trees onto the overpass, the car gleamed like polished black pearl in the sunlight. The inside smelled like fine tooled leather and…new technology. Booker took the entrance ramp onto Route 50 and hit the gas. Everyone gasped and their bodies melted like a cold hand in the warm glove of the seat.

"Wow, fast," said Booker.

"Seven speed automatic," answered the salesman.

"Four wheel?"

"All the time. This baby can go anywhere on any terrain."

"Talk safety."

"Sure," he paused, evaluating Booker. "I get it. Security it is. It comes standard with infrared remote, selective unlock, rollover sensor, driver recognition sensor, and run-flat tires with steel rims." Booker heard a second's hesitation. "We have a contract company that can install double fuel tanks for distance, add a steel plate on the chassis and armor plate the perimeter. You can even have the windows bullet-proofed. Is this a government contract?"

"No."

The tone changed. Suddenly, it was 20 questions as the button down shirt in the front passenger seat tried to qualify the black man behind the steering wheel. Booker was having none of it and became more and more noncommittal, his hands played over the two tone steering wheel, his eyes on the road ahead.

Finally, the man asked, "Do you plan on purchasing today?"

"Only if I get a good price," answered Booker.

"We have excellent financing but depending on your down payment, you'd be looking at a monthly payment over $3000.00."

"Uh-huh. We can talk money later. The engine?"

"It's a V-8, 528 horsepower. Comes with six months free concierge service for any event booking you need. Concerts, hotels, flights…even dinner at The Inn at Little Washington. And it's versatile. It can haul a 7,000 lb. fishing boat. A lot of our clients spend time on the Chesapeake. Do you need this for your boat?"

"Might."

"Are you in sports, Mr. Solomon? I thought I've seen you before."

"I ended my football days years ago. How fast?"

"It's a biturbo, 0 to 60 in 5.2 seconds but I guess you figured that out back there on the entrance ramp."

They were passing the dealership on the wrong side of the highway when, from behind him, Claire patted Booker's shoulder. "Food, honey. We need to get something to eat. Can you stop at the Wendy's drive thru and I'll order a quick burger and shake?"

The salesman turned on her and in a studied voice, said, "Ma'am, I often see people get hungry when they drive one of these. Get's your juices going, I suspect. But if you don't mind, let's save the drive thru for after this little spin."

"Oh. I didn't mean I'd have to eat in the car, for goodness sake. I just thought we could save some time picking it up and I can eat when we get back to the dealership."

"Why don't we take this exit and head back to the dealership now," said the rep. "That way you all can go eat at Wendy's and if you're still interested come back later. We're open till eight tonight."

The brushoff. Booker caught Claire's eyes in the rearview mirror. She gave him an almost imperceptible nod. She nestled into the seat again and asked, "What kind of gas mileage does this thing get anyway?"

The salesman laughed and not bothering to turn around,

he flipped the visor down against the late afternoon sun. "Believe me, our clients who purchase vehicles like this baby aren't worried about gas mileage."

With studied patience, Booker pulled into the dealer lot and parked in front. Being familiar with the shut down that white folk give black folk who ask for things they can't have, he recognized this line of thinking but was surprised that it was directed at his wife.

Being a forgiving man, he decided not to be too harsh. "You know, if my wife here really wanted this truck and she felt that the gas mileage was too high for her tastes, I'd have your V-8, 528 horsepower engine torn out and put in a hybrid engine to keep her happy. Don't care how slow it drives. And I'd have it done in a week so she could take it to any Wendy's she wanted for any chocolate shake she desires, if you get my drift?"

"W-wh-why, of course, sir. I didn't mean she couldn't eat in the car. I-I'll tell you what. Why don't the three of you come inside, give me your order and I'll send someone over to Wendy's to pick it up? My treat."

Booker smiled and jumped down from the car. Wendy's, huh? He opened the back door and gave Claire a hand as she climbed out. Sam soared around the rear and hung on Bookers arm. "Are you getting it, Booker. Are you?"

Claire looked up at her husband and said, "If you want it, let's give him a check, my man. You look good in it."

"Well, you need a car, too," he said.

"I don't care. I just want a burger and a shake. Get me a hybrid off the lot. Something comfortable. Don't make me have to drive it home. Ask them to deliver it. We had these growing up, although I must say, Dad never bought a black refrigerator on wheels," she said patting the side of the SUV.

Claire walked inside the bright and airy glass walled dealership. Sam loped along behind her and Booker threw his hand on the salesman's back. "Get her a double cheeseburger, fries and a shake. That should hold her till we're done, if we're lucky."

It was everyone's lucky day. By 7:30, the fourth and final hour, they were ensconced in the black pearl refrigerator on wheels, rolling east over the bridge. Claire had made a nest in the front seat out of a sweater, his jacket and Sam's backpack. She was already half asleep. Sam busied himself in the backseat playing with any technology in arms reach. Booker scanned the pink water, glowing from the sunset behind them, the seagulls doing barrel rolls in wind currents and the triangles of sailboats bobbing below. A slow grin spread on his face. Ahh, baby, baby, you so fine, he thought. It's all mine. *I've arrived.*

*****

14 CLAIRE

We might have lost each other in a sweaty 10X12 foot box. Cambridge U-Store was one of those fenced concrete fields on the outskirts of town reached by a sandy road snaking into dying pinewoods. I had never seen a whole forest of conifers brushed red at their tops and green toward the ground. Some trunks were surrounded with what looked like coffee grounds and their bark was riddled with red sap. "Bark beetles," said Booker and I didn't ask more. Spring had been short and summer's heat was upon us. Insects everywhere. Spiderwebs in the morning, midges at night, and dragonflies all day long. It was only the middle of June.

The storage complex was so far from civilization that I wondered how the owner made a go of it. Another of my famous misconceptions. Everyone has something they want to keep. Inside the gates, we found the perimeter lined with forgotten boats and RVs and each unit was padlocked. A downed pine had crashed through the top of the fence and come to rest on an ancient trawler that rested on cinderblocks.

We drove down row upon row of aluminum warehouses as if searching the bookshelves in the Library of Congress. Yet, the location system was haphazard. Large alphabet letters labeled some end rows but were missing on others. Twice we drove past storage line "H," and once we made the correct turn, we realized many individual units were missing numbers, including Velma's. Booker and I pointed and counted like two preschoolers until we came to what we thought was her unit, H-23.

The padlock was rusted, so Booker, ever resourceful, sprayed WD40 into the keyhole. It clicked and he bent to raise the garage door in one fluid move. We had agreed he would do the lifting and I would do the sorting but the rat's nest that met our eyes deflated our bubble of anticipation before we began.

"Why are we doing this again?" he asked, scowling.

"Because she's old and infirm and she trusts me. Besides, there's something shady about her past."

"Not good enough. You said she had plenty of money. Hire somebody. You're her attorney. Let's go."

"Nope. You're not getting off the hook that easy. This is good practice for dealing with all your mom's stuff."

"Exactly. I'm related to Mom. I'm no kin of Velma's."

"But you're married to me, right?" He had worn a black muscle shirt emblazoned with a skull and some head banger death tribute that must've been left over from his undercover days. I bet he was hot. Too hot. I passed him my water bottle and he put it to his lips downing the contents. I didn't want to come back with hired help just yet. I just wanted to organize and take stock—and see if I was wrong to trust Velma.

He squinted at me in the sunlight. "Okay. We got two hours. Let's see if we can do some damage."

He began by wrangling the dresser, highboy and bedstead against the back wall and laid the rug on top of an ancient dining table. Three TVs of the last century had him cursing under his breath, they were so heavy. I swept clumps of dead bark beetles under the table while he created two rows of boxes on the right wall. At least fifty, they were all marked in black letters. Two of "Good Crystal," five of "Good China," three "knick knacks," "pots/pans," "Melamine," "Fred's Navy." "Photography" and "albums" had a box each, and then there was one that gave me pause, "Baby Stuff." Booker set the last four on the dining table and handed me the box cutter. I pulled my phone from my purse to take notes.

The photography box was filled with expensive but outdated equipment. Cameras, light meters, lenses and a collapsible tripod. I didn't know if there was a resale market but an auctioneer could deal with it. Booker had opened Fred's box and threw an enlisted man's dark wool U.S. Navy dress shirt on the table. "Thought Fred was an officer."

"That's what Velma told me. She has a really poor memory." That wasn't the way I had seen dementia work. But maybe she made up stuff when she couldn't remember the reality.

He rummaged around and pulled out a gun, holding it upside down by one finger in the trigger. It was tagged by the Maryland State Police. "Colt 45. They don't use these anymore. Some collector would like to have this."

"It's just a service revolver, right?" Then, I realized it was probably the gun that Fred used in his suicide. "Did I tell you her husband killed himself maybe 40 years ago?"

"There'll be records of that. Newspaper articles. Do a search. *Salisbury Times* and *Eastern Shore Democrat*. You sure it was a suicide? Maybe old Velma did it."

"Oh, stop. She's bossy but she wouldn't hurt a flea."

Booker grunted and opened the baby box. "You should be looking in this one. Might find some baby bell-bottoms." He stirred around as if it were a pot of sauce on the stove and drew out a picture frame. Holding it out, the bright sunlight from the garage door glared on the surface of the glass, so I grabbed it from him and laid it on the table. Two boys, seated together, their hands intertwined in their laps stared back at us. One, the bigger of the two, was solemn—the younger one was erupting in a giggle. There was no resemblance between the two but the younger boy's resemblance to Velma was unmistakable.

"She said she had two sons. But she told me one wasn't hers and he didn't come live with her until he was a teenager." I pointed to the older boy. "He's what, maybe five and this one's three."

"You don't know if they're brothers, or cousins or just friends, Claire. Don't make assumptions. Elementary mistake in investigations."

"Well, there's no mistaking this one is Velma's. He looks just like her right down to the forehead."

"You're worried about an unknown claiming her

inheritance?"

"I better be. She wants to leave it all to the Catholic Church. Two priests whom I've never even met; I've just spoken to on the phone."

"Sounds like it's time for a sit-down with them."

He reached in the bottom of the baby box and pulled out a brass box, the size of a five cup coffee pot. Its surface had browned from lack of polish but I could still make out the religious engraving of a church's poor box. On closer look, we read out loud in unison, "St. Joseph Labre, Patron Saint of the Homeless."

"Wow. Let's take that with us," I said. "It must have some sentimental value since she worked for that church in Cambridge for decades."

"Listen, Claire. My two hours were up before we got here. You got me working too hard," said Booker, wiping his forehead with the tail of his shirt and flashing me some of that six pack. I thought, yep. I want to go home, shower and lay on the bed in the air conditioning. I needed me some cuddle time.

"Let's put these boxes in the truck and head out," he said. "Sam will be getting home from school and I want to have a little talk with him out on the boat."

So much for cuddling. "What about?" I asked.

"Nun-ya," he responded as we headed to the black hulk parked out front.

We bypassed Cambridge on the way home and I pleaded with Booker to return on a day when we had more time. "Really, it'll be fun exploring another little town," I said. He grumbled, but the air conditioning in his new four-wheel guzzler blasted, cooling him off. I drummed my fingers on the armrest. Schedules make for missed opportunities, but so does squeezing in a round of good sex when you should be keeping our eye on what matters. I swore after Sam's kidnapping, that it wasn't just your heritage that could be uprooted, but your family in the process.

The ancestral home of the McIntosh family is on the Tred Avon River in Oxford, Maryland, a mere half hour from Cambridge and further north on the western shore of the Chesapeake Bay. It's a sleepy little village that has some powerful colonial history: home of Robert Morris, financier of the Revolution, and such. There was tobacco, slavery, indentured servitude and eventually abandonment of the settlement in favor of better money.

Early Cambridge might be the redheaded stepchild to that kind of history, but nevertheless, some bad history went down there in the '60s during the struggle for civil rights. I was curious about what Velma would remember of that time, if anything. Sometimes you think you know where you live and you really don't.

On the way home, traveling the back roads to the ocean, the sky grew progressively darker. The weather report that morning had predicted late afternoon showers but no tongue lashing from Mother Nature. I switched from paid satellite jazz to local news and Booker asked me why I was worried. Because, I said, we have a teenager and we always need to be worried when he's not with us.

He blinked and frowned, his nostrils pinched. "Claire,

when are you going to give it up? Sam's safe at home. He doesn't take risks outside of what he's searching on the internet. That's the *real* problem."

"Oh, and that's what *he* said, ba-dump-bump," I deadpanned and stared out the window at the squall from the east.

*****

15 THE GRIST MILL

Davis watched the clouds unfurl above the gray water. Frothy spits of foam stirred in the air and waves drove against the sawgrass embankment. To the west, patches of blue sky gave way to encroaching darkness. His chest resounded with the first clap of thunder and Davis gazed eastward, rubbing his eyes in disbelief.

In the middle of the broad creek a half-mile away, a skiff appeared, bobbing. Two figures huddled, one low over the bow, the other in back, a hand extended to the steering tiller. He shook his head.

Underpowered engine.

Too far from land.

They were a stripped screw spinning in a channel, useless against the force of the wind's fetch over water. They were headed in his direction.

Standing next to the waterwheel, Davis studied the energy of creek water against the shoreline. He had stored four armfuls of cut phrags in the mill's storage closet to eat, burning the rest so as not to leave evidence that he was squatting on borrowed land. Scanning the heightened vista, he thought his work had paid off until now. Below his boots, the brackish creek water surged into the stalk filled mud with each successive push of wind. He estimated it was a foot deep as the wave receded.

He was patient. When the salt water drew back and the skies cleared, a trickle of clean creek water would reappear from the west. He could dig out the embankment to channel fresh water, creating a pond for his personal use. He would need to find stones for filtering and ultimately he would have to start building fires to boil water and cook. He grimaced, as he was wary of fire. It could draw attention.

He was even more afraid of dark water and felt secure with his feet planted on land. Davis was a careful poacher, squatting on earth of no use to others and he loved its feel. Water, in his book, was meant to be useful; land was meant to glorify mankind and make wealth. Water could destroy the hard labor of whole families, erasing decades of fruitful work. Whether it came from the skies or rose from the creeks and rivers, water could not be trusted. Folk were always stealing land from one another but you never heard about them stealing water. No, whoever was in the boat, didn't respect the force of water. And that dumb fault was theirs. He decided he wouldn't help them.

Davis picked his way from the shoreline, his thick matt of hair blowing in a twirling rope down his back. Rain soaked him in great sheets, but he wasn't bothered. Rangy and lean, with forearms the size of ham legs, he had commandeered the four square walls of the grist mill. He strode to the door, righting his chair blown on its side against the stone threshold. To his right, the wind had battered the interior, soaking the wood floor, pouring through the roof holes and glassless windows. His bowl and spoon had scattered, spilling the remainder of a thin gruel he ground daily from the phrag seeds. He regretted this. It was past the full moon and his next supply of goods from the ranger was still days away. He had added a pinch of sugar and shake of cinnamon to make the meal palatable and now it was wasted. He shrugged. There were bigger disappointments in life.

He crossed the room. To his left stood a closet the width of the entire wall that provided support for the sagging roof. It was dry here. Before the rain began, he had run miles on the backcountry roads and now it was time to open the storage closet and remove his framework.

Over the expanding hours of spring's evening sunlight, he had measured wood, cut with a bow saw, and assembled using a motley collection of delicate screws and nails. His project was nearing its finish. The sturdy wood base was four-sided, measuring three by three with an X connecting the four corners for stability. He pushed a metal rod into a narrow steel cup at the center of the X and because he didn't like how it wobbled he screwed the rod into two angled pieces, making an equilateral triangle that reached his waist at the top. A wood rod fit into the end of the hollow metal pole and extended upward another three feet.

When assembled, the entire structure was nearly six feet

high. At the top he suspended a circular wire like a hangman's noose. The only thing he hadn't nailed was a crossbar at shoulder height. He stood back, imagining the finished piece and it struck him that it was similar to a crucifix.

He thought this would please the solicitor general, the man who had ordered the framework, because upon introductions he had held Davis' hand between his, admiring the tiny crosses tattooed on his knuckles. They had prayed. Davis splayed his fingers in an array before the framework, counting all ten of the tiny crosses—a memory of his time in lockup. Quickly, he balled his fists and seeing an appartiton flying about the grist mill, he pummeled the air.

Torrents of rain beat against the mill while an orchestra played in his head a four part children's fugue,

Row, row, row your boat,
Gently down the stream,
Merrily, merrily, merrily, merrily,
Life is but a dream.

It wasn't until he heard a shout that he stopped his boxing dance. That boat, he thought. They've come for me. He disassembled the framework and pushed it into the back of the closet, throwing the double doors closed and dropping the rusted metal slider into its hook. Involuntarily, he uttered, "Ghya, ghya."

"Hey man," came a familiar voice.

Davis turned to look at the figure pushing through the door. A man was draped in a clear plastic poncho and he thought that might be something he wanted. The figure drew his hand across the hood revealing the face of the older kid, the one who had befriended him. He couldn't remember what the kid wanted from him but remembered their talk had been pleasant.

"Hey man," the kid said again.

Davis swallowed hard. "Hey."

"We were going out fishing and got caught in this squall. It pushed us up the creek, here. Hope we ain't bothering you but we thought we'd come in and say hi!"

A smaller, rain soaked figure in bright blue hovered over the threshold, one foot in, one foot out. Davis knew he was supposed to invite them inside and offer them something. He swallowed again. "Ghya, ghya," he whispered.

"I was telling my friend here, Sam, that you got a fox skeleton. What'd you call it? Articlated? He really wanted to see it."

"Articulated," answered Davis, finding his voice.

With that, the other figure came through the door but hung behind the taller one. Davis hesitated, trying to control the noises in his throat and then walked to his closet, pausing now and again to eye the boys up and down. That was it. He had given some bones to the older boy so he could learn how to assemble.

Interest. The older boy had shown interest and wanted more. He was supposed to teach him. Davis nodded vigorously. He had given him old human bones that would never match. Possibly, they were left over from another life in the hardware store.

He cleared his throat. "Stand here," he said, pointing to

the wall near a closet door. When he swung the door open the boys craned their necks around it but Davis blocked their view. He scanned the shelving with an objective eye. A tub of sugar, his cinnamon, two gallons of water and his dried phrags tied neatly in bundles. He rummaged below and dragged a cardboard box across the floor, shut the closet and opened the box. The boys huddled around, dripping into it. Davis raised his arm, pushing them away.

"No, no, you'll get it wet," he said.

"Sorry, man. Sorry," said the tall one.

"Come on," said the younger boy. "Let's go. We can walk back. I'll get the boat later."

"No," said the older boy. "You wanted to see this. We didn't come over here in this storm just to go home."

"Okay, okay. But we gotta go fast. At this rate mom and dad are going to be looking for me."

Davis heard the worry in the younger kid's voice. He didn't want him to get in trouble. He remembered now. He had seen this boy once before and he was attracted to his curiosity and remembered that he lived near the black man. The one he wanted; the reason he had chosen to come to the creek. It occurred to him that the parents might punish the boy.

With great reverence, he drew the skeleton from the box and raised it up in the air between them, like a priest consecrating the host on the altar. "Carnivora, canidae, vulpes. The red fox," he said. The polished yellow bones gleamed even in the low light and the animal's essence appeared ready to run through the air.

The Grist Mill Bone

The boys stood back, heads up. "Cool," said the younger one as he took a step in for a closer look. The air seemed to electrify, followed by a low rumble nearby. The hair on Davis' arms rose and he counted mentally, *one one thousand, two one thousand...* A clap of thunder shook the grist mill. The boys ducked.

In an awe-struck voice, the younger one asked, "They move. How long did it take you to connect all those bones?"

"It's a work of art. Time doesn't matter," said Davis.

"You got some more, man?" asked the older kid.

"What is your name again?" asked Davis.

"John, man. You know me. I'm John, for God's sake."

"I don't hand out bones like candy. Especially human bones. You should respect them. I gave them to you so you could learn."

"Right." John grabbed the other boy's arm and pulled him away.

He wanted to be first. Davis understood that this boy, John, with the pronounced forehead, wanted to be ascendant. But the younger boy—what was his name—Sam. He wanted to learn.

"Well, if you got some more human bones stashed around here, I'll pay you for them. Or I can bring you food," said John.

The boy, Sam, broke in, "Can't you see he doesn't want to give away his creations? These are like museum pieces, John. Like in the Natural History Museum." He turned to Davis and said, "Look, he doesn't mean to be rude. We just thought it was cool after we saw the box of human bones, like something we'd like to try—maybe it's like building a model of the Millenium Falcon, you know?"

The younger boy continued as if they were in conversation outside church on Sunday morning, "No, of course you don't know. Anyway, somebody stole the bones from John and buried them by my grandmother's driveway. It sure caused a scene. But, don't worry. We're keeping our mouths shut about it 'cause we don't want to get you in any trouble. Nobody knows you're here. You're safe. We won't tell."

Davis dwelled on the boy's face. He was still soft around the gills, no down yet but below his blue eyes his cheekbones had the sharp edge of the man he would become soon. His hair was wet, tousled across his forehead, and his eyes held the sincerity of a child's soul.

"Ghya, ghya," said Davis as he laid the articulated bones in the box. His voice raspy, he said, "I can give you some bones of a vole to assemble. If you come back, I will show you how to drill the holes, how to wire it together."

"Look, I don't want to bother unless you want us to come back. I can come in my boat so as not to draw attention and I'll bring you some food," said the boy, Sam. Then to the older boy, who stood sullen, one hand on his hip, he said, "Come on John. Let's start walking. It's going to take us an hour to run home."

"I ain't running. You crazy?" asked John.

Davis didn't like where the conversation was headed all of a sudden. Why wouldn't he want to run? Was the younger boy crazy? He stood up and moved toward John, his hands at the ready. John backed away and stumbled out the door into the rain. "Okay, okay. I get it. Come on, Sam. Asshole crazy shit."

Sam followed him into the rain and Davis watched as the boys retreated down the path toward the road, leaving their skiff wedged onto the embankment by the waterwheel. He followed them a few steps and watched as John punched Sam's shoulder, saying, "What'd you wanna go tell him about the bones getting stolen for? That was a secret between you and me."

"Do you think it matters?" said Sam. "That's the lonesomest man I've ever seen. Who's he going to tell anyway?"

***

"Sam," I yelled. "Come on down. We're going to pick up Odessa for an early dinner." I stood with a foot on the bottom step, one arm on the bannister supporting myself. I was tired, my legs felt like lead and I had no desire to climb the stairs. Compass was jumping around behind me and obviously hadn't been let out. Sam was going to lose his allowance this time. I slapped the banister. He was either taking a nap or had his headset on playing Dark Souls and couldn't hear me. Just as I was gearing up to go after him, Booker appeared in the doorway to the kitchen holding the binoculars.

"He's not here. The skiff's gone. So are the keys."

"What? It's gone? In this storm? Oh, my God, Booker."

"I looked up and down the shore. I can't see him anywhere but then there's no visibility." He was frustrated.

I zoomed into hysteria. "He could die out there. Should we call DNREC? Maybe they have a boat."

"They won't send an officer out in this mess. Let's get back in the truck."

"Why would he do that?" I grabbed my purse and followed him down the hall I had just come in. "He's knows what the rules are. He knows he's not allowed to take that boat out without our permission!"

"Well there's no use talking about it, now. It's a done deal." He was ten steps ahead of me. I just couldn't move that fast.

I ran through the porch, leaving the screen door flapping in the wind. Rain, thick and blinding, battered us. Compass bounded ahead of Booker to stop and pee on a rosebush. Booker called him into the truck. Once settled, my seatbelt locked over my four-month belly, I sighed and asked, "Which way? You think he went out toward the bay or up the creek?"

"I don't think he has much choice. The wind is pushing west up the creek. Let's go by Ma's driveway and down Old Mill Bridge. Maybe he's stuck in the back creek area. He'll never make it home in the boat."

I fiddled with the sound system until an announcer's voice came, "...vicinity of southern Delaware, thunderstorms carrying microbursts. Residents are advised to take shelter..." I looked up. The sky roiled and churned.

Booker slapped my hand away, decided better, and tucked it into his lap. "Not now, Claire. Not now." He turned the radio off. Compass panted in the back seat and my heart beat in my ears. We drove through the trailer park to Lighthouse

Road, not wanting to alert Odessa to Sam's disappearance.

Out on the main drag, the lights at the gas station flickered and went out, the blackout continuing down the line of businesses. I was sure we had lost power at our house and Odessa's as well. Her rambler on the short rise above the creek had a back up generator and a collection of century old hurricane lamps on her shelves. Odessa was old school. She wouldn't flick the switch for alternate power; she'd strike wooden kitchen matches and set her lamps around the house.

The rain let up a bit but not the wind. Seabirds floated in the air looking for shelter. Traffic had thinned to nothing. Booker jerked the truck, avoiding a trashcan rolling in the street. We took the turn onto Old Mill Bridge and watched out the front windshield as the oak trees swayed in every direction under mushrooming, graphite clouds.

"You take that side. I'll take this side," he said nodding. He clicked the headlights on bright as if the beam could penetrate sideways into the woods. I gripped the armrest and prayed to see Sam traipsing along the road, wet but safe. As we passed Odessa's entrance I noticed a ribbon of yellow police tape billowing and wondered if the State had ever called Booker with the results of the investigation. We were both so busy, we never had time to follow up... we were just too busy...

16 CLAIRE

I know never to take my eyes off my child. These days, he's a windsock turning in a storm. Sometimes engaged, laughing, eyes teasing…my son. Other days, he's taciturn, vindictive, and ready to lay blame at my feet for every perceived slight.

"You didn't wash my soccer uniform…

"You never have anything good to eat in the fridge…

"Why can't I get more allowance…

"Did you check the history on my computer again? Stay out of my room…"

I get so aggravated about the time he spends playing those damn video games but then I think, at least he's sitting at his desk, safe in his room.

The right side of the road was all Solomon property and densely forested. The drainage ditch that parallels the road ran with rushing rainwater, overflowing into shallow woodland, creating misty pools of water. There was no Sam, no signs of any life.

We reached the south side of the bridge where rising creek water had submerged the grasses and was encroaching on the road when a clap of thunder struck and the rain came down in sheets again. Booker slowed and we both leaned forward in our seats to scan the whitecaps rolling in from the east. We couldn't see much, perhaps 150 yards but on the far shore, I thought I saw an outline of the skiff, cockeyed against the reeds. The ruins of the old grist mill were barely visible behind it.

"Booker, do you see that?"

"U-huh. Looks like it's pushed down all the phrags in that spot." His brown eyes caught mine, his face so stern. "We're crossing the bridge. Undo your seatbelt and crack the window a quarter inch."

"Why?"

"Just do what I ask for once."

He unlocked the doors. Compass stood on all fours and pushed his face between our seats, his panting fogging the windshield. I glanced out the window and watched in horror as an enormous black cloud formed in two shelved layers chugging toward us. Lightning strikes knifed through them hitting the brackish water below. I felt a jerk and realized Booker was checking the four-wheel as we rolled slowly onto the bridge, high water creeping around its edges. I knew we would get across before it rose enough to sweep us away, but would we be able to cross back over to home?

We nosed through, the rain pelting the windshield and I scanned the edges of the bridge wild with fear that Sam was floating face down in the water below. The trees surrounding the grist mill shivered as if in some magical trance. It was then that we both saw Sam.

"There he is," shouted Booker.

"Oh my God, Booker. Look at him."

Sam was struggling down the path that led to the road, a bright blue exclamation point in the darkness. I had gotten him a wet suit of bib overalls and matching hooded slicker for Christmas. He was embarrassed by the color, saying he would never wear it and told me to send it back. Today, he'd found a use for it.

The truck, buffeted by the storm, seemed to tilt despite its weight. Top heavy, it felt like it might roll. I screamed at Booker, "Hurry," just as I caught sight of another person who was taller, following Sam at a distance. Walking slowly, he stopped at the edge of the woods beside an ancient oak that was mostly dead. Sam was fifteen feet in front of him, close enough he might have heard me if I yelled. I recognized the pudgy outline of Little John.

Lightening struck close and with an involuntarily duck, I looked over my shoulder at the water by the bridge. It was rising fast. Hood up, clutching it around his face, Sam was keeping his eyes on his feet.

Booker hit the accelerator and we took the small rise in the road. Then, just as suddenly, Booker jammed on the brakes and the truck reared. I pressed both hands against the dash and my eyes were drawn to Little John who casually leaned against the oak tree as if he was waiting for a bus. Time froze. He shifted, laying both palms against the tree and pushed hard, his face determined. I heard a crack and for a minute, couldn't tell if it was thunder or the tree. I screamed again as the tree broke free of the forest.

Throwing the door open I jumped from the truck. Water rose around my feet, up to my shins and I grabbed at the bumper to steady myself.

"Sam, Sam. We're here," I yelled but the winds took my words and flung them back at me. Leaving the safety of the truck, I slogged through the water and in the increasing dark, another figure separated from the trees, racing toward Sam. He ran spring-loaded, a winged Hermes, head down, arms pumping. He passed Little John unnoticed and tackled Sam from the side, throwing him over his shoulder as the tree toppled into the path. Sam and his savior were devoured in the branches and leaves as Little John watched from safety.

Finding my legs, I ran from the truck, Booker following in my tracks.

"Sam, are you all right? Where are you?" We neared the mound of tree and stumbled through the sea of downed limbs, both of us yelling in unison. Compass bounded from the truck and began his own search. Rustling through the dead leaves, the dog's fur blended in and he eventually crawled into a section of shiny green. A leafy hump moved as if alive and Sam emerged, slickered in blue. He tumbled into Booker's arms and then mine. I clutched him to me as we fell to our knees.

"Mom, where have you been? I knew you'd come."

"Oh my God, Sam. You can't take chances like this. What were you thinking?" My hands cupped his face, level with mine and I searched his eyes. Bruised and tender, his filled momentarily before he blinked back the tears.

"I—I'm sorry, Mom."

From somewhere behind Sam, I heard Booker yell, "What's the matter with you? You stupid or just trying to kill your friend over there?"

He had leaped over the downed tree and grabbed John by the scruff of his neck as he tried to escape. His other arm wrapped around the boy's midsection and he slammed John against another tree. The wind blew his words about but no one could mistake that kind of anger. My husband had lost control. He scowled inches from John's face, wired in his own power. "You know, you belong in prison and one day, that's where I'm gonna put you."

"Booker! That's enough," I said, scurrying as fast as I could around the felled oak. "We'll talk this out in the car. We need to get out of here before the bridge is flooded."

My hand rested on his forearm, his muscle flexed and he relented.

"Get in the truck. Now," he said to John. He stood back to let the boy pass and John glanced at me. The look on his face! He was seething, not at all sorry. Quickly, he turned away as if I had seen too much.

Booker and I climbed around the downed tree and he pulled branches away from the trunk calling for the man who had carried Sam out of it's path. We thought we knew where he had landed but there was no one crumpled beneath it and no one answered our shouts. The rain was so heavy our voices were muffled to our own ears.

Frustrated, we headed to the truck, entering on the

leeward side. Sam climbed in first across the seat in back, and me in front. He cuddled Compass who pawed him as if he hadn't seen him in a week. Little John glanced warily into the rearview mirror at Booker who remained impassive. The engine hummed and Booker wheeled us around facing the bridge. Again, he unlocked the truck doors and cracked the windows. Rain ran inside.

"Booker, shut the windows. I'm getting wet," said Sam.

"Like you aren't already? You better sit and be quiet, Sam. Don't question your father," I said.

Creek water rushed across the bridge and Booker drove slowly into it, eyes locked on the road ahead. John craned his neck but unable to see out the window at the water, he leaned back.

"Damn. You're gonna drown us, man."

"John," I snapped. "Be quiet."

"I'm just saying. Just 'cause you got an expensive truck, don't make you God."

I'd had enough. "John, you can shut up or get out of the car and walk home." Staring at him, I continued, "Do you get it now?"

Sam piped up from the back seat. "What happened to the other dude? The one who grabbed me from the tree? Did anybody see him?"

"For Christ's sake, Sam," said Booker. "Did you hear your mother?"

The truck inched forward, waves splashing against the left door panels and over the hood. I could hear water rushing underneath us. A gust howled, winding out eerily like the

McIntosh banshee, a screech my father's mother imitated when I was too young to know of such things. She called it keening, a mournful wail that announced the death of our kin, particularly a woman in childbirth when in reality, it was just a crazy old woman scaring her grandchild.

I clenched my teeth, gripped Booker's thigh and prayed. I am not given over to lengthy recitations but this time it rushed from my soul and winnowed my thoughts to a phrase... "to thee do we cry, poor banished children of Eve..."

"Jesus, Claire. You're drawing blood."

"Sorry. It's the prenatals." With all that calcium in the baby vitamins, I had grown claws. I gripped the seat instead but it wasn't nearly as satisfying as Booker's flesh.

I felt another wave push against us and the wheels lost contact with the road as I sucked air over John's whining. We floated in a diagonal toward the railing where the front right bumper made contact with a *thunk* and the truck came to rest. The engine chortled then failed.

Booker dropped his hands in his lap, his eyes darting over the dashboard and I stared into the swirling water. As I watched, a river of rain washed down the windshield. In slow motion, the brackish creek crested below the truck windows, below the engine, only as high as the bumpers. My heart thumped in my chest and the baby stirred. I wrapped my hands around my belly, willing us to safety, whispering a Hail Mary. In seconds the wave subsided giving us traction.

Booker tried the engine and it caught. He accelerated and we cleared the bridge, creeping above the widening creek. Only the tips of the wetland grasses tickled the light of day, submerged with each new surge of salt water. We watched, incredulous, as hail fell like diamonds from the skies, spitting at the turbulence below. Now that we were safe, I could see the beauty.

He closed the windows and threw John a towel, saying, "Wipe it down back there and hand it back to Claire."

"Booker, we should stop in at Odessa's and make sure she's all right," I said. "The power's probably been off for hours."

"Uh-huh. Call Trixie and tell her we have John."

The windshield wipers beat back and forth at a furious pace and the pounding of hail on the truck's roof echoed inside. I called, yelling at Trixie that we would return John once the rain let up. Her voice was surprised, but she thanked me saying she thought John was working at the nursing home.

"Figures," said John. He was wedged into the corner of the back seat, soaking wet in his rumpled, plastic poncho. His black Metallica T-shirt and worn jeans left me feeling as forlorn as he looked.

I could not imagine what Sam saw in this unlikely friendship but I couldn't say that to Booker. It seemed to me that all they shared were video games. But then, Sam always was a sucker for helping the underdog over his own personal needs. Looking at John's dower expression I wondered if Sam knew when the law of averages would win out. I leaned into my seat and looked into the visor mirror. My hair was plastered to my face and mascara streaked my cheeks. I wasn't wowing any pageant hashtag on Instagram either. But appearances weren't the issue.

Was Little John totally clueless leaning against the tree? Worse, was I right that he had actually pushed against it? Maybe I was just too frightened in the moment. Surely he saw that it was dead, the trunk whitened and stripped of bark. Maybe he hadn't put together that his bulk could topple it.

And then I wondered what the boys were doing by the ruins of the grist mill anyway. What could be so pressing that Sam broke a standing rule that he could only use the skiff with permission? Living on the water as we do, it wasn't like Booker and I hadn't had many stern conversations with him about weather and boats.

I wiped my eyes with a damp tissue thinking the biggest conundrum was identifying the man with the dreadlock ponytail. He came out of nowhere and saved my son from, if not death, at the very least, broken bones. I blew my nose. We were headed to Odessa's, a woman who knew everyone in the community. I'd ask her.

We drove past the excavation on the driveway where the police investigators had removed all the odd bones.

"I haven't had time to call about it," said Booker thinking the same thing as me.

"Maybe they've notified your mom with the results."

"Doubt it. Investigators don't put anything out for public consumption until it's a done deal or headed to court."

"But your mom isn't the public. She's the property owner. She has a right to know what they found on her land."

"Well, she's probably sitting with her hurricane lamps singing *Nearer My God To Thee*. I'll turn the generator on and we can go get something to eat. I'm starved."

"Me too," said Sam.

"Me too," said John, suddenly grateful to be in our company.

"Yeah, well. You know I can always eat a table leg," I answered.

Booker and I were overdue for a Sam conference. One of those 'do you see the consequences of your behavior?' conversations that always lead to sullen faces and slammed doors these days. Or maybe I had it wrong. Didn't he wrap his arms around me and say he knew we'd come for him?

We pulled under the portico by the front door. There were no lights visible but Odessa always sat by the great room fireplace, alternately watching the creek and at this hour, *Wheel of Fortune* on TV. I didn't want us to startle her so I picked up my phone again and called to say we were coming in. There was no answer.

We entered. The house was dark inside, no hurricane lamps to light the way.

"Ma," Booker shouted, "We came to get you for dinner. Want to go the pizza den? I'm sure they got power."

The boys were dripping wet and I told them to remove their raingear at the door. Odessa was meticulous about her floors. Booker had hung his on the hook and strode down the short hall into the family room.

"Ma?"

Sam was struggling to get out of his slicker. I pulled on his jacket and watched as Booker passed through the kitchen still calling. He disappeared from sight. I had Sam's jacket halfway off when I heard Booker groan.

Then I raised my head as he called out, "Claire, call 911. Ma's down. And don't come in here. Stay with the boys."

***

Sam didn't leave his room for three days. On the first day, I sat outside his door and listened to his strangled crying. On the second day, he mumbled in answer to my pleas to open up but left me frustrated and silent. He waited to use the bathroom when I wasn't upstairs and wouldn't answer Booker who stood at the bedroom door as helpless as I. On the third day, he opened the door in time for the funeral, dressed in the suit he had worn for his high school interview. He was ashen…and nearly immobile. I broke down in tears and he walked away from me. We rode in silence to the Freeman's Baptist Church.

It seemed like all of Sussex showed up, but to me, they were all faceless. We parked in the rear of the church and took our seats in the front row. A sign greeted us at the altar: *Odessa Solomon, a Celebration of Life.* The assistant choir director nodded to the organist and she struck the opening chords. Something about reaching the other side of the *Chilly Jordan* sung in three-part harmony, no less. Miss Lydia, Odessa's longtime friend, sang *The Battle Is Not Yours* with a rousing chorus to "hold your head up high." Booker's baldhead remained bowed throughout. I held his hand, and Sam leaned against his father's shoulder, drained of tears.

I glanced to my right and paused over a line of cabbage-faced older white males in suits. The state senator and his lackeys stuck out from the rest. Elbowing Booker, I nodded in their direction and he whispered, "County council. Election year—looking for votes, I guess." I suspect Sam and I were pretty noticeable, too, sitting alongside Booker. If people didn't know we had an interracial marriage before, they did now.

There were other church leaders, each one taking a turn at the podium as part of the Christian Charities Network that Odessa help start back in her heyday. Then, Odessa's minister gave a resounding eulogy recalling the Solomon family legacy that she was "a Christian woman who held our hearts in her hands with her husband who shepherded our lives over the generations." He anchored each stanza with "I remember the day…" as if calling up stories from the Old Testament.

Words extolled their veterinary service of large animals on local farms and their great grandparents who supported black tenant farmers who would've starved without access to Solomon land. Shouts of *Amen* rose from the congregation. The minister called out to "Remember the day of the grist mill, how it ground corn for our free black ancestors, then wheat for our community and even bone meal for fertilizer on our early farms." Heads nodded and murmurs spread like they were all alive over a hundred years ago. I was pretty sure family memories hinged on those stories told around the dinner table. I thought if that had been my heritage, I would have been proud to share it too. My colonial family were tobacco farmers, poor, indentured servants, who rose up on the backs of black slaves to make their fortune. Not as noble an existence. I have guilt. Booker teases me and tells me to pay up in bed.

He leaned back in his seat, threw his arm across the chair behind me and raised his eyes to the ceiling trying, no doubt, to shake the weight of Solomons dead and gone. He was ready to leave this world behind for the call of—what had Odessa said—"government lucre?"

In the end, we marched down the aisle to a single earthy voice singing *Be Still My Soul* and all I could see were hands reaching to touch Booker. He stopped here and there to hug family friends and Sam I and I stood motionless, waiting for him to lead us out. It took forever. I was aware of our place, our whiteness, our recent belonging, which somehow seemed in question now that Odessa was gone.

Outside the church, Booker and I invited them to lunch at the fire hall. It wasn't lost on me that I had expected the next funeral I attended to be Velma Owens' but she was still hail if not hearty. At the fire hall I wandered around uttering conventions. After the umpteenth 'thoughts and prayers' a familiar numbness invaded my bones and I remembered my father's funeral. Different but the same.

Sam led us to the fried chicken, baked beans and coleslaw. But having no appetite, the three of us sucked down sweet tea. Later, I wandered into the kitchen to get some more ice. I laid the ice bucket on the top of the machine and bent down to open the door. That's when I heard them, a group of white ladies of a certain age, standing in a circle by the plated desserts.

"You know she stole him from every good black girl down here. They don't like her. It was only 'cause they all respected Odessa they never said nothin' to him."

"I heard his last girlfriend did. Brenda Mack's daughter, Queenie. She gave him holy hell for selling out."

"I hear Miss High Horse lost her big city money in the recession. That's why she's working as an attorney in Georgetown for next to nothing. Must be a real comeuppance after how she been born and bred."

"Ain't got nothin' to do with money. She's just like every other western shore come-here: out to change us. Think they know it all. Paint us all like some kind of country bumpkins."

I stood up and the door to the ice machine slid shut with a bang. They all turned in my direction. With studied care, I tossed my auburn hair like a runway model and held the ice bucket over my bellypudge. I smiled.

"Wow. Just a laundry list of Eastern Shore meanness? 'Cause none of the black folk around here talk about me like that. Wonder how you ladies will feel when I spit out Booker's ginger baby?" I scanned the shock on their faces. "Only five more months to wait and you can let loose on that!" I stalked out of the kitchen.

Booker was talking to an elderly woman with a walker. I leaned over and whispered, "Who *are* they?"

He glanced into the kitchen and waved. "Don't pay them any mind, Claire. What?" he said amused. "They just got your goat? Chalk it up to the ladies auxiliary."

After two more hours we dragged our tails home to Odessa's and began to organize all the donated food. Sam couldn't complain that I never had anything to eat in the fridge.

We had no sooner arrived and finished hauling in the aluminum foil trays to the kitchen than the doorbell rang. Sam was in the den watching TV and I was up to my elbows in macaroni and cheese and deviled eggs. I answered the door, dishtowel in hand. I recognized the face.

"Ms. Solomon? I'm Natalie Messick. I'm looking for Mr. Solomon."

The woman was small, smaller than me but she looked like someone who had only recently made it out of grade school. Short, dark hair and an unfocused look in her eyes. She pushed her glasses up her nose and adjusted a briefcase under her arm.

"He's out at the boat right now. May I tell him what this is about?"

She hesitated and pawed the stone. "I met you all earlier last month when the investigation began on this property. I'm forensics with the major crimes unit, Delaware State Police. I'd like to speak to him privately… and off the record."

"Sure, I remember. Please come in and have a seat. I'll just be a minute getting him." I planted her in the family room next to Odessa's hideous grain pot and tore out on the deck to call him. In the glow of afternoon light, my man seemed ethereal, almost supernatural. He walked up the hillside and asked me what I wanted now. His attitude changed when I told him Natalie Messick was waiting. He strode inside.

"Mr. Solomon, I'm sorry to bother you at such a difficult time. I wanted to speak with you before a detective shows up at your door. I hope you'll keep my presence between us?"

The Grist Mill Bone

She looked at me sideways. A direct woman, plain speaking, she wasn't wasting our time.

"Of course we will. Claire and I are a team." He sat down across from her on the couch and leaned in, elbows on knees. I folded my towel on the kitchen counter and joined him.

"I'm giving you a copy of my report to the state's attorney about the dig on your property. Basically, I'm going out on a limb providing you this ahead of time but I have my reasons." She blinked hard and started again. "It says that none of the bones have matching DNA, except two." Lacing her fingers together, she tried to focus on Booker but I guessed his spring-loaded intensity was too much for her. She looked down. "The bones all appear to be in museum quality preservation. The femur and the fingertips found in the gun case belong to the same person."

Booker was glancing through the report. He didn't raise his eyes from the page. I put my hand on his for the third time that afternoon. He looked at me, then Messick. "I'm sorry," he said. "What was that about the fingertips?"

"Yeah. They belong to a black man, Matthew Williams, who was murdered on the Eastern Shore in 1931. He was lynched by a mob and then his body was burned. The crowd cut off his fingers and toes as souvenirs."

Booker squinted back at her. I could tell he was wondering what this all had to do with us. "I know the story. Go on," he said.

"Salisbury. Happened in Salisbury. The sheriff reclaimed what was left of the body that night for the family but it's an unsolved murder. The sheriff kept some of the toes. The DNA is on record for any of us forensic people to match."

"Jesus, Mary and Joseph," said Booker. "If you're black, this is like a Bible story. Ma's father was there that night. I remember she said it was a good thing we didn't live in Wicomico County. It's a good thing we have our community here in Sussex." He rolled the report closed, I suspect not wanting to see anymore. "And what does this have to do with us?"

"The bones were planted here. With a gun case, a Browning pocket pistol, and the fingers. Why?"

"Because someone's got it in for me." It wasn't a question. He was resigned to the fact. I looked at him in disbelief. He always told me not to assume and here was a case of him saying and not doing.

"Maybe. But it's clumsy," said Messick. "The question is why would you, a black property owner, have evidence from a black lynching in the 1930s and plant it near your own driveway?"

"Because I'm saving it for posterity? I don't know. You tell me."

"Your fingerprints don't show up on any of the evidence. That's why this is so clumsy, like a kid's prank. But, the fingerprints on the gun case have a match in the NCIC database."

"Whose database is that?" I asked, hoping the 'N' stood for 'national.'

"National Crime Information Center. FBI," she said.

"Who's the match?" asked Booker.

"A man named Davis Vickers. He was put away in

The Grist Mill Bone

Delaware on circumstantial evidence for killing a black farmer and creating a display of his skeleton back in the 90s. Thing was that the skeleton wasn't one single person and some of the bones matched Matthew Williams DNA. It was all questionable evidence."

"A bone cache? To make a display? That's a sicko," said Booker, throwing Messick's report on the coffee table.

"Maybe. Or maybe he took the heat for somebody else. The guy's too young to have participated in the lynching. We'll never know how he got them. Matthew Williams' fingers and toes were hacked off before he was burned to a crisp. The mob threw his digits on the doorsteps of black homes that night as a warning." Messick waved a hand in the air. "We know the fingerprints on the outside of the gun case match Vickers. Could somebody think you're the right person to solve a cold case?"

"Not that cold. More than likely somebody wants my hide. 1931? Things haven't changed that much for a black man like me who's made it in the world. Hate's just a little more subtle."

Booker stood up. His normal looseness was gone, his body rigid. He poured himself some tea from a jug and then left the glass on the counter without taking a sip.

"There's always a story for public consumption and then there's the real story," he began. "Matthew Williams worked for a white lumberyard owner and had saved a big 50 bucks. That was a lot of money back in the '30s. The owner's son wanted a loan from that black boy and when his father sided with Williams, the son shot his father and wounded Williams to make it look like he was the perpetrator. That very same night, a white mob tanked themselves up and stole that black boy from the hospital, lynched him on Salisbury's courthouse lawn before attaching him to the back of a car and dragging him down Isabella Street. They doused him in 40 gallons of gas and lit him up like a funeral pyre.

"Nobody ever found his killers but funny thing is 1000 people came from all over the peninsula to watch it happen. They tossed those fingers and toes on the porches and lawns of black folk as a warning."

"Barbaric," I said.

"No one ever found his money either," said Messick.

Booker looked at me, lips pressed for a second and said, "Poverty, the root of all evil. H. L. Mencken in the *Baltimore Sun*."

"What?" asked Messick.

"Mencken wrote in an article, 'The common argument that crime is caused by poverty is a kind of slander on the poor,' " I answered.

"He was a racist at heart. Even with the Scopes Monkey Trial," said Booker.

"Yeah, and he was also guilty of binary thinking."

"Right. Black or white. Monkeys or Creationism."

"Evolution or the Bible," I said.

"Oh, I get it," interjected Messick. "Fundamentalists or atheists. Whatever. I feel like I'm still fighting these battles. Race biology has surfaced again as a theory—like cranial size indicates inferiority. And you know what happens? Somebody's always trying to tamper with the evidence.

That's why I'm here."

"Here at my house or here at your job? What're you getting at?" asked Booker looking annoyed.

"Your house. The facts are what they are. There were over 4000 lynchings in this country between the Civil War and the early '30s, and seven recorded right here on the peninsula."

"You're going to have to be more explicit. What does that have to do with my mother's death?"

"This kind of hate might be more subtle today but it's how the 'powers that be' use the facts to get what they want."

"And that is, Ms. Messick?" asked Booker.

"Your land," said Natalie.

It was an enlightening conversation. Odessa's land, at the cheapest price they could get, meant millions. And that meant buy it early before Booker got it appraised. Or, having a naturally suspicious mind, I thought: *steal it from him*.

Messick claimed powerful men were turning a blind eye, building personal wealth down the line: county legislators, developers, and the landowners, many of whom were the same people in different positions. I knew that nobody gave a goodgoddamn about the consequences of building all these beach houses on sinking land that flooded with each nor'easter. But then Messick's next words fell like a stone in Odessa's family room.

"If they can tie you up in a criminal case, they figure you'll have to sell the land to support your defense," she said, stroking her neck like a general at war brushed his beard.

"Whoa! That's a pretty damning accusation," said

Booker.

"Yeah, well. I never thought their greed went so far to ruin a good man's reputation, but anything goes for money."

I gripped the arms of Odessa's rocker and leaned back remembering Mencken's editorial on the Eastern Shore lynching "kultur." I was in first year law school when I read it. People didn't expect much from the local police and media back then. But when all was said and done, even the arm of justice hid the truth, never trying anyone for Matthew Williams' murder. Mencken had excoriated the people on the peninsula from the safety of Baltimore and they answered with threats to his life. Williams' lynching was followed by another brutal murder in Salisbury, a bludgeoning of a black man's skull and again two years later by a lynching in Princess Anne, a Maryland County near the Virginia border. Years ago they were a breed apart, but surely those sentiments had died out.

I knew what I wanted. I wasn't up for any ugliness and Messick told us to be prepared, it was coming. She had overheard a conversation as a group of detectives left her forensics lab the day before.

As we escorted her to the front door, she said, "There's something else. I have the preliminary results of the autopsy on your mom, too. They asked me to hold off writing the report until they completed their investigation. They have to follow up with Vickers and his case. But you should know about your mother. The heart attack was triggered by electrocution. Her left fingertips were pink and blistered."

Booker's eyes widened in shock and he fell back against

The Grist Mill Bone

the hall table, rocking it against the wall. Recovering, he asked, "Who asked you to hold off on your report?"

"Lowery."

Booker cursed and Messick said nothing, just waited patiently. I thanked her and shook her hand. As the door closed behind her, Booker looked at me briefly. "The laundry room," he said and bolted.

I followed. He grabbed a pair of plastic gloves beneath the sink and stretched them on. "Got your phone?" he asked.

"Yep."

"Take notes for me."

He flipped on the overhead lights and the room burst into sterile awareness. Two stainless steel racks against the left wall contained a jumble of flowerpots, detergents, and large baking pans packed in tight, Odessa style. The indoor recycling bins were tucked in the corner next to the washer, dryer and utility sink. A corkboard full of faded family pictures hung on the wall next to the light switch. Next to it was the door that led to the garage.

Booker grabbed a flashlight from the shelf and walked over to the sink. He shone the light behind the washer and opened the lid. "Empty."

"The dryer?" I asked.

He opened its door and one of Odessa's bright yellow cotton tops fell to the slate floor like a fallen bird. The rest of her clothes bunched in a small hill inside the dryer.

"She never opened the dryer door," he said. He leaned one hand on the stainless steel sink and followed his thought, turning to look at his hand. He raised it and put it back a couple of times. I thumbed some words into the notes application on my phone. Silently, he raised the flashlight to a square metal box installed on the wall above the dryer. In the middle of the box was a brass button. A ribbed metal cable snaked from the box into a rubberized service hole that accessed the outside.

"What does that go to?" I asked.

"The generator she never uses," he said.

Booker trained the flashlight on the black supply cord to the dryer and followed it, bending down below the sink.

"Come here," he said to me.

I laid my phone on the nearest shelf and slipped in beside him keeping my baby bump out of the way.

"Hold the light," he said.

I held it and followed his gloved hand as he pulled the supply cord out, running his fingers the length until it disappeared under the sink.

"What the hell!" he said.

We both peered up and there at the back we could plainly see the cord was wrapped tightly around the rear leg of the sink. Booker tugged on it, pulling it loose. The light wavered in my hand and he took it from me, training it on the cord where a half inch notch had been cut fresh out of the black rubber skin, exposing two red and black wires twisted loosely together. Booker swore again.

"The power wires are exposed. Intentionally wound against the steel table leg. If she touched the sink she completed the loop."

"What loop?" I asked.

The Grist Mill Bone

"The generator to the dryer to the sink and back to the generator. It only worked if the power was off and she wanted to start the generator."

"So it can't shock us now because the generator isn't on? There's got to be more evidence than that."

"Hop up," he said. "I got to go look in the garage."

I pushed up out of his way, not very gracefully. I was so tired and just wanted the day to be over. My heart was thumping hard and I felt dizzy as Booker pushed past me to the garage. I stumbled after him and hung onto the doorjamb with a shaky hand. In the light from the laundry room, he stood in front of the electric box running his fingers down the breakers. He clicked one back and forth. I flipped the lights on in the garage.

"Number 13. The dryer," he said.

"What?" I asked still dizzy, my knees weak.

"It's popped. Somebody planned this. Ma was murdered."

The overhead garage lights swayed back and forth. I lost my grip on the doorjamb and my knees buckled. Ever so slowly, I slid down against the wall and called out. I heard my voice in a tunnel far away, "Booook—er, I...I..."

*****

17 THE GRIST MILL

Davis sat cross-legged on the splintered wood floor, an orange tabby languishing in his lap. He listened to the rise of the cicadas' song and the cat's purr that subsided in a valley of quiet as his hand moved mechanically across its fur. He watched with secret delight as the tip of its tail flicked like a light switch. Finally, he had the peace he yearned for while living in prison commotion. It had arrived on the creek where he was able to work alone, eat alone, sleep in quiet, and *now* he had earned a pet of his own.

Only this hot summer morning he had been polishing and sorting his collection of skulls when the cat slipped into his space, taking ownership of his mattress. He had fed it milk from his new cooler, a gift from the solicitor general and the cat decided to stay, rolling about on the floor, watching him, watching it.

Davis raised his head at the sound of tires scuffing the sandy stone outside and his hand tightened around the cat's ribs. It hissed and sprung away. His moment of reprieve lost, he gathered the skulls and laid them carefully in a large plastic box, another gift. Intending to store it in his closet that had grown conspicuously crowded in recent days, he paused when he heard the car engine burble and cut in front of the mill. A door creaked open and a voice came, "Boon. Are you here? I brought a visitor. Come out." He recognized the voice.

Boon. Boon. Why had the solicitor general dubbed him that? He couldn't remember but he knew it was a compliment. He would have to ask the young man and hope it wouldn't anger him. Davis had watched the man inspect his skulls on an earlier visit, but there was another reason he had come today. What was it? Why had he thought to be so familiar that it was his right to bring company?

He wasn't used to all these visitors. They brought obligations. The boys appeared first, coming back stupidly in the storm, and then the black man with the pretty white woman, which confused him. The only explanation was he thought the two must work together and were forced by circumstance and the rains to ride in the same car. They left that day in the black man's vehicle, but not before the black man threatened to catch John. Catch him and put him away for years, repeating the sentence he had given Davis. John, an innocent boy, one who only wanted the respect he was due.

And then there was the matter of the red haired boy who had survived the tree falling with nary a scratch. Standing in the doorway of the grist mill, Davis had heard the tree crack with John's weight and knew what would happen. His quick rescue had earned himself a deep bruise across his lower back that had caused him to limp for a week. He had escaped, unnoticed. But barely. He couldn't take that risk again.

"Boon? We want to see the progress on your assignment. Come out."

The assignment. The afternoon light cut an oblique angle through the window casings and Davis hung back in the shadows, craning his neck to see outside. He swatted at a lazy honeybee that wove lackadaisically in the sunlight near his face. The solicitor general, a name the young man had used in his formal introduction, was tall and bulky, still soft in the middle, like a child. His face was round, his cheeks smooth and clean as a baby's ass. He must have grown his thin line of mustache to prove his age. The young man, the solicitor general, stood under a tree looking inside.

The sun glinted off the hood of the car and haloed in Davis' view, nearly blinding him as he stepped outside. Squinting, he shielded his eyes with his arm, extending his other hand warily. The solicitor general grabbed it and shook enthusiastically. Feeling an odd thickness, Davis turned the boy-man's hand in his, and saw that the ring and pinkie were formed in one, leaving him three instead of four fingers on his right hand. He wondered what the bone would look like stripped of its skin and sinew. The solicitor general pulled away, wiping his hand on his pant leg. Davis stepped back under the tree to remove the glare from his view. He rubbed his eyes and was surprised the other man was much older.

He glanced, careful not to stare because he found the man's blue eyes intense. Stringy hair was combed over a bald pate, marked by brown moles. The folds of his skin around his mouth were thick and his lips moved in small words that Davis didn't understand, attuned as he was to the cicadas' song. The man's heavy gut hung over his belt and the buttons on his lower shirt were stretched near to popping. Davis knew this man from a former time, and yet, he didn't know him. He sensed that he needed to be careful.

"This is Glower, a friend of mine. He wants to help you, Boon."

The man spoke and saved Davis from having to embarrass himself with the question. "And how did this guy get the name 'Boon'?" asked Glower, clapping the solicitor general on the back.

In his boy-man voice, the solicitor general answered, "Well, we was sharing our love of our fellow man and the perfection of the human race and how it must be preserved for the white man to proliferate. And Boon here, he knows something about that preservation. He knows how to make sure our brotherhood remains strong. He comes from a long line of baboon hunters. His father hunted before him and that's how Boon learned to preserve the skeletons of those who're imperfect so we can teach our children what the deviant ones look like underneath their dark skin. So, as the solicitor general, in charge of registering new names to our cause, Boon here is listed as 'Baboon Hunter,' in charge of keeping skeletons."

"Well, that's mighty fine," said Glower. His tie ruffled in a short breeze and fell across his protruding gut. He wiped his forehead of sweat as the afternoon sun bore down on the threesome like a sizzling grill press. Davis watched as he patted his tie flat in an effort to hide his shirt buttons. It was a ragged blue tie, painted with a silver marlin, breaking above an ocean wave. Davis understood the man had given up caring about his appearance and wondered what other battles he had lost. The men waited and he realized it was his turn to speak.

He cleared his throat. "Come in. I'll have to get it from the closet."

They bowed their heads, stepping under the door's slate lintel that was held in place by two oak beams on either side, saving the outer wall from complete collapse. The two men were quiet, almost reverent the way Davis had seen his father bow on Sunday before the altar. And sure enough, Davis, or Boon, as he was in their company, hoped that they would judge him worthy, as he knew he was different. Not remembering their coming, he hadn't dressed in his button-down-Sunday morning, his one and only good white shirt. It hung on a nail beneath the clear plastic rain poncho, a gift from John.

He looked around, trying to see his surroundings from their eyes. Like the ancient Christian monks who his father said were persecuted by the Romans, he had learned to stay ordered and spare while in prison, not accumulating much since jealousy and grift could put his life at risk. He knew better than to be impressed with their glad tidings, as sweet words were often a cover for pain to come. Someone always wanted to strip you to the bone. Still, he hoped to impress them with what little he had accomplished.

A covered mattress lay against the solid wall opposite the

water wheel outside. The millstones were gone in the floor's center, relics of a bygone age, and newer wood filled their hole. He had structured shelving out of broken cinderblock and garnered planks that had floated by in the last flooding. His toothbrush, a draped washcloth, chipped dishes, two aluminum pots, and three plastic jugs of water lined the wall. Polished animal skulls, small and large, decorated the shelves. Satisfied, Boon walked to his storage closet and threw back the slide lock, swinging open one of the doors. The unassembled framework stood inside a large wooden box, oddly reminding him of his time on the stand during his trial many years ago.

"Boon, what you waiting for, man?" asked Glower.

"He's thinking," said the solicitor general.

"What makes him freeze like that?"

"Don't know. Ask him."

"Boon, why you freeze like that when we're waiting on you?" asked Glower again.

Davis turned and looked at Glower. He took a step in the man's direction, thinking he remembered a detail. Glower's hands went up and he backed away, a movement Davis knew.

He saw Glower in the courtroom decades ago, sitting on the stand, a man of importance in a police uniform who talked with much confidence, spreading lies about Davis. He held pictures of a black man, burned past recognition and accused Davis of saving his skeleton in the basement of the hardware store in Cambridge. It wasn't Davis's skeleton. It was one of his father's. Davis felt the courtroom's silence like his dead father's eyes staring at him and the old man's words rankled from the grave, *the sins of the father will be visited upon the son*. Davis cleared his throat but nothing came out.

Another police officer had wheeled a mysterious standing drape down the courtroom aisle and pulled back the gray material to reveal a human skeleton, perfectly articulated as if ready to scare children on Halloween. The courtroom gasped and the judge's gavel banged away.

Davis' mind had whirled in confusion. It was his handiwork done under his father's bidding, a skeleton that no longer hung in the cellar in Cambridge but had made its way to Delaware. A farmer, the prosecutor said, one of our own good black farmers had disappeared and only through the determined resourcefulness of Glower and his assistant did they find proof of his death. It hung before the judge's bench, before Davis' guilty bowed head, a complete skeleton but for his missing fingers and toes. Davis heard the farmer's name, one he didn't recognize. Knowing his future, he had leapt from his seat at the defense table and charged at the witness stand. Glower's hand rose in defense and he backed away, knocking down his chair before Davis was subdued.

The solicitor general moved between Glower and Davis, his arm spread wide in protection. "Whoa, there Boon. Glower don't have no beef with you. Calm down."

Davis decided he didn't like the name Boon. He decided he didn't like Glower but there was a reason to continue dealing with the man. He struggled to remember and it came to him. His personal goal to rid the world of black men who accuse white men of crimes they didn't commit. That was it. Glower's assistant was behind everything that happened that

The Grist Mill Bone

day. He was young then but Davis knew him. The police officer who had wheeled the skeleton into the courtroom was the black man who drove the expensive black truck. Younger than Glower, he was the same one that Davis wanted for his scaffold, the black man with the pretty white woman and the boy he had saved from the tree.

"Stand back there, man. Don't come any closer," said Glower, raising the point of a pistol to his face. Davis stopped. "You go sit down on that old mattress of yours where Beavens can watch you, I'm gonna take a look at what you got here."

The solicitor general whispered heatedly, "You said we wouldn't use our real names. What'd you go and say my name for?"

"Shut up," said Glower. "He's such a retard he's not going to remember nothing anyhow. Keep your eye on him though. I don't trust him to sit there."

The boy-man followed Davis over to his mattress and stood in front of him, blocking his view of the closet. Davis began to mumble to himself, repeating words in an effort to retain his thoughts. "Glowerie, Soulman, Glowerie, Soulman, ... jail. Beavens."

The solicitor general glanced over his shoulder at Glower who pulled the structure from the closet. With a few grunts and whistles, the portly old man had partially assembled the framework when he called out, "Boon, now you get yourself over here and help me put the rest of this thing together."

Davis stood and shoved Beavens out of the way. He sidled up to Glower, shielding his handiwork from the man's attempt to put the wrong piece into the backbone of the framework. Davis assembled the remaining pieces and stood back, looking at his work with pride. He advanced and put both hands on the cross piece, weighing it down. "I35 pounds, the average weight of a six foot skeleton. That's what it can hold," he said. He reached in the box for the noose and attached it to the top of the framework where it hung waiting to grab a neck.

"Well, well, well," said Glower. "You got yourself an impressive start. Now all it needs are the bones."

Boon couldn't handle the excitement and out slipped a, "Ghya, ghya."

"What's that you say?" asked Glower.

"Nothing," answered the solicitor general. "He has a tic is all. He don't mean nothin' by it. We gonna invite him now that you seen it?"

"Sure. Boon you come to a meeting with some of our friends. We have a plan we want to share with you. It's a way for you to reckon with that black man who stole all those years of your life, sending you up to Smyrna to the penitentiary for something I know you didn't do."

Davis nodded, wondering what shape their idea of reckoning took. He had never killed a man outright and wasn't about to start. He would burn in the devil's hell fires for an eternity. He just wanted the natural law of God to take shape.

They brought in foodstuffs, cans of beans and spaghetti, stuff his father fed him during the workweek, living in the hardware store's cellar as a boy. They brought him two

Walmart bags, one full of clean socks and underwear, the other contained a small camp burner with a propane attachment, luxuries in his book. Lastly, they presented a pair of work boots, smelling of new plastic.

His visitors left, and Boon followed them out toward the car. They hailed him a hero to the cause and as they walked to the car, he heard Bevens say, "Crazy asshole. Did you see those bug bites all over him?"

Glower answered, "The guy's not all there. Very useful to the cause."

Inside, Davis dragged his mattress away from the wall, got out his penknife and carved into the wood floor: **glowrie soulman bevens jale**. He blew away the sawdust, studying the words. There to trigger his memory, like a lover's heart on a tree. Above it were the names, **sam** and **jon**.

*****

18 CLAIRE

"Pembroke, are you in there? I have to take off this afternoon for a doctor's appointment," I shouted. "What the—you just got here!"

I walked in his seedy wood paneled office to find him sitting behind his desk piled high with immigration papers. His desk light was on, the shades were pulled against the heat and it smelled like the moldy law books that lined the shelves behind his head. Even the big name law offices of the county seat worked out of dilapidated turn of the century Victorians and bungalows, or, if they were lucky, strip mall spaces. I like to call it Local Law. Pembroke's Spanish is much better than mine. I'm still thankful for our division of labor, me on elder law and he on immigration. He gave me that after Sam's kidnapping. I was sweating from the humidity outside and I pulled my damp bangs over my forehead to cover a bruise. Damn blood thinners.

"Booker drove me in for a meeting with Father Caulfield, Velma's priest friend." I took a seat in one of the two walnut armchairs that sat in front of his desk. "He's coming back to get me for the doctor."

"Poor Booker. Now that's a man who's going to have a learning curve. My first kid busted my balls for lack of sleep."

Colorful, my boss is colorful. He threw a file on a stack to the right and grabbed another one. Our secretary was on summer vacation with her family and Pembroke was doing it all. "Where'd you meet the priest? He's from Wilmington, right?"

"He drove down and we met over at the library. I walked over here."

"Lord, have mercy. In this heat?"

"Yeah, but my office is too cramped for a meeting."

He ignored this and asked, "Did you find out if she has another heir?"

Pembroke ran his fingers through his graying locks. I always suspected it was a bad toupee taped to the crown of his head. It curled behind his ears. Real hair or no, it stuck. He barely took his puffy eyes off his work. The man clocked some long hours for next to nothing.

"Not yet. It shouldn't be this hard but she's so secretive. I think Father Caulfield stands to become a very rich man." I started to cross my legs and stopped. There was another bruise, a bad one on my left knee.

"Isn't there another priest in her will?"

"Yep. Father Chilcott who—get this—is in a nursing home up in Wilmington."

"Nearing death's door? Caulfield could inherit it all. He

can't be motivated to tell you of an unknown heir."

"Caulfield says there's a charity."

"Well, there you go. Crazy, demented Velma has a soft heart in the end. Bet she's leaving it to the Daughters of the Confederacy." He looked up at me finally. "That takes care of your concern—that the priests would lose half of it to taxes. What's the charity?"

I pulled a file out of my tote bag and opened it up. It was hefty, the first pages were records and diagrams of her investment stocks. The miracle of compounding interest. "I haven't plowed through all this yet. Caulfield didn't have a lot of time. Said he had to go visit her in the nursing home before he headed back to Wilmington." I fanned the pages until one word caught my eye. Scholarship.

"What is it?" asked Pembroke.

"Unbelievable. There are two scholarship funds." Scanning, I pointed to a paragraph buried third in a letter with a Catholic Charities logo. "It says college scholarships for 'worthy black students on Delmarva who attend a historically black college.' " I walked around his desk and laid the papers on the only clear spot.

"That's not Velma's charity. Isn't she a latent racist?"

"I can't tell what she is. Dementia is a terrible thing. Look," I said, spreading them out. "There's a current use donation agreement and a contract with the Community Foundation of Delmarva. Says they're the selection committee. And here's Catholic Charities as the umbrella organization. If she has all this, why does she need another trust in the priest's name?" I picked up one of the scholarship

The Grist Mill Bone

descriptions. "Criteria maintaining a 3.0 over four years, majoring in any science related field. It's $10,000.00 a year and doesn't mention Velma's name anywhere."

"What's it titled?"

"The George Calvert Family Scholarship."

Recognition passed over his face. "No way!" he said, never missing a beat. Pembroke knows everyone around here.

"Who is that?"

"George Calvert—Velma's from Cambridge, right? That's the homeless dude who tried to save a priest in the Cambridge church fire way back in the 70s. I'll never forget it. Some folk were all up in arms about it being the homeless guy's fault but after the 60s riots that burned the town, that old mayor finally had some sense and called in a Baltimore FBI forensics team. *They* said it was an accident.

"I was in my late 20s and just starting out in law. We hoped the ACLU would take the mother's case and sue the church for child support. Her husband, this Calvert guy, was a famous etymologist working down here with the University of Maryland. Grant work, if I remember. He got laid off, in my opinion, for no apparent other reason than he was black.

"Insecting while black. That's a new one."

Pembroke erupted in that singular explosive laugh he's so famous for in court. I could never do that. He always gets away with it.

"What's the other scholarship?"

I read it out loud. "The Matthew Williams Memorial Scholarship."

Pembroke leaned back in his chair with his hands behind

his head and looked up at me. "Now that's reaching back into history. I think Matthew Williams was one of the last African Americans lynched on the peninsula. They strung him up in Salisbury during the Depression." His pushed his desk chair back and stood up. I had his attention.

"You need to wrap up Velma's case." He flicked his pen back and forth in the air between us.

There was something else on his mind. He wouldn't look me in the eye. "I know, I know," I said. "I just have one more thing to check out."

"I'm interviewing for your job. You're moving to D.C. soon and I need somebody who can work full time. I'm not pushing you out on any schedule, mind you, but we agreed Velma was your last case."

I was stunned. The Offices of Pembroke Law have been a second home for me, ... intimate, folksy, and respected. I blinked in surprise a couple of times and sat down. My mind tripped trying to number up what steps came next. Pembroke was jumping the human resources gun—my gun.

I was surprised, like the freshman who comes home for Thanksgiving and finds their bedroom turned into a gym. I'm a good attorney who covers all the bases and I wasn't done yet. I'm also cheap and not bringing in any money. Yet, I wasn't going to make excuses for my pregnancy, or moving for that matter. My baby was my business. Moving is just a hassle. Yet, Pembroke wasn't laying me off. *'not pushing you out on any schedule.'* Of course he was overwhelmed with immigration cases, and I had been completely oblivious. It was unfair of me to assume that with all the new clients he had that I was going to fill the void. I hadn't even offered.

"Sure. I understand. I could help out more. I could take some of the immigration work again."

"I appreciate that, Claire. I really do, but we both know you don't want it. And you won't have time with the baby coming and packing up your house. With Booker's mom gone, you have even more to do. Let me be clear. I just want your *office* for the new person. You can work on the extra desk out front until you're ready to go."

My shoulders sank and I looked down at my growing belly. I had told him I was leaving but this felt wrong. I had popped out. 20 weeks and I was nearly irrelevant. In a rush, I was back on the Georgetown campus, in a conversation with a law professor who told me I wasn't eligible for an internship with the D.C. Court of Appeals. Second in my class and the word ineligible was hanging in the air. The only thing standing in my way was my pregnancy and the professor who was white, male and stale. In the big wide world, I have learned that every woman fears becoming invisible behind the baby bump.

I hadn't seen Velma since before Odessa's funeral and I knew she would have some smartass comment to make upon seeing me. In a phone call to her a week ago I had shouted so she could hear that there was a death in my family and that I would be back to finish her trust, that I have more questions for her to answer this time. She had answered, "Solomon, you get your butt over here and take care of me. I'm paying you to deal with that storage unit."

Now I had become a moving company. It was amazing

how clear headed she could be about the things she wanted but silent on the things that counted. I mean, why does she need to be so stubborn? I wasn't going to finalize everything until I knew who was the little blonde boy in the picture.

"I'm almost finished with Velma anyway," I said to Pembroke. "I can be out of here in a week, ten days. No worries." I smiled at him. "See ya later. I have to get going." Gathering Father Caulfield's file on Velma, I strode out of his office as fast as my short little legs could carry me through the front door.

Booker should have been waiting but he wasn't. Our office was one block off The Circle where the county courthouse and legislative hall take up half the landscape. On the opposite side is the Brick Hotel, a Victorian landmark. Working on a one-way street, I often found myself going round the circle more than once looking for a parking place. Parking is tight, especially for the monstrosity Booker was driving. I waited, watching cars circle. A black, unmarked SUV stood out from the field of older pickups. Delaware State SUVs are usually dark blue. This one looked like one of the secret service vehicles that prowled D.C. I was wrong. It was FBI.

I stepped back into the doorway of our office and watched as Brent Fowler emerged. Dressed in a gray suit and tie he looked trim and full of business. He stood rather conspicuously, leaning against a tree trunk. Well, it was conspicuous to me. He had investigated Sam's disappearance four years ago and when it was all over, he was the FBI contact that urged Booker to apply, saying they needed him because of interstate crime on the peninsula. Booker declined to my surprise.

I debated going over to say hello when I saw a familiar figure approach him from behind. Pembroke. He looked distracted, glancing around as if he was afraid of being watched. And well he should. I took in everything. Pembroke handed Fowler a thin manila file and what appeared to be a thumbdrive. Fowler asked some questions and Pembroke was quite adamant, his hands waving in the air. He shook his head and I saw him mouth *No, No!* before he took off down the back alley to the office.

A horn tooted and Booker pulled in his black refrigerator-on-wheels that had a distinctive scratch on the front right bumper.

"Did you get your tags?" I asked. He was holding the door open for me, ready to help me up.

"Yep, they came in as ordered. Wanna see?"

I walked around the rear of the truck. There, on his blue and gold plate was were two words, "BLK * NEC."

"Nice. Making a statement for your new FBI job?"

"Ma's right, I ain't gonna work for The Man. I got Tosh behind me."

"That so?" I asked. "Then how come I just saw Brent Fowler over there on The Circle? He was talking to Pembroke."

Booker took up the sidewalk, his hands on his hips as he watched the black SUV move into traffic. The license plate was government. Federal government.

"Not very secret of him, right?"

"I'd say not. Although it's nothing but us dumb Sussex lawyers walking around here. And you."

***

"Claire, your INR is 3.8. Are you eating too much broccoli again?"

I heard his voice but was so unfocused after my conversation with Pembroke, blinded by the white coat, white cabinets, and white blinds. For relief, my eyes fell to the beige tiled floor. I sat on the examining table, an unripe plum, bruised and tender. My veins were pumping thinned red blood, pushing white cells, and too few platelets. My fortitude was gone. This is my M.O. I can pull together for everyone else in a crisis but after the wailing and anger are over, I fall apart. Especially if I'm suddenly the object of attention.

He pushed my white paper drape aside revealing my knee and thigh streaked in a purple bruise. He brushed my hair away to study my forehead above my right eye where a blackened bump had taken up residence after my fall.

He nodded. "That's going to spread like a rainbow below your eye in the next few days. Better have some good make up. You aren't drinking, are you?"

"I'd love a gallon of pinot right about now, but no, alcohol has not passed my lips since I found out I was pregnant."

"That's exactly what you need to keep doing. I'm giving you two weeks to straighten this out on your own. No alcohol, no cranberry juice. Limit your leafy green vegetables. Eat red meat and chicken, no liver. I'll have the nurse give you a copy of the diet again. Are you doing your shots every day on schedule?"

"You want to see my belly? It looks like target practice with a bb gun. I just need to draw the circles"

"Why'd you faint and hit your head?" he said.

"I fell backward into a metal mop bucket and banged my head on the corner of the door jamb. Just clumsy, I guess."

"Well fainting leaves the ballerina out. You're blood pressure's low. Are you having dizzy spells?"

"Nope. I didn't have time to eat that day. Things just got ahead of me later on."

"What got ahead of you?"

"Everything's okay with the baby, right? There's nothing wrong?"

"The baby's fine."

I looked past his bespectacled face to the light glowing around the window shade. It was so hot outside and the air conditioning blasted away. I could hear the hum of the unit through the wall, sighing and whining as it cycled off. That's what I wanted to do—cycle off. Coming here with Booker meant the trip home would be 20 questions. Could I just go home to bed and take a long summer nap? I was irritated after the morning's events.

"What got ahead of you?" he asked again.

"My mother in law," I said. "She died before I could take her home with me, before I could, … before I could, …"

"What?"

"Protect her," I said, shivering.

His hand was on my knee, a familiar touch and warm. Dr.

Burton was a country doctor, had delivered a thousand babies at his age, and I didn't worry about his touch. A tear escaped and splotched my paper dress.

"You left your husband in the waiting room. I like to meet the dads around 35 weeks but this isn't too early. Why don't you get dressed and meet us in my office? That okay with you?"

"What, the men are going to discuss the little lady in her absence? Naw. You're not talking to Booker without me in there."

"Okey dokey, then. I'll have him wait in the chair outside the door until you're ready."

I dressed, taking extra time to brush my hair. When I opened the door, I found Booker sitting down the hall with his legs crossed, knee jiggling away. He followed me into the office and we sat across from Dr. Burton. In his windowless room, lined with medical tomes and diplomas, I felt like I might suffocate.

"Dr. Burton, nice to meet you." Booker extended a long arm across the desk to shake hands. "How's Claire doing?"

I swear if I hadn't already been pissed off about the possibility of being tagged teamed by the two of them I might not have noticed the look on Dr. Burton's face. He was seriously dumbstruck for a second. Guess he hadn't pegged me as being married to a black man. He jumped right in though.

"She's a pro. You understand the reason she's taking a blood thinner?"

"Yeah. Genetics, right? The potential for blood clots

increases with a pregnancy."

"Uh-huh. She's positive for Leiden on both sides of her family tree making this a high risk pregnancy."

"Dr. Burton," I interrupted a little sharply. "Booker knows all this. It's been discussed, he's researched ad nauseum and he's read your handouts. He's a little nervous about the bruising. I told him I won't let it happen again." I widened my eyes and nodded slightly to make sure the point got across. Seemed like it didn't matter.

He ignored me and looked at Booker. "Her blood is too thin right now and she needs to watch her diet. Sometimes cultural traditions are hard to overcome for people. Limit the greens and no alcohol."

Really. I stood up and they both looked at me, waiting. Booker grabbed my arm and pulled me down into the chair. "Dr. Burton," he began laughing that Booker chortle, "I may be African American, but we don't all eat greens and drink wine every night. Nor does Claire do the cooking for dinner. We have a housekeeper who's a little heavy on the beans and rice, not greens and wine. And while Claire likes to say she's not going to faint or fall again, that's not the issue. The issue, sir, is what happens if she does have an accident again and develops a blood clot?"

Dr. Burton erupted in a little high-pitched squeal. "That's just where I was going," he said, smiling and happy to move the conversation along. "If there's a catastrophic accident and Claire's transported, if she's bleeding, the EMT's should be told right away that she's on heparin, or say, a blood thinner if you don't remember. They have ways to reverse a bleeding situation. It's another story if a blood clot develops on its own, either from being too sedentary or a blow to the body, excuse me, like falling into a mop bucket and striking your head on the door jamb. If one develops in a leg or arm, there'll be swelling, the skin will be red, feel warm and, Claire, you'll feel pain in the area. Call me, or if it's the weekend, go to the emergency room and they'll call me."

I stood back up. Now, all of this was directed to Booker except the very end. There was a hierarchy to his instruction. Booker came first and I was the afterthought only capable of judging my own pain. The man had made a good impression on me up until now. I was heated, I'll admit, and I let him have it. "Dr. Burton, I'm sure you are a man with great medical experience and knowledge. I'm sure the very first thing the hospital wants to do is call you about your patients. I'm sure Booker needs to know what to do or say in an emergency, but there won't be an emergency. I'm not taking any risks, engaging in any risky behavior, and I'm extremely guarded in dealing with others. This pregnancy is going along just fine and if I can get out of here, I'll get a healthy lunch, go home and do an evening shot in my tummy like I do every goddamned day." I grabbed my purse off the chair and walked out of his office with any shred of dignity I hoped my body still afforded me.

Outside, I yanked the door to Booker's big-black-refrigerator-on-wheels, and realized, of course, that it was locked. I flung my purse against the door, cursing. A pregnant woman lumbering to the office entrance, frowned and said, "Ain't it just a pisser? I just had an all out fight with the mailman for using my office bathroom when I needed it. I mean can't he go to a gas station?"

She was huge, ready to drop at any minute. God help the man who got in her way, I thought. Then, I wondered if I was going to get that big. Suddenly, it all seemed too much. Like I wanted the baby to go away, Booker to go away and for Sam and me to have our own lives bumbling around D.C., the Tosh heirs, doing whatever we wanted.

The car locks beeped twice and I opened the door, grabbed the short people bar and stepped on the foot rail. It was all I could do to haul myself in and I wasn't that big—yet. This situation was not going to get better. I plunked down in my seat and watched, chin up as Booker exited the building, papers in one hand, the key in the other.

We rode in silence for a long way. Finally, he said, "You want to go get a drink and some greens?"

I burst out laughing, a belly laugh that brought tears to my eyes. He laughed and grabbed my hand laying it on his thigh under his, like he always does. I sat back and looked out the window.

"The baby's okay. You're okay. That's all that counts, Woman."

He called me Woman. He hadn't called me that in ages. The baby started to show and Booker didn't look at me the same way. I had become some china doll that belonged on one of his mama's tchotchke shelves. I squeezed his hand and leaned my head on his shoulder. His lips brushed my forehead and I sat up saying, "Careful, that's a little bruised there."

He sighed. I said, "Dr. Burton gave me the order for our next ultrasound. Want to find out the sex?"

"Hail yeah, I wanna know."

"What if I said I don't?" I asked.

"I'd say you don't get to decide. You already had one and got to find out it was Sam ahead of time. This is my first go around. I get to decide."

"You bossy, controlling daddy-to-be."

"Yep. Get used to it."

I laughed again and he nodded. Big Cheese Booker.

We turned on to Old Mill Bridge and at a distance I saw a man running. He wore cutoffs and a jeans shirt, the sleeves and collar torn out, no colorful athletic gear for him. His shoes had seen better days, too. He was in a trance, head down, watching each step he took, his arms pumping away. Brown as a nut, he had thick, curly bleached hair on his arms and legs. I rose up in my seat and looked out the tinted side windows. His hair was matted into a single thick tail that ran past his shoulders. It was the man who had saved Sam in the storm.

"Booker, turn around. That's him. I want to thank him. Give him some money."

"Claire, if the man wanted something from us, he would've found us. Everybody knows where we live." Booker patted my hand on his thigh. "Look, we'll see him again when we have the time. And he gets gift certificates, not money. Besides, you need some lunch right now. It's almost three."

The baby was throwing karate kicks and I was overcome

with hunger pangs thinking of the roast beef sandwich I could make from last night's dinner. Nearing the creek, the frothy tops of the phragmites blew in a light breeze and a cloud opened up spinning sunlight across their dusty fronds. I wavered, remembering myself and that the tiny being inside deserved more of me, and my consciousness. Booker reached in the glove compartment and pulled out an energy bar for me. My beloved man was more attuned to the constancy of our existence, to the bounds of our family and nurturance. The baby was healthy, Sam was okay, and my anger was gone. I looked at Booker's profile and asked God to forgive me for being such a wingnut.

I didn't object as we took the driveway into Odessa's house. It was so much more comfortable than the farmhouse in the summer because of the central air. I had spent a couple of days boxing up her personal things—clothes, shoes, even her lavish hats for donation. I lingered over her simple jewelry, laying it out across her dresser. The silver and gold crosses, the St. Anthony medal, it's gold edges worn, and beaded baby bracelets, Booker's in blue and white and Olivia's, his sister's, in pink and white. The collection was so modest compared to that of my mother's it squeezed me with tenderness and I stopped for the day, going out on the deck for air.

There I found Booker sitting in a chair, staring at the shoreline. He was making slow progress on her desk and I guessed he'd had enough as well. My hand brushed his shoulder and he grabbed it pulling me into his lap. He rested his broad hand on my roundness and for the sake of his warm touch and our loss, the baby moved. He bent his head and kissed the spot, saying, "I will make the world better for you, child. Just like my Mama did for me." I wrapped my arms around him and tucked my head near his, kissing his neck.

It had been ten weeks since her death and Booker, Sam and I had spent the night in the extra bedrooms when the nights were so hot that the window units didn't cool the farmhouse down. Even the crickets sounded hoarse in the heat. Upon waking the first morning, I found myself waiting to hear her voice. I thought I was handling things well until I walked into the family room and my gaze fell on the grain face pot and I remembered her delight the day we told her about the baby. I had to move the pot, dragging it behind the sofa for fear of the tears that overcame me. We have so much. Except her. My heart hurts.

Rosa has been working in Odessa's kitchen, cleaning out cabinets when she isn't working her shift at the DelAire chicken plant. Booker asked her again to quit, telling her we could make her a Tosh employee, pay her health insurance, and set up a retirement trust. Last night, she and Baby Bessie stayed over as well. Rosa said she would consider the offer.

It's all coming together with the exception of the investigation into Odessa's death. There isn't one, although Booker called Lowery a week ago to give him the evidence in the laundry room and garage. That old coot said he wrote everything down and that he was waiting for the forensics report, that it was delayed for some reason. He was manipulating us for what purpose, but there was nothing we could do except go over his head. Booker said to give it a little more time to let him play his hand. And then, he did.

***

We pulled up to Odessa's front door and, wearily I climbed the four stone steps, my arm entwined in Booker's. Putting the key in the lock, he pulled back as the front door swung wide of its own. He pushed me behind him and reached under his shirt for his gun. Old habits firmly rooted for a retired detective. Nine days out of ten, he wears it, concealed. He called out, "You got some business in my house you think you can just walk right in?"

Around the corner from Odessa's family room came Lowery, a smirk planted on his face as big as the Cheshire Cat's. Two uniforms followed him, hats in hand. "Well, we're real sorry for entering your mama's house when you weren't here but we got a search warrant to look for the evidence you alerted us about. Ms. McIntosh, nice to see you again," he said nodding to me.

"Lowery, you common bastard. You could've called me. Where'd you park your cars?" asked Booker, holstering his gun.

"I could arrest you, Solomon. Be careful what you call me. You got a permit for that gun?"

I spoke up, "Detective. Nice to see you. It's Ms. Solomon now. Mr. Solomon can call you anything he likes as his speech is as protected as mine, or yours for that matter. And you need to show me that warrant immediately. I'm pretty hungry, so your paperwork better be in order."

Lowery glared at me, stern, unmoved, and then upon

seeing my intent, he huffed and mouthed something to the uniform who handed me the papers. Judge Schofield, had signed the warrant. All legal. I nodded to Booker. This man had intimidated me once, long ago. He had intimidated both of us and I was going to make sure, if he had forgotten, that we could burn him.

We walked into the laundry room and found Messick sprawled across the floor, holding a field camera and snapping pictures under the sink. She was all over the electric cable from every angle. Dressed in her white jump suit, all business, she didn't look up.

Lowery said, "You remember Ms. Messick?"

There wasn't enough space in the laundry room for us all to squeeze in there. It was obvious that they had made it another crime scene. I heard the generator humming in the background. Somebody else must've been around back of the house. The side garage door was open and we followed Lowery and the uniforms outside where an undercover SUV, a squad car, and the forensics truck were parked next to the house, hiding from us. They had strung yellow tape around the generator and the HVAC unit. A technician huddled overtop, his forensic case sitting atop Booker's upturned duck boat.

I wanted to yell, to scream at them all to leave but I receded into the background and watched. It was all so professional, tidy, and unforgiving. They even took pictures of the garage door lockset covered in blue tape where it had been jimmied, I guessed to make it show up better in the photos. Thorough.

"You're going to need to come down to the station in Georgetown," said Lowery, looking at Booker warily.

"Why's that?" asked my husband leaning against the doorjamb.

"We have some questions."

"Go ahead. Ask."

"I'll give you a few minutes to look in your records on that generator. Bill of sale, any work orders that were completed."

"And then what?" asked Booker.

"Messick's going to stay here and finish up. Has to dust for fingerprints. We want to eliminate yours."

"Uh-hmm. Fingerprints. You can get mine from Maryland State. They're on file. Major crimes lead detective on Delmarva, remember? Or has that slipped your mind?"

"No, what I remember is a ghetto do-rag pretending to be a cop. You need to get your file on that generator and come with us."

"Or what?"

"I'm asking you nicely, Solomon. Get the file and come with Officer Beavens and there won't be a problem."

"Do your job, Lowery. Are you detaining me or arresting me?"

It was all moving so fast. I couldn't ask Booker to calm down. He was calm. I couldn't ask him to stop taunting Lowery. The man deserved it. I couldn't ask him to walk away, either. He was on his own damn property.

"I'm not doing either, Solomon. I need your cooperation any way I can get it. You know this is a crime scene. Now get in Beavens' squad car and we'll find the records ourselves."

"Lowery, you can stick your gumshoe up Beavens' whiter than white ass before I'll get in a car with any of you."

"That's it. I'm arresting you, Booker Solomon on suspicion of murder of Odessa Solomon. Beavens, read him his rights and cuff him."

And so it went. Beavens' words evaporated in the air like a trite Monday night Five-O detective series. But in some sense, it was a heavy footed do-si-do—they were serious as they danced around Booker, careful not to bait the black man into what could've been a civil rights gaffe. The video was recording on my phone, held beneath my shoulder bag and I was hoping against all hope that they would make a mistake.

Booker forfeited his gun. Beavens grabbed his wrist only to back off inches from Booker's scowl. The other uniform held open the back door of the squad car. I cleared my throat. Lowery said again, "Mirandize him. *I'm* arresting the bastard."

And Booker looked at me with a smile. "Get some lunch, Woman. I'll call you if I need your services."

Beavens gestured to Booker. He climbed in the car. They took off, leaving me, staring down the driveway at their dust. Then, I remembered Messick and her assistant. I found her in the dark, inside the garage, waiting.

"Well, I guess you had that one nailed," I said.

"They can't hold him. They have probable cause but not enough evidence unless they planted something."

"Would they do that? Wait, we're talking Lowery. Did he take anything with him?

"Your mother-in-law's file cabinet—before you got here. He knew Mr. Solomon wouldn't cooperate."

"Son of a bitch. I'm calling my boss, Pembroke. He'll find out when they plan to arraign him."

"You might need to call in the big guns from D.C. This feels bigger than anything I've ever experienced on the shore."

I began to shake and leaned over to hug Messick. It was too much for her—the intimacy.

"Okay. Okay. Science person here. Not a stuffed animal."

"Sorry," I said, separating myself. "Did you see anything else I should know about before I call?"

"There are footprints around the generator and the boat. It was pouring rain that day."

"Gangbusters."

"It's a partial but I can cast it. Unusual pattern in the sole. I'll take a soil sample as well."

"Will they interfere in your research?"

"Not if I do it tonight after the lab closes. Also, Odessa Solomon had long black hair," she said holding up a plastic bag.

I squinted. "Yeah, she did."

"Well, let's see if this is a match."

*****

19 THE GRIST MILL

The evening was steamy and singing with the drone of insects. Even the setting sun over the ridge of trees to the west gave no reprieve from the humidity, baking the grit of a west wind into his forearms. It blew farmland dust and black flies toward the bay. Davis trudged up the sandy path and around the felled oak to the grist mill. He had grown braver, and ran that day in a more populated area, suffering the glances of out of towners hell bent on beach fun. They had thrown empty miniatures of flavored vodka at him from their car, and shouted insults, as they roared off in laughter. The plastic bottles bounced off him into the run-off ditches.

Only one encounter disturbed him. The big black truck driven by the black man held the white woman by his side. The truck had slowed on passing him but he didn't turn in its direction. He heard her voice, heard her say, *that's him*. They were together. Again. He began to think there was more reason than their work.

He might be able to use her, he thought. A pure woman was sacrosanct and should be revered like the Blessed Mother, but this one was risking her life riding around with the black man. Planning outcomes was difficult and he hoped the gathering of friends might help him decide. He heard wings flapping above and raised his eyes to the yellow sky where a pair of gulls sailed about. They called to him in laughter.

He stood next to the rain bucket and stripped naked. He added his washcloth and a sliver of soap. He dipped a cup in the rain bucket and poured fresh water over his head to soak his matted hair. He worked the cloth into a lather and pushed it back and forth over his knobby skull with both hands until his hair became a matted halo. He scrubbed the rest of himself, ignoring the cuts and scrapes, the swollen insect bites and scars from a rough childhood. Leaning against the door he raised his face to train rainwater over his sore eyes, down his neck—a waterfall that splashed his chest. He smelled under his arms. Satisfied, he took a towel from the window ledge and dried off. The fur on his arms and legs fluffed and he rubbed his lean stomach that rippled and tightened like cogs in a wheel as he bent to wipe between his toes. His hair fell, dripping in a twisted tail down his sunburned back.

Baptism.

Before entering the mill, he stared at the slice of orange sun hanging above the dark trees, the last light of day. The solicitor general would appear soon and open the door of his car. Boon would get in, would ride in his car, wearing clean khakis, a white button down shirt and new work boots.

The cat meowed from his mattress and he hurried inside to pour a saucer of milk from his cooler.

*****

20 CLAIRE

Messick finished with the footprint outside and I heard their diesel truck chug away. I stood at the kitchen sink, wolfing down the roast beef sandwich with my phone to my ear. I was on hold, waiting for my closest Tosh exec—Dean Campbell. He was a fixer, a confidante, a man who had a vision for the corporation decades out into the future. He was my father's man and now mine. Loyalty. We paid people for it and Dean was true to us.

"Claire. What's up? Did you find a house you want?"

"No. Listen, Dean. This isn't about a house. I'm calling because Booker's been arrested and, and, Jesus. I'm an attorney and—I don't know what to do!" I sobbed, suddenly stunned at my own inadequacy, my inability to have seen this coming. I crumpled over the sink and leaned my elbows onto the counter's edge. Odessa was gone, murdered, and Booker was being blamed for it.

"My God! Booker? What do they have him on?"

"They're accusing him of murdering his own mother."

In a breath, there was dead silence at the other end of the phone.

"Claire, that reeks of behind the scenes dealings. I'll be down tonight. In the meantime, you know what to do. You're just a little rattled."

"Yep. I'm alone. It's me and Sam. I need some back up."

"Remember what your father would say in a situation like this, 'If the wolves are circling, separate them with a line of fire and hem them in.' "

"Right. More of that. I need a Tosh pep talk," I answered.

"I'm bringing Ross. He'll start an investigation before we leave here," he said. "Go down to the courthouse and post bail. Get him out. Don't speak to anyone else until we get there."

"Yeah, I know. I—I don't know how complicit the judges are around here. It's money, Dean. Real estate. Outside developers. They have to let him out. He's not a flight risk for God's sake."

"Outside developers? Well, they got nothing on Tosh, my girl. And you're right—Booker's not a flight risk. See, you're already arguing the rationale. You know what to do."

I stared at Odessa's white plate, smeared with brown mustard from my sandwich. I swiped my finger across the plate and licked it. So spicy, my head cleared.

"I do. Just had a moment of doubt. Won't let it happen again," I said and walked over to the couch to shove it with my hip, not caring if my thinned blood left a bruise. It shifted enough for me to see the grain pot, the googly eyes laughing back at me. I sighed. I wasn't alone. "I'll see you tonight,

Dean. Hopefully, Booker will be here too. Are you flying in?"

"Sure. Nobody uses the plane since your dad's gone. Unnecessary expense. Except it's the fastest way to get to you. Once you move back, we'll unload it."

"Yeah. Once we move back," I said.

"Yes. You and Booker and Sam. The family. Once you all move back."

I didn't say anything to Sam before I left. Just that I had to run an errand in Georgetown and I'd be back late. I called Trixie and she said to bring him over for dinner. He grumbled some at having to go to her house, having to leave his precious video game for a house that only had a TV. I didn't tell him that Little John was working at the nursing home for fear he wouldn't go at all, that he would insist on staying by himself at the farmhouse. He knows he can't stay alone. I guess he could see the determination in my face and I felt it too, deep in my bones. My game face was back, as if I was striding the halls of my old office on K Street.

Booker wasn't released that night. Arraignment was set for the next day at 1:00 before a judge, not a magistrate. I drove home without him and went to get Sam in the trailer park. I looked through the storm door to see Sam wrestling with Trixie's three young foster kids on the living room floor in front of an ancient big screen TV. I stepped inside and called for Trixie. Sam and the kids froze in a tumble of puppy energy to look at me surprised. He didn't notice the desperation on my face.

Trixie barreled down the hall from the kitchen, her black

eyes smiling as she wiped her apron-covered breasts with wet hands. I was always delighted to see Trix in a new flowered apron, like an Italian grandmother who carried a small pistol in the pocket for emergencies.

"What's going on chickie? You not looking so happy to see me," she asked giving me a hug.

"Let's go in the kitchen."

I spilled the whole story as she poured red wine into her jelly glass. Her eyes were wide with disbelief, then anger. She patted my hand.

"Well now, this shit's not going down on our watch. I got friends I can call. You need to find out who we got to turn around here."

"Trixie this isn't some corrective Philly mob action you can take. This is court. We have to play it out between the lawyers, the judge and the jury."

"The hell we do! I wasn't brought up a southside girl to let all that talent go to waste here at the beach. You get me the information and I'll get these ridiculous charges dropped. They need to find Odessa's killer. Booker's a good man!"

"I know. I know. I have my people coming in tonight. They'll have it covered. We'll get Booker out. But thanks. I mean I really love you for the offer. I love you, Trix."

I hugged her and she went to her fridge to get a container of her Italian red sauce, her 'gravy,' and said, "You got pasta at home? I'll give you some home made Capellini."

Later, as Sam was getting ready for bed, his mouth full of toothpaste, he stood in the hallway outside our bathroom and asked where Booker was.

The Grist Mill Bone

"Did he have to go over the bridge, Mom?"

"Yep," I lied. "He'll be back tomorrow, I think."

Satisfied, Sam crawled in and I kissed him goodnight.

"Booker said he was gonna take me fishing this weekend. Said the mahi mahi are good a few miles out from Ocean City. I hope he comes home so we can go."

"I'm sure he will, Sam. Booker doesn't go back on his promises unless something really big derails his plans. He's been wanting to spend some time with you."

When Sam got up the next morning for school, he was unaware that Dean, Ross and I had stayed up past midnight preparing for the next day in court. I told them everything and only stopped to run in the kitchen and do a shot of blood thinner. Sam left at eight and I called Dean to pick me up. We were meeting a Wilmington attorney at my office in Georgetown.

Pembroke hadn't hired anyone for my job, so for the time being my office was still mine. Looking as disheveled as ever, his hair askew and his shirt stained, he greeted us at the door. I could see the worry in his eyes but I didn't utter a word of my private business. He stood back as Thomas Whitten, Esquire, passed him with a polished smile and dismissive handshake. I didn't have time to worry if Pembroke was offended. I shut and locked my office door and closed the blinds. We had three hours to prepare. Halfway through I ordered a hamburger and fries from the diner next to the courthouse. I wasn't going to faint in the courtroom. At 12:15 we drove to the hearing rooms behind the state police barracks. I was freezing from the office air conditioning and the sudden heat hit me like a sauna. I grabbed Dean's arm and he turned to look at me.

"Claire, you can go home if you want. Take the car. We can handle this."

"No way. I want Lowery to see me with you. I want him to know what he's up against."

The hearing room was small, 1950s knotty pine paneled, chipped tile on the floor as if the space was a world of imperatives in need of a response. Booker walked in to sit at the defense table looking worn, exhausted really. I tried to catch his eye, to send encouragement but he never looked my way. Beige prison scrubs washed him out, leaving his eyes dull and unresponsive. I couldn't believe one night in the county jail had done this to him.

The evidence against him was hollow but Messick was right. They planted some and the rest was fabricated. Fingerprints to start. His were all over the sliced wiring despite the fact that he wore plastic gloves the day we cased it out. But then, it was his mother's house on Solomon family property. Where else would they easily find a treasure trove of his fingerprints? They had the original bill of sale for the generator—recent enough, but that in itself wasn't incriminating. A good son would want his mother's home to be protected in case of a power outage.

No, it was the testimony of witnesses carefully built over the last month, many of them innocent church friends who made statements that Odessa and Booker's relationship had always been contentious in the way of most families. Lydia, Odessa's good friend stated that Odessa expressed doubts about moving and if it weren't for a baby, her first grandchild coming, she wouldn't have considered it. Four or five choir members agreed that Odessa had a great fear of ending up at a nursing home and they all thought it a good solution that she would move with us.

All normal, I whispered heatedly to Dean who sat with me behind the defense table looking at Booker's slumped shoulders and bowed head. And then the district attorney, George Farqhuar, read a statement of finding from Glory Bender, a local realtor and landowner, who said that Booker had been negotiating the sale of Solomon property for the express purpose of funding his mother's nursing home care. She said that he had no intention of taking Odessa with us but that Booker stated he was going to plant his mother at Fairhaven. Farqhuar submitted an estimate of the worth of the Solomon property from a surveying company, ordered and signed by Booker. $347,000 for 183 acres. The statement read that it was swampland, not suitable for building and that the only high ground was where Odessa's house stood.

That was the clincher. Not one single piece of evidence tilted the scale. It was the body of evidence, the damn fingerprints, the recent installation of the generator, Glory Bender's statement, and the estimate. Booker's attorney asked to see his signature and showed it to Booker. We both knew it wasn't his.

And so it finally happened. The set up he had always expected—only instead of it coming from a criminal he had put in jail, it was coming from the unknown—developers maybe, who wanted his land at the cheapest price they could get, to create a fire sale to pay for his legal defense. I thought we needed to do some investigation of the only lead we had.

Who the hell was Glory Bender anyway?

My nerves were justified but in the end, we won. The judge released Booker and scolded the D.A. and police for having only circumstantial evidence, knowing, I suspect, that Tosh would fight the case into eternity. Booker and I climbed in the back seat of Dean's rental and my man laid his head in my shortened lap and kissed my belly.

"Hello, baby," he said. "You be a Solomon and a survivor, just like your daddy."

He straightened up and asked to no one in particular, "Who's this Glory Bender woman? Anybody know?"

Ross turned his bullet head and said in that coffee grinder voice I remember from my childhood, "She's a man. Lives outside Annapolis and runs four hate groups in the eastern side of the state. Neo Nazi, White Supremacists, Klan, anti Muslim. Has an online blog and goes after young recruits on college campuses. His money comes from rural area residents on both sides of the bay and now, I suspect, some low life from Bear, Delaware who's organizing activities in Sussex."

"Is it just a bunch of rednecks with an axe to grind who found some money laying around?" I asked.

"Not if you believe there are identified hate groups operating right under your nose. These guys are serious about taking back the U.S. for the white man. That begins with guns and real estate."

*****

21 THE RELIANCE WOOD

"Boon," called Glowery, "I have somebody I want you to meet."

Davis looked across the grassy field where Beavens had parked his car. It had been a long ride from the grist mill, more than an hour, more than the bus ride from his trial in Georgetown upstate to prison. Then as now, he felt confined, trapped and unable to breathe. He was restless and, exiting the car, he found himself pacing back and forth trying to find his equilibrium. Davis scrunched his eyes in the evening's dim light to see who called his name. Try as he might to hold back, his soft, repeated 'ghya, ghya' burbled from his throat. The man's voice was familiar. Beavens grabbed Davis by the elbow to pull him into the woods and Davis yanked free of his grip, stopping to stare wordlessly at his solicitor general.

"Okay, okay," said Beavens. "I'm not gonna rush you. We're gonna get over here to the picnic table to sign in and then we're gonna take a walk down that path over there."

Beavens nodded, his palm with its fat little finger raised toward the forest opening as if to grant a blessing to the proceedings. "Now, you don't have a problem with that, do you, Boon? 'Cause you seen all the cars parked here in the field? We have a gathering of some of the best folk in the tri-state area who want to meet you here in the Reliance Wood."

Davis eyed the cars and the woods. His blurry gaze fell on the table that was manned by two women of indistinguishable age, beyond their fertile years, dressed in white, their faces shadowed in pastel beach visors. He drew closer to them and one smiled and put out her hand, a round paw with delicate pink nails. Her hair was short, shaved on one side like a man and longer on the other. He took her fingertips in his with a shake.

"This is our new recruit, I hear," she said. "You can sign in right here with the name of your rebirth that we have provided."

The florescent pink spike tapped at the wavy black line on a clipboard. Beavens handed Davis a pen. "You just write Baboon Hunter, like we discussed and jot your initials after."

She tapped again and Davis bent down, his eyes five inches off the page. He gripped the pen and did as instructed, spelling correctly, writing in his best cursive with a flourish on the 'B' and 'H.' He followed with his initials, 'D.O.V." for Davis O. Vickers. It had been many years since he had autographed anything and he felt a jolt of importance in his core come from a Sunday morning social of his youth.

The other woman stood and asked him to extend his arm. She was large and soft and kindly and he willingly put out his arm for her to wrap his wrist in a blue paper tape. She gave him a black bandanna and instructed him to wear it around his neck, "You are in the army of security, those who protect and defend the rest. It also says you paid up for dinner." After she wrapped Beavens' wrist in the blue tape, she gave him a red bandanna and greeted him, "Welcome Solicitor General, we look forward to hearing more about your new recruit."

Davis was unsure of their strange language but not wholly put off, for his father often spoke with vague words from which he only learned their true meaning over time. He was in no rush. If he didn't like what he saw tonight, he would leave the grist mill and all his new possessions and wander. Only the abandoned cat would leave him with slight regret.

He followed Beavens and Glowery down a forest lane, rutted with a century of wagon tracks where the temperature fell ten degrees. Cicadas chirped in a rise and fall like crashing ocean waves. The bare barked tall pine, eaten away by bark beetles, gave way to a thick canopy of leafed trees, dappled with a yellow glow from the evening sun. Soon, they reached the glade where bench rows lined with the backs of seated attendees faced a gray wooden structure, one story, capped with wood roofing shingles on which grew heavy green moss. In the interior of a wooded cathedral, evening light glowed. The Gathering. The ground had been trampled bare and was worn in grooves between the bench rows.

This place had a history the likes of generations. Davis squinted at the structure, for a word was painted in white over the door that he had trouble deciphering. He drifted away from Glowery and Beavens. From a good distance and over the chattering of the crowd, he heard their whispered conversation as they huddled with a group of old men who had not taken their seats, men who wore purple, green and gold bandannas over their white shirts. Davis kept his head down, drawing close to the edge of the wood and looked away.

"How you gonna get her back here in a wheelchair?" asked the green bandanna.

"They picked her up in one of those assisted vans."

"You driving that back here? Them damn things is heavy. Not much clearance," said the gold bandanna.

"I had the ditches filled with gravel."

"Gravel? You crazy asshole. That's a sure sign to the Feds that we're active. You just leadin' them in here."

"After the van pulls out tonight, we got a team to cover it up with dirt and pine needles. Besides, if the Feds come to Seaford, nobody gonna breathe a word of the first Gathering in 12 years."

"Better not," said the gold bandanna. "There's 'nuff trampled grass from them parked cars to build suspicion."

"Family picnic is all," answered the green bandanna.

"Too much labor. I got some men who can transfer her to the back of my pickup."

Davis stole a glance and noted that the tall, thin man with the purple bandanna reserved comment, and strode toward the path to wait for the coming. Davis resumed meandering but with a hidden purpose. As he neared the large shack, he could see that it leaned on its foundation, the walls repaired poorly with pieces of trash wood. He thought the end of his grist mill was in better shape than this dilapidated mess.

The air cooled on his warm skin and he shivered, his slight sweat chilling him. Deep in the wood he heard a black bird caw. He was aware of eyes following him but he was drawn to the building as if it were a place of holiness.

The door hung on its hinges and as Davis stepped onto the curled wood of the shed's porch, he read the sign over the door painted in a crude print. Cannon.

He stepped in. Darkness engulfed him and he could barely make out a stone hearth and fireplace big enough to burn a tree stump. A crude iron grate sat inside and his nose filled with the damp acridness of burnt firewood but he was soon overcome by the smell of rotting flesh. The floor was potholed and squinting, he heard the scurry of forest rodents receding into their depths.

A decaying animal, perhaps a small dog or a wolf near the hearth became the object of his attention. He drew closer, his poor eyesight adjusting as he made out its form. Crusted blood covered the black fur and the stomach cavity was hollowed, spilling its contents in a muddy red across the floor. The head lolled, oddly twisted at the neck, the eyes sightless marbles.

"Boon, where'd ya go?"

What was left of the light that came from the door opening was blocked and the interior space fell into almost total darkness. The figure entered and Davis uttered an involuntary, "Ghya, ghya." A splinter of light shot over the man's shoulder toward the hearth.

"Jesus, it stinks in here."

And then, as if taking in the scene for the first time, the man Davis knew as Lowery pawed the wood with his shoe and said, "That's a shame. You don't need to look at it. A young coyote come in here to die. Sometimes the mother abandons them and they're kinda defenseless in the wild."

Davis didn't know what to say. The fat man felt compassion the way he felt responsible for his cat.

"Come out," said Lowery. "We got a lady we want you to meet. One of the originals."

Dutifully, Davis followed him onto the porch. Folding tables covered with brightly covered cloths and laden with bowls and platters of picnic food lined the edge of the glade. Folks, paper plates in one hand and cans of beer in the other, waited in line joking and laughing. Younger men, their hair shorn on the sides and their parts off center, some with shaved heads and tattoos had joined the picnic now that the sun was so low in the sky and a few torches lit the glade. He counted the tattoos of eagles, swastikas, AB for Aryan Brotherhood that wrapped around arms and necks, and AYAK ran down a man's calf asking anyone who followed him, 'Are You A Klansman?' His other calf testified AKAI, 'A Klansman I Am.'

Davis recalled the force with which he was drafted by competing groups while in prison, everyone wanting him to join their effort, the indoctrination, the readings and lectures on racial purity held slight differences in orientation. The message was all the same: the white man needed to rise up. He had resisted tattooing because of the thick fur he grew on his body and they had laughed at the impossibility of labeling him. His sight might have faded but his memory of their artwork had not.

A small band of children, dressed in white tunics ran past him carrying tiny Confederate flags, their faces red with exertion and excitement. Davis heard the sound of a diesel truck engine that thrummed over the bustle of gatherers. Lowery waved his hand and Davis walked behind him, avoiding the stares of others.

A tailgate opened and he stopped behind a small crowd of men who parted as they lifted the sides of a wheelchair, passing it and its contents to rest the wheels in the packed dirt. The chair held a profusion of pink, green, and yellow, cushioned below a wrinkled face wrapped in gold lamé. She peered up at him, two piercing blue eyes above distorted cheek bones were barely visible below a jutting brow. An old woman opened her mouth, her heavy chin hanging down while she planned her words. She spoke.

"The world has not been kind to you, son."

"Miss Velma," shouted the man with the purple bandanna as he bent near her ear, "this is Boon, our newest recruit and a member of our security team. He's got a talent nobody else has."

The turban shifted slightly as she took in the purple bandanna from head to toe. "Glory," she said, "shut up. You don't have to tell me who this is. I know."

Davis was thrown. He didn't recognize this woman and although he hadn't been able to trust his near sight lately, he surely would've remembered a person who dressed like this.

"Your name isn't Boon," she said looking at him with an intensity he hadn't felt in many years. "Your name is Davis Vickers. You're the son of a hateful man, Theodore Vickers, who died mercifully in 1973 and left you with me when you were barely a teenager."

Davis shifted on his feet. He rubbed his palms up and down his pant legs and tossed his hair like a pony ready to gallop away. "Ghya, ghya," came out of him loud and clear.

"I remember when you started that tic after your father hit you in the throat one too many times. Broke my heart," she said, shaking her head.

The canopy of trees began to spin, the lightness and darkness whirling together in a yin and yang color wheel until Davis found himself on the ground. He groveled at her feet swaying his head back and forth like a dog trying to shake loose a soda can from its tongue. "Ghya, ghya, ghya," he said until she commanded him.

"Now git yourself up boy. That's no way for your new friends to see you. Don't you see you got their respect?"

Davis groaned slightly and stood. He put out his hand to grab hers and it was dry and whispery in his. He leaned down to her ear and asked so no one else could hear, "Is it you? Are you my mother?"

"Do you remember your brother who died?"

"Yes. He was older."

"By two years. He was your half brother. God stole him from me and Theodore stole you." She patted his hand and out of the side of his eye, Davis saw the purple bandanna nearing. The man called Glory. He moved aside.

The Grist Mill Bone

"Enough whispering, our dear Lotie. We got food to eat and another guest to introduce that Boon is going to enjoy."

"Glory," shouted Davis' mother, "Don't you go calling me no Lady Of The Invisible Empire. Those days are long gone."

The assemblage had mostly taken their seats, some on benches, others on folding lawn chairs. Chattering, only a few grew aware that Glory Bender had taken up residence on the porch step and was shouting over the crowd.

"Greetings All. Good evening. Please take your seats. We have a full program tonight. Thank you. Do I have your attention? I want thank all parties who contributed to this event. George Henley from the American Free Press provided the beer. The Confederate White Knights of Unionville in Maryland, Identity Evropa and the Be Active Front here on the peninsula provided all the food. Jon Kirkly of Refugee Resettlement Watch provided all the paper goods, tables and porto-potties. Can't go without the porto-potties, folks. And of course, I want to introduce myself. I am Glory Bender of ACT for Delaware and the Imperial Wizard of our own peninsula-wide White Knights of the Klu Klux Klan."

Applause rose from the center of the crowd and sprinkled about the group. Davis wondered if this was the first time so many different groups had met. He wondered if it was wise because, in his experience, if you gave a man a motto and a badge he would soon want all other men to have the same.

"You all traveled from near and far to build our enthusiasm and organize for the coming racial holy war. We share a belief that the white man's civilization is doomed in today's world. These United States of America are devolving into a third world country with the proliferation of illegal immigrants and the slavish adoration of political correctness that chains our freedoms. The Jews and their socialist ideals have control of Hollywood and our economic future. Our government is being run secretly by a Muslim cabal and they are driving us into trillions of dollars of debt. The historic contract between the Jews and the Negro will take over our world as we, the purest of the pure, decline in numbers. We are at historic lows in world population: only 9%. We, the Christian white folk of America, suffer poverty, liberal tyranny and the power of unseen forces while our government hides under the yoke of Muslim beliefs. We must rise up and take our country back for the our children's future, for this nation is white, Christian and the soil belongs to us."

Davis stood behind a tree and watched as a skinhead in the middle of the crowd stood and shouted with a fist raised, "Blood and soil! Blood and soil." Soon a chant began and he could no longer hear the insects chirping as the human voices rose in power. Several younger men with the odd haircuts, carried lit torches to the edge of the woods and plunged them into the ground creating an eerie glow on the glistening faces.

Glory Bender called the skinhead to the front. Davis moved closer, unnoticed by the crowd. The man was dressed in a wife beater, not appropriate wear for a social gathering, he thought, but he speculated that it was an effort to show off his bulging muscles. He had only seen such massive arms before on a black man in the prison yard. No one ever messed with the man, a member of a black gang, The Crips. A swastika was plastered in red and black on this man's shoulder and a spider web on his elbow. Davis could barely make out the words, Blood & Soil across his collarbone.

Singlehandedly, the man bent before a log on the ground and dead lifted it to his waist, whereupon he shifted his grip and threw it above his head to catch it above his shoulder. He tilted against its weight and Davis could see now that it was a huge cross that the man walked upright to a standing position, 12 feet high. People came to assist, leveling the cross in its hole and filling in dirt around its base.

A chant began again in earnest, "14/88, 14/88," and the assembly stood thrusting their arms upward in unison. It was familiar refrain to Davis, the "Fourteen Words—because the beauty of the White Aryan Woman must not perish from the earth," were drilled into his head as he walked the prison yard. 88 stood for the eighth letter of the alphabet, a salute, "Heil Hitler." It had been more subtle at Smyrna, although with so few prison guards they were allowed to get away with whatever they wanted, since a few were sympathetic to the cause and wary of the black inmates.

Glory's voice rang out. "This Nation was created by us, settled by us and we will carry on the memory of Virginia Dare, the first white baby born on this soil. She was born here for the sake of all white children and all others will be expelled. The dirty masses who come to our shores will be driven away and we will retain our purity for the longevity of our country."

Davis searched the fevered crowd for the only face that mattered but he could not see her. She had been swallowed up in their furor and as he gazed at their messianic faces, he realized he had lost her to the proceedings. He ran the edges of the crowd, back and forth and decided that he would have a better chance if he waited at the entrance path where she had arrived in the back of the pick up. Just as he pushed his way through the crowd, they became uncontrollable at the sight of the cross, burning, its flame reaching upward in a blue light to the dark heavens. They pushed against him and he squeezed through, bursting forth onto the path only to find that the pickup was gone. Davis groaned and slapped his arms against his sides, when he realized the crowd behind him had calmed and Glory's voice rang out again.

"Tonight I bring you a man with great talent. Where is he? Our solicitor general has recruited someone with years of experience and outstanding lineage. He was trained by the father of the KKK on the peninsula, Theodore Vickers, who as a very young man engineered the lynching of Matthew Williams, the nigger who killed a white businessman in Salisbury in the 1930s and who paid for his heinous crime with his life. This is a message to you young people who are here tonight that your power is great. We want you to unite your forces. Use your media skills, operate in unknown cells, and build our legions. Create an ironclad organization that works together for our goal is the same. Tonight I bring you our Baboon Hunter! Where is he, where is our Baboon Hunter?"

A single high-pitched noise in his head took over Davis' hearing and he froze as Beavens and another man strode to him, their arms waving. He was helpless to their strength as

The Grist Mill Bone

they led him to the front of the crowd whose chant had changed from "14/88" to "Baboon Hunter, Baboon Hunter." As Davis slid behind Glory who stood on the top step of the Cannon cabin, he saw a man he had never seen bring forth from inside his framework, fully assembled. He rested it next to Glory who opened a box at his feet, and with the other's help, rummaged about to produce for everyone a polished rib cage, a spinal column and human skull.

"Here he is people. This is the Baboon Hunter, Davis Vickers, who will assemble for posterity the skeleton of that very nigger so that we can all see the elements of our destruction and know that it must be erased from our Nation."

Glory grabbed Davis' arm and extended it up in the air as if he was a prizefighter being introduced to the Boxing Hall of Fame. In his other hand he held the skull. Davis was sickened that his framework was public, sickened that they all knew his name and that expectations of him had been built. He shook and trembled in the spotlight and wished he could disappear.

His hearing returned bit by bit and the siren pitch in his brain subsided as the crowd's lasting applause surfaced. He gazed over their heads as he stood between Glory and the skinhead with the huge arms. More people gathered behind him and soon they lined up to greet him and shake his hand. He muttered beneath his breath and every so often a "ghya, ghya," slipped out unnoticed. Face after face wished him well, asked if they could assist him in the assembly of the skeleton or offered a space for his work. Some suggested they go out for dinner and drinks, a convention that he had never known and was afraid to experience. Just as the last of the greeters shook his hand and the crowd began to break up, he heard the diesel engine of the pick up truck at a distance. He wondered if she had returned, if he would have a chance to speak with her again and ask what she meant about his brother. His memory was so splintered. He could not recall his childhood but realized she was the key. She had said she was his mother but when he asked, he only meant to question whether she was the woman who had taken him in after his father had died in the church that day. It seemed she knew more. She knew from where he came.

The engine was the same diesel pickup but it carried a different prize. The driver pulled it up next to the burning cross. As Davis shook the last hand and Glory dumped the bones in the box, the man with the green bandanna slammed the driver's door and ran to the tailgate. He pulled a black balaclava over his head and hollered from the bed of the truck.

Everyone's eyes turned as he shouted, "I got me one and Patty Cannon would be proud." He wrestled a short figure from the bed, a man with his arms tied behind his back, and his head covered in a hood. Throwing him on the ground, others surrounded him and pulled him to his feet. The man with the green bandanna dragged him to the foot of the cross where he unceremoniously ripped the hood from his head. The poor man's eyes filled with terror as looked from face to face and back to the burning cross. "No. Déjame ir. Por favor!"

Glory ran over to him. "No, no. We aren't heathens here.

We're not burning people on the cross. If this man should be judged we need to form a jury and decide. We will not invoke Patty Cannon whose ideals were noble but whose methods of burning children in her fireplace were far from modern. People, you need to armor up."

With that, those who stood by the prisoner pulled on a balaclava and the other quickly extinguished the torches casting the area into darkness. Boon figured it was as good a time as any to make his escape and he started down the path mingling with parents and children who were the first to leave. As the path opened onto the field of parked cars and trucks, one family asked Davis if he had a ride home. He looked them over and deciding them harmless, he accepted. They made their way to an old Chevy and Davis piled in the back with the two school age children. He could smell the children's sweat, a grassy smell coupled with the sweetness of their breath. One had a ring of purple around his mouth and still toyed with his Confederate flag. He looked up at the hairy man next to him, wary at first and when Davis smiled down at him, he warmed and poked Davis' thigh with the tip of the flag. Soon he piped up and asked a question that must have been burning his lips.

"Mommy, who is the Patty lady? Did he say she burned children in her fireplace?"

The mother turned around and, looking at Boon and then her small child, she said, "Oh my honey. That's not for you to worry about. Patty Cannon's dead and gone 200 years. And she didn't burn up good little kids like you anyway. She only burned up wicked little nigger kids that didn't make good slaves."

The car was silent and Davis could hear the children's breathing with the rise and fall of their chests beneath their white tunics. The woman turned to stare out the windshield into the headlights. He watched as her arm fell across her husband's shoulder and her fingers stroked his head as if he were her child. Davis wondered if this was what it was like to have parents and be loved by them.

*****

22 CLAIRE

"Ms. Solomon, I'm not sure Mrs. Owens is capable of meeting with you today."

I stood at Fairhaven's reception desk, balancing a box of Velma's belongings from the storage unit on its edge. It was nine in the morning and I had an appointment with her, made the previous afternoon. She had sounded fine on the phone, chipper. She was excited about some friends picking her up for an evening out.

"My goodness. Is Velma okay? Is she sick?"

"She's very depressed this morning. Refuses to get out of bed and is complaining that her joints hurt. They hurt all the time so we've called the doctor to see if we can get her in for an appointment. They haven't called back yet."

I whipped out my cell phone as she spoke. "Why don't I call upstairs and see if she still wants to meet with me?"

The receptionist huffed a moment and gave in. I'm not hawking subscription magazines, for God's sake. I'm her attorney. If her health was taking a turn for the worse I needed to get the paperwork done.

It rang twice and she answered the phone. "I forgot you were coming, Solomon. I'm not dressed, but you can come up."

I took the stairs rather than wait for the slow elevator. Good for me to get my blood moving in the morning, especially carrying a box. At the top of the second flight I was out of breath from the extra baby weight. I had really popped and there would be no hiding it from Velma this morning. I had on a gray capped sleeved summer top over black gabardine maternity slacks. Nice pearls, low black heels. But baby was unmistakable. Nervous, I put down the box on the step and pulled my hair up on top of my head to stab the bun with a pen. It held.

No one was in the hallway. I pushed the door open gingerly and called, "Velma, can I come in?"

The wheelchair was empty in front of the table. Letters were piled up unopened, the first sign that I might need to take over her correspondence and banking. The social worker from Fairhaven had not called to alert me, so this had to be a new behavior. I stepped further into her room and looked around the corner.

Velma lay in bed, the last bird in the nest, a round white hump in rumpled linens. Stripped of her outlandish wrapping, she had shrunk to the size of an egg, except for her head. At the sight of me, it wobbled and she tugged and prodded a terry cloth shower turban, trying to cover her boney skull. In her hurry, she was unable to hide the overgrowth of bone that ridged above her eye, her forehead, and bulged like Hags

Head at the Cliffs of Moher. Wisps of dry white hair could do nothing to soften her appearance. The turban was bunched up, her tug was too weak and she was embarrassed.

I put down the box, sat on the edge of the bed and asked, "May I help you?"

She nodded silently and I reached out to gently unroll the turban and pull it down over her ear. "There," I said. "Now where's your brooch so we can clip it on and make you a little more festive?"

She pointed to the bedside table where amidst the profusion of creams, tissues, and earrings, was her favorite—a cameo profile of a young Victorian woman, delicate, her hair piled on her head and framed in gold filigree. It had been fashioned into a clip back and I carefully wedged it into her sad little turban. I sat back and smiled. In a weak attempt, the corners of her lips turned up with no delight.

"You aren't feeling well today."

"Don't want to live no more, Solomon."

"I see you're pretty despondent. You don't even want to get dressed? Did you eat anything today?'

"I et last night. Pretty fires, ever-where. Don't add up to nothing—don't make the worl' a better place."

"You went somewhere with friends and they had a fire?" I was choosing my words carefully, humoring her, for who on earth would have a fire in this July heat wave? Surely, she couldn't have been to a beach bonfire. They're few and far between and have to be permitted these days.

"Not my friends no more."

"Oh, I'm so sorry, Velma. I hope something bad didn't

happen."

"Dumb folk, think they know me. Field of 'em wearin' white. Give it up, ... the fight over."

"That's a good observation." I spoke slowly to match her words. "Seems like there are a lot of people like that these days." I wasn't sure what she meant but I thought the best thing to do was agree with her.

"Solomon, you got a brain. Look at those folk—thinkin' pert near a horse with blinders on."

I didn't know what to say. She had reverted completely to a previous time in her life, and although I'd heard bits of eastern shore colloquialisms, I'd never heard that twang from her. This was a tough morning and I was angry that something had upset her during her evening out.

"Oh Velma, don't take it so hard. People resist change. It makes folks uncomfortable. You're an enlightened lady who's lived a long time and have the benefit of years of wisdom." I wasn't holding my tongue in my cheek. I suddenly realized that she had the benefit of retrospect—that her old class driven beliefs had surfaced in the nursing home—bossing Tyneice and the head nurse, but she wasn't wedded to those beliefs. It was dementia that robbed her of her better sensibilities.

She snorted. "Fat lot of good all these yers are doin' me. I don' know howter make new friends and the old ones are despicable human be-in's."

"Well, you made a friend of me."

She looked at me hard and for the first time since I sat on the bed she seemed to come out of her misery a tad. She patted my hand.

"I did. We are." She looked me over and continued, "What's that you got there, Solomon? I not seen you in a while. Looks like you been up to somethin'."

"I have. We're going to have a baby in the Solomon household come October. Are you coming to the baptism?"

She smiled merrily then. Almost like the smile I could have seen on Odessa's face if they hadn't been so far apart in looks and culture. Still, it was the same goodwill that babies always bring, especially to old women.

"I won't be here then and you know'd it, girl. I just want you to git the future solved fer me."

"I do too. Do you feel up to talking today because I went to your storage unit in Cambridge and brought back some things I thought you'd want here in your room?"

Her head fell back against the pillows and I could see without saying a word, she had resigned herself to whatever came next. I pulled the framed photo of the two small boys from my briefcase. I had taken it home and wiped the mildew from the glass, but its faded glossy surface was pockmarked with spots of mold. The boys' faces were unharmed. The dark haired older one looked so serious, his hand resting on the toddler's thigh as if to prevent him from hopping off the bench to play with the photographer. I wondered if she had snapped the picture and could just see Velma watching the two boys and hoping the camera would capture their frivolity before it all evaporated. I passed it to her waiting hand.

She held it out and said nothing. Her eyes filled briefly and she blinked back the tears. Then, she said, "They were so different."

"Your sons?"

"Yes. Different but doomed. I shoulda never had 'em. Either of 'em. I only brought 'em pain."

I was alert. Was this a moment of clarity? Was I on the verge of finding out the truth? "Why do you say that, Velma. Why were they both doomed?"

Her hand passed over the photo and she was quiet as if she was considering the secret. "I'm not goin' to be here so it don't matter. If I cain't tell you there was no use in keeping it a secret. Besides, he's alive. And I got to change things again. I already spoke to Father Caulfield."

Father Caulfield. What did that old man know that he wouldn't tell me? The only thing I could think was it had to be a confessional secret.

Velma pointed to the older boy. "That's Fred's son, my husband who up and killed himself a long time ago. He were a weak man. Couldn't handle the truth but men are like that when their ego's hurt. You see, I had let the boys out in the front yard to play that afternoon. They was maybe seven and five. I told Christopher to watch out. Play tag and run around, I said. You know children are like dogs. They'll follow a ball into traffic and back if they're lucky. They both listened that day. It weren't their fault.

"We had a neighbor spent all day in the bar a few blocks down the street. He'd come home for dinner, driving up the street, bouncin' off the parked cars. We all kept our children inside but on that day, he come home early, hit a car opp'sit our house and drove right into our front yard, through the fence, and hit Christopher square on. He was deader than a doornail right there in front of that little one's eyes.

"My husband and I both went into a decline after that and we kind of ignored the second born. Me, out of guilt and my husband out of grief. Rumor started around the church that we weren't taking care of him because he wasn't Fred's child. An old bitty on the altar society spread it, saying that our little boy was this man Vickers' child and don't you know, my husband believed it. Wasn't long before he got outta bed one morning, walked down the basement steps and killed himself. Shot himself in the chest.

"Well, it was all true. I made my confession to Father Ingle. I told him that I had committed adultery in the church sacristy with Vickers. See, Vickers and I had worked on some stuff together, got too close in those days, thinkin' we could change the world, make it like it used to be. We'd done some bad things and I knew I needed to make up fer it, so when the money finally arrived from the insurance company over Chris' death, I set up a fund to pay for the education of children on the peninsula. Private school to college, in perpetuity.

"You don't know about that investment fund. It's a whole lot more than the amount you have in your briefcase because it includes Vickers' money. He were a skinflint and it's right and just that his money bein' used to educate little black kids."

I was stunned. She was making sense of her universe and finally confessing it to me. Velma raised her gaze from the photo of her sons and looked at me, then looked out the window. The sky was white hot, the July temperature blistering outside but in her 350 square feet of airconditioned space, I was too warm. I picked up her file and fanned myself. "Do I need to get that fund into the trust?"

"No, Solomon. The Catholic Church in Wilmington services those scholarships. I don't even know who wins the money but them schools send me pictures of students and they list the scholarships ever' year in their publications."

I had never heard her be so clear, so matter of fact and without judgment. If no one knew she was doing this, possibly she had never been recognized for it. "Velma," I said squinting, "do you want the community to know about your philanthropy?"

"Heavens, no. Are you crazy girl? There are forces out there that'd take great delight in disassembling this structure, no matter how sure we are of its future."

"What happened to the son you had with Vickers? Is that the same young man who lived with you later but ended up in jail?"

"That's him. I'm sorry to tell you, Solomon, that he's alive. Saw him last night. I always thought he would have good luck because he was born with a veil and the birth caul is so rare. But that's just an old superstition. Davis was a good child, happy and smart. He was so little when Vickers took him away and I never saw much of him, 'ceptin' at church on Sundays. He forgot who I was over time. But I would recognize him anywhere. As he got older, he began to look like me. Not as bad as this, but he had my forehead. Blonde. He was there last night at the cross burning. They got him indoctrinated. He looks like a skeleton with hair."

"Cross burning? That was the fire you attended?" I wanted to shriek those words but they came out little more than a whisper. She didn't hear me.

"He may be a worthless piece of shit but I told him who I was. I think he understood. I want you to set up a fund for him, so's he gets money by the month. Just enough to live on and it come from the church, not me. If he find out there's more, he might go after the scholarships."

"Do you know where he lives? I'd need his phone and social security number and the name on his birth certificate to get started."

"I don't know any of that, 'ceptin his name. I got a birth certificate 'round here somewheres that say his name is Davis Owens Vickers. You can start with that."

Velma laid the photograph on her bed and reached for a glass of water on her nightstand. She groaned, stretching her joints, and I reached for it too. Our hands touched and hers fell back into the linens. I stood to put the glass to her lips and she gently took a sip, then more.

"That's 'nuff," she said. I put the glass down and she asked, "What else you got in your box?"

"I brought your photo albums. I wiped the mold off, the ones from St. Aloysius. I thought you'd enjoy looking at them."

"Put them on my bed here and I can look at 'em this mornin' before they come in with more pills."

I lifted the container and turned it on its side on the bed so she could reach in. The albums slid out and revealed the cast metal poor box dedicated to St. Benedict. I shook the container and it landed in Velma's lap. I didn't know its significance. I assumed it had special meaning for Velma. I should've known what happens when I assume something about my client.

"What's that thing doin' on my bed. Get it offa here! Right now!"

"Oh, my goodness, Velma. Of course. Don't get all upset. I'll take it home with me."

"You take it!" she said, pushing it away. "I don't want no more reminders of that skinflint, murdering son o' a bitch! He ruined countless lives and died without ever sufferin' for it. Left me to do his clean up."

"Who, Velma? Who left you to do his clean up?"

"Vickers, girl. His spirit alive today. Why them dumb white folks might as well be prayin' to him and Patty Cannon in the same breath!"

***

Later that day, I headed home early to the farmhouse with the poor box on the front passenger seat. I ran my fingers over its cool, marbled surface that was cast with a contemplative profile of the beggar man, Benedict Labre. I had searched for his info on my phone. Sure enough, a homeless dude from the 18th Century who earned his sainthood performing miracles after his death. I always love how that happens in the Catholic Church. Like they give licenses for making saints. He sure had Velma's panties in knot. I called Pembroke from the car.

"Hey, do you have a minute?" I asked.

"For you, I have three," he answered.

"Velma's got an heir. She's asked me to write him a trust. Dicey information, Pembroke. I think she was involved with the Klan in a previous life."

"No question, Claire. You need to write Velma's shit up, get her signature and get out quick. The Feds are involved. They want information on Velma but I wouldn't give it to them without a warrant. I called Gloria Richardson in New York yesterday to see what she remembers."

"Gloria Richardson, the civil rights icon? Isn't she the woman who stood up to the police during the Cambridge riots back in the '60s?"

"The same. And I wouldn't call what happened in '67 riots anymore. The media conveniently labeled it such to sell news. Richardson didn't remember Velma. We talked about the possibility of a very active KKK at the time in Cambridge. Old white dudes in power who had an agenda to burn out the black section of town since they were shaking up the town council and making Cambridge a national issue."

"Okay. Then it's all probably true. But listen, it sounds like they're meeting around here now. Velma was confused but she may have attended a cross burning last night."

"There you have it. Now, you know why the FBI is snooping around."

My mind was awhirl. "Pembroke—all the murders of those homeless guys. They're all people of color."

There was silence on the other end of the phone. "I told Brent Fowler you were handling Velma's case. You might want to call him," he said. "Screw the warrant."

I hung up, now even more worried as I entered the Solomon property through Odessa's shaded drive on Old Mill Bridge. I didn't have the energy to risk a conversation with Trixie by going in the back way through the trailer park. The police had removed the yellow tape at the entrance where the bones had been found that fateful day I first met Velma. It seemed like eons had passed since then and now, I wasn't sure I would ever complete her legacy.

I passed Odessa's house, silent and dark, where the second wrap of police tape was still strewn around the generator and the HVAC unit. Messick had not returned calls to her cell phone and I worried that she would lose her job, or worse, be forced to alter her report about Odessa's death.

After the rains had rutted the path through the stand of beech trees between our houses, Booker had one of his Sussex construction contacts widen it, grade it, and gravel it, so that his new truck could make it through without another scratch. My Mercedes handled it like a dream and I thought again that a car was much more a symbol of power in D.C. than it was on the shore. Power and character. My shoulders knotted with tension and I realized my jaw was clenched. Our move, the baby coming, our new life seemed so distant and no longer held that joyful anticipation.

Yoga. I needed a good yoga session on the lawn to peel away the stress.

I also needed time to think. That morning at breakfast, Booker had said he was staying home till ten, skyping with Ross who was back at Tosh collecting evidence for his defense. After, he had a three hour drive to Wilmington for a meeting with his attorney. He wouldn't be back till late. I made a stack of blueberry pancakes and Sam wolfed his down, carb loading for soccer camp that lasted till early afternoon. I threw the dishes in the sink and I told them both I would be home by two.

I was arriving early and happy I'd have a couple hours to myself. As the car broke through the stand of beech trees, the sun hit me square in the face, blinding me. A figure broke free of the trees, hailing me down. It was Little John.

I put my window down, wondering why he was walking around our land when none of us were home.

"John. Can I help you?" I asked, seeing the concern on his face.

"Claire, Mrs. Solomon, Trixie sent me over to find you. She couldn't get you on the phone. Booker, I mean, Mr. Solomon called her."

The kid was having trouble figuring out what to call us. We had always been on a first name basis but I assumed it was the influence of his new job and having to address everyone by their last name. I was a little charmed by the change in him.

"Is everything okay? Was there a message?"

"He's broken down over by the old mill. He called Trixie to say he was going to see if he could give the guy who's living there some money and thank him for helping us out in the flood. His new truck won't start back up."

I looked at my watch. Booker's appointment was at two in Wilmington and this was going to make him at least an hour late. What was he thinking? Apparently, not much, and I panicked, worried he had bad news from Ross. I was on my phone all that time with Pembroke and he couldn't reach me. I hate call waiting and had deactivated it on my cell. He argued with me about that and I guess now he could say, I told you so.

"Over by the old mill, you say? Okay, listen, I'll go pick him up but we're going to have to head up to Wilmington. Can you ask Trixie to take Sam this afternoon when he gets home from soccer practice? We won't be home till late but tell her I'll make it up to her."

"Yeah, sure. She likes having Sam around. He helps with the little kids. I gotta get to work, now. See ya later, Ms. Solomon."

John walked toward the trailer park and I wondered if Trixie was driving him to work every day or if he walked. I didn't think Trixie would be real flexible in driving him back and forth. In this heat, the kid would need a shower when he arrived. I put the window up, did a U-turn, dusting up the oyster shells on the driveway, and drove back through the stand of beech trees to the road. I could be there in five minutes. I was ready to call Booker when my phone rang again. It was the social worker at Fairhaven.

"Listen, can I call you back in a half hour?" I asked.

"I'll be quick, Ms. Solomon. Mrs. Owens is failing. Her breathing's become irregular and we've called the ambulance to take her to the hospital. I thought you'd want to know since you're medical power of attorney."

"Okay. Thank you. I hate to ask, since I just left there not

The Grist Mill Bone

an hour ago. Is this serious?"

"I'm not a nurse, Ma'am. I'm sure the doctors will get up with you if it is. Her blood pressure is up and she wasn't making sense. Could be a stroke, ... I just don't know. We sent her paperwork with the ambulance."

"All right. Yes. I'll see if they call. Thanks." I pressed the button on my steering wheel and hung up. I couldn't do anything at the moment. I wanted to get to Booker. If all else failed we could reschedule the appointment with the attorney but only if it was a last resort. I sped across the bridge, not even looking out at the water I was in such a hurry, but I didn't see his black truck anywhere near the mill. The fallen tree was mostly cleared and I pulled in. I got out, slammed the door and called out, "Booker, are you here?"

There was no response. Strange. I had never been inside the mill, never been curious enough to check it out. Where the hell was he? Maybe he got that miserable truck running and took off. That'd be a relief. I walked up the short path and peered inside the mill, my phone raised in my hand. It was ringing for him.

And then it was snatched from me, and heavy arms wrapped around my body from behind as I was lifted up and over the doorstep. He was a big man, soft around the middle but I was high in the air—he was so tall. I screamed once and a rag was stuffed in my mouth before a rough cloth over my head plunged me into blackness. Disoriented, I stiffened and gagged as I doubled over. The man's arm slid below the baby and the other came across my chest pinning my arms to my sides. I kicked furiously and slammed my head back into his.

He dropped me to the floor and I tried to get to my feet and pull the hood off, but hands grabbed mine from the front, and I realized with a sinking feeling that I was dealing with two people.

When he yanked my one hand behind my back, I knew I had to catch a glimpse of my attackers if I'd ever identify them. I tugged at the hood with my other hand, getting it halfway off. I saw boots, black ones, polished, and blue pants before it was pulled down, blinding me again. Someone grabbed my other hand and drove it up behind me, and dragging me to my feet, I was pitched forward.

This was good. With all the force I could muster, I stamped my spiked heel repeatedly into his foot. This man wasn't wearing boots, maybe leather shoes, not canvas. He let one arm go and I drew my fist up under the baby and flung it backward into soft flesh. I made contact with his balls but his gut was in the way and it jammed my elbow. He groaned and let go. I was free for mere seconds and I turned to run toward the light as I pulled the hood away and the rag from my mouth.

I could see trees in front of me through the doorway and heard my car being started. I screamed "Nooooo!" and ran, hands outstretched right into the rat-tailed man who had saved Sam. "Oh please, please, help me," I yelled. I glanced over my shoulder but pushed into the safety of his arms as someone whacked me over the head. My sight began to slip and I heard a distant garbled voice say, "Ghya. Stop, she's the Madonna." I was gone.

I woke later on a thin mattress. My head pounded and I

fingered the spot beneath my hair, locating a lump the size of a large lemon. My hands were free and I could see just fine, a bit blurry, but things took shape. I was too scared to move for fear my attackers would leap out of the shadows. My watch was gone from my wrist but it seemed from the sunlight streaming in low through the window opening that it was probably late afternoon. Maybe three hours had passed. I had to pee.

I could feel the rough cotton duck of the mattress, buttons sewn into it and a selvage edge of thick tape. My head was sweaty and I wiped my brow with my hand. It came back bloodied, sticky, … *Great*.

Slowly I turned my head to see a man standing outside the doorway. He must have been watching me because he stepped inside, blocking the light. I turned back to the window where a smattering of small, winged bugs floated silvery in its beam of light. I moved my leg out from under the other and realized they were tied around the ankles. Raising my head to look, the pain was too sharp, and I fell back into the mattress.

I passed my hand over the baby and felt a kick. I sucked back a sob so my captor wouldn't see me weaken.

"I hear the baby," he said. "It moved with you."

He was crazy.

"I need to pee."

"Okay," he said.

I thought he would untie me and take me to an outhouse or somewhere in the woods. No such luck. He wandered out of sight and was gone so long, I wondered if he forgot. I heard a footstep nearby on the wood and he put a small cooler on the floor next to the mattress, removing the lid.

"Can you get up?" he asked.

"That's what you want me to use? A cooler?" I asked with no small degree of indignation.

"It's all I have. I'll turn my back," he said.

"You bet your damned ass you will."

I struggled to sit up and a wave of nausea hit me. My feet were tethered by ropes to an eyehook in the wall. The ropes were long and if I could rise, maybe I could walk a little. If he wasn't watching, maybe I could loosen them.

In my confusion, I didn't see him nearing me. His hands came up under my armpits and lifted me in a steady grip. He bent over behind me and said quietly in my ear, "Can you pull your pants down?"

I was surprised by his gentleness. I tugged at the maternity pants that rolled right off my belly and slid to the floor, entangling my feet. I struggled to reach my panties under my long shirt and his one hand reached and pulled them from my fanny. He sat me on the cooler and turned his back. I peed a long time, wobbling on the cooler. Blood dripped down my face and onto my gray shirt. I cast about, looking at the mattress and realized it was stained with blood. When I was done, he handed me some toilet paper. Confused, I didn't know what to do with it once I used it.

He glanced furtively and said, "Throw it in the cooler. I'll get it."

I did. He turned and said, "You ready?"

"Uh-huh." I tried to stand and he was right there, one

hand under my armpit again, the other pulling my underwear up, then my gabardine pants. They were ruined, a big hole in the knee, and it was then I realized that my knee was skinned and bleeding too. The heparin was doing a number on me.

He laid me carefully on the mattress and I heard a strange, "Ghya, ghya" as he moved. He was an odd one but my fear had dissipated some. He wasn't going to kill me. At least not right away.

"I told them not to hurt you. I told them it wouldn't go well."

I was quiet. I could hear the cicadas' song, rising and falling outside. At least I was alive and the baby was kicking. "Who is 'they'?" I asked.

"No one."

"Why are you doing this?"

"They said he'll come for you."

"Booker? You're damn right he will. You think he's coming for one? He's coming for two and you're just prison fodder to him."

"He already sent me once."

I didn't respond. He was a criminal then, escaped or released and bent on retribution. I wasn't the target, Booker was. It was then I thought we could both die.

That is, if I didn't bleed to death before Booker found me.

"I need some gauze or a clean towel for compression. I'm going to keep bleeding and then what use will I be?"

He had been sitting opposite me on a rickety chair and he got up to open double doors under the eaves. It was a closet, chock full of stuff packed on shelves. He pulled out a beach towel, a bandsaw and a broomstick. "Why are you bleeding still?" he asked.

"Because I'm taking blood thinners to keep me from miscarrying the baby. What are you doing with that saw?"

He must have seen the fear return to my eyes. "No, no," he said, "I won't hurt you. It's the others. I'm going to make a tourniquet for your leg and patch your head."

I had propped myself on one elbow and the blood was still pumping across the mattress in a swath. He ripped the towel in a long piece and folding a clean washcloth in quarters, he knelt under my shoulders, leaning me against his thighs and pressed it onto the head wound. He told me to hold the cloth while he wrapped the strip around it, tying it up neatly under my hair. The blood poured like dark syrup from my knee and he cut a three inch piece from the broomstick, tied another strip of towel around my knee and inserted the stick, twisting tight until the bleeding slowed. He moved a wooden box onto the end of the mattress, layered the rest of the beach towel over its edge and propped my leg on it. He knew his stuff. He wasn't an idiot and he wasn't crazy. Or maybe only a little.

"Who are you?" I asked.

"It doesn't matter. I'm here to carry out a project. Are you hungry?"

"That's ridiculous. How could I be thinking about food?" He was staring at the baby and I had the strangest feeling that's what he meant: feed the child. "I'm really thirsty," I said.

He took the width of the floor in three steps and reaching

a makeshift shelf, he grabbed a coffee mug and a gallon jug of water. He returned to the chair, poured the water and handed it to me. He set the gallon next to him but didn't drink himself. I propped myself up and tried to sip but the water sloshed, so he knelt before me to hold the rim to my lips. I paused and took a good look at him before I swallowed.

He sat. He was a hairy, big boned animal. Huge arms and hands. Tight, runner's chest. The muscle in his upper arm was ribbed with ropey veins. His hairline was receding but what fell down the middle of his back was a thick matted mess of graying blonde hair. His forearms were covered in thick, curly fur. Blonde, a large forehead. Light blue eyes: Velma.

"I know who you are," I said. "You're Davis Vickers. I know your mother."

He almost fell off the chair. His fist pummeled his chest, as if he was trying to shock his lungs into taking a breath. He stood up and his chair fell behind him. He paced back and forth. I had really upset him.

"I—I'm sorry. I didn't mean to scare you, Davis. Your mother is Velma Owens and she's a lovely person."

"Ghya, ghya, ghya," he said, and went to the doorway to spit. He returned, his hand over his chest, rubbing it now. He leaned down to me and asked, "How do you know my mother? I only met her last night."

His breath smelled odd, not mint but—root beer. Close up like that, I saw that his sunburned neck was misshapen, that his Adam's apple had been split.

"I'm her friend," I said. "I visit her regularly. She told me about you this morning." Was that right? It seemed like it was yesterday. "She was a little upset to see you with your companions."

"I thought she'd like them."

"Oh, on the contrary. She was repulsed by the event last night. Especially the cross burning."

He was quiet, considering this. I hoped he didn't think I was lying but my hopes were realized with his next question.

"I want to see her. Can you take me to her?"

I laughed a hard little laugh and raised my hand in a question. "How am I going to do that? Is my car outside?" I ripple of anger coursed through my bones and I quickly looked away from him.

"No, it's gone. They drove it away."

"How's Booker going to know I'm here then?"

"Someone will send him here. They're watching your house to see when the lights go on. He won't find you home and will be concerned."

Little John. That's who's watching the house. Who else could it be? He had sent me here and now he was going to send Booker.

Davis stumbled over his words and couldn't get his thought out. His face contorted, calmed and contorted again. His mouth worked in unheard words and finally, he said, "Why are you his?"

"His?"

"Why are you with him? He will defile you. His skin will defile you."

Oh my ever loving God. He was a full-on whack job.

How could I feed into him, get him to trust me? He didn't

know the baby was Booker's. Maybe he didn't know we were married. "Oh, Booker works for me," I said. "He won't defile me. I'm safe." Placate him once, placate him again.

"Your manservant, then? He takes care of you and the boy? They said he's no longer a police officer."

He knows Sam! Fear rose from my gut and I began to breathe very quickly. Would they take Sam, too? "That's right. Booker's retired. All he does now is take good care of my son and me."

He nodded and seemed satisfied with this, that I wasn't betraying the white madonnas of Sussex County. *Manservant?* What century was this cretin from?

"You can find another to serve your family. He filled the prisons with innocent white men during his time. He's going to pay for his crimes."

The mug of water rolled off the mattress. I slid into my sticky brown blood and closed my eyes.

I woke in darkness to cold on my knee. My right eye was swollen nearly shut and I was floating. I raised my head for it had fallen backward and realized I was being carried. A single candle flame glowed, reflecting off a wall. The grist mill. The attack. I ached and my arm felt like lead, pulled downward by the force of gravity. I had no substance, no will. Davis was taking me somewhere. I glimpsed his large head above me, his hair falling over his face as he bent to lower me onto something soft. I gave in and slept.

*****

23 BOOKER

When Booker Solomon cleared the grove of beech trees he hit the brake, studying his farmhouse at the end of the drive. He strummed his fingers on the steering wheel and cocked his head. The timer had turned on the living room light but all the other windows were dark. Claire's car was gone. He had called her repeatedly as he drove Rt. 95 from Wilmington but there had been no answer. He told himself she had misplaced her phone, that she had taken Sam to the movies and turned it off, that she had gone to the gym for an evening yoga class. None of the answers seemed as plausible as his one instinct that the whole world was very shortly going to explode.

But he wasn't going to enter an ambush like he had that day at his Ma's house. He put the car in park, killed the headlamps and called Trixie.

"Booker, hey man! I was wondering when youse guys were gonna call. Sam's here. We went over to pick up Compass, so's the dog's been fed and walked. You about home?"

"I'm sitting in front of the farmhouse."

"What's up with that? Come on in for a plate of puttanesca."

"Have you heard from Claire?"

"I thought she was with you," said Trixie her voice rising. "She wanted me to pick Sam up from the soccer bus; said you two were headed up to Wilmington. At least that's what John told me."

"John? He's involved in this?" Booker asked, pulling his gun from his shoulder holster. "Look, I can't find Claire." He could hear the kids fighting in the background. "Trixie, are you listening? Where's John?"

"At work."

"You haven't seen anybody hanging around the farmhouse?"

"No. What's going on?" she asked.

"I didn't want to worry you or I would've let you in on this earlier. Ma didn't die of a heart attack. She was murdered. I can't explain it all right now. What does John know?"

"Lord, Booker. Claire already told me. Are you sure?"

He heard the TV and a child began to cry. "Sure as the gun I'm holding in my hand right now."

"Alrighty then—I was just going to take the kids for ice cream," said Trixie. "I guess I could stop by Fairhaven and talk to John. He can't take phone calls while he's working."

"I'm going to search the property. If you find John, ask him what exactly Claire said to him."

Trixie's voice rose. "Oh my God, Booker, I'm just putting all this together. There's some seriously bad karma around here. They found another body today. Some Hispanic guy, shot and dumped off Rt. 54 in the Great Cypress Swamp. All his organs were removed."

"Trixie, don't go off the deep end. Claire doesn't have anything to do with the homeless killings and neither does Ma."

"Don't be so sure. You want I should call the police?"

"Not yet. Call me Trixie. Call me," he said, hoping she was wrong as he hung up. He threw the truck into reverse, backed into the glade of beech trees and got ready.

Unbuckling his shoulder harness, he stepped out, laid the SIG Sauer on the seat, pulled on his tactical vest and a black nylon utility belt that carried extra magazines, a flashlight and combat knife. He holstered the gun at his waist before he walked to the truck's rear gate. Inside, he opened a large gun case and assembled his AR-15 with the night scope. He raised it, took a bead on a yard flag fluttering by the Gronski's driveway at 400 yards and was deeply satisfied. He scanned the farmhouse and seeing nothing, bent to attach an ankle holster for his Glock 27. Locking the truck, he darted out of the woods, nimbly keeping to the shadows as he entered the house, waterside, from the screened porch.

It was a quick search. Nothing had changed since breakfast. Dishes in the sink, pancake griddle on the burner. The smell of bacon frying lingered in the air. Neither Claire nor Sam had come home. He kicked one of Compass' plastic squeaky balls that cluttered the kitchen floor, a sure sign the dog had grown bored. Booker flipped on the kitchen light, put down his rifle, and sat down at the table to think, squeezing a ball in his hand.

There was no reason to connect any of the murders to Claire's silence but he knew the first few hours were critical to finding a missing person. If he reported her disappearance, he would be stuck for hours at the farmhouse answering questions, imprisoned by the local police. They'd waste time establishing her status, that she wasn't visiting a friend, that she wasn't having an affair, that she wasn't under stress and left on a vacation. And there was always the possibility that Lowery would be the first detective assigned. He would have the devil of a time getting another investigator quickly. No, it was better to call Agent Fowler.

He explained their investigation.

"Nice. Ya coulda said something earlier," said Booker.

"I didn't want to prejudice you into taking the law into your own hands. You have a history with that, you know."

"Add the fact that Claire's missing. It hasn't stopped you from wanting me to join your ranks, now has it?" answered Booker.

"No. But we can't have you interfering in this investigation even if Claire is involved. You aren't law enforcement anymore."

"Well, how 'bout you deputize me over the phone.

Fowler ignored him. "The reason I had that conversation with Alfred Pembroke is your wife's client, Velma Owens, is part of the investigation. Turns out she has some interesting contacts on the peninsula."

"Let me guess."

"She's former KKK. Too old to be anything but a poster grandma now."

"You got anything on her?" asked Booker.

"There was a cross burning last night out in Reliance. KKK field party. We got an undercover agent planted. The old lady was there for a short piece but left early before things got cooking."

"What you mean cooking, agent?" asked Booker as an image of Matthew Williams' lynching flashed in his mind.

"They didn't string up the homeless dude last night, but nobody can find him either. We don't even have a name."

Booker threw Compass' ball across the room and hung up but it was seconds before the phone buzzed in his hand. He cursed seeing it was Trixie, not Claire.

"Booker," she said, "I'm here at the nursing home. They said John's not on the schedule today. Claire was here this morning visiting with some client she has, a Mrs. Owens. Now get this, the old lady's in the hospital. They called Claire so maybe that's where she went?"

"She hasn't answered her phone for six hours, Trixie. I don't think she likes Velma that much, but I'll call the hospital."

"Whatja want me to do? I got to get these kids ice cream and back home for bed."

"Let me talk to Sam." He heard Trixie shout. There was a pause and Sam's voice came strangled with concern.

"I have to explain something to you, Booker. I—I think I really screwed up. I'm really scared for Mom." He began to cry.

"What is it, Sam. What do you know?" asked Booker but Sam heaved and sobbed at the same time, drowning his words. Trixie's voice returned.

"Booker, he's having a panic attack. I'm getting these kids outta here." Then to someone else, he heard her shout, "You got a paper bag he can breathe into? A lunch bag or something? For God's sake, aren't you people nurses?"

Booker yelled over the phone, "Trixie, just stay there. I'm coming to you."

"Well get your ass in gear. They don't look real happy with me."

Booker arrived at Fairhaven minutes later and pulled onto the sidewalk at the front entrance. The nurse was watching the door and buzzed him in the second his hand hit the door handle. The lobby was utter bedlam. Residents had come from dinner and the game room and crowded around Trixie's kids who were laughing and putting on a show for the old folks. Compass was on a short leash, sitting primly, and as one of Trixie's kids held forth on his talents the old and infirm petted him. By the desk, the head nurse held a crumpled paper bag in one hand and Sam's wrist in the other, timing his heart rate as he sat in a rolling office chair that slid across the tiled floor. "Put your foot on that brake under the seat or he's going to fall off!" she shouted and returned to lecturing Trixie about bringing so many visitors but didn't have anyone to visit. "We aren't your amusement park!" Trixie's arms flew about as she defended herself and her kids.

Booker scooped up the dog, first grabbing his leash before ordering the four rambunctious kids to get in the car. He glided up to Trixie and speaking low, wrapped an arm around her waist as he moved her to the doors. "Trixie, you done your best, girl," he said. He slapped the loose bills he had in his pocket on the desk, nodded to the head nurse and in a quick evaluation of Sam's color and alertness, ordered, "Let's go, boy."

As he herded his brood in front of him, he noticed the faces of the elderly residents, stunned, mouths open, some smiling and waving at the big black man in a dress suit who had taken charge. A wizened lady, sat hunched near the exit. "Excuse me," she asked holding a handkerchief in the air, "Are you the detective on that *Criminal Minds* show?" she whispered.

Booker frowned and then it came to him. "No, Ma'am. I'm no actor. I'm not even a detective." He nodded to Trixie and pushed them outside, the kids running to Trixie's van, while Sam waited next to the truck.

Trixie's eyes were wild with drama. "I never found John. Not answering his phone either! I got one more month with that kid before he's emancipated from the State and it can't come too soon." She hugged Booker and hollered for the kids to put on the seatbelts as she started the car. "If you need me to help with Sam, you can drop him off after I get the kids to bed. Too much excitement for one night." She took off, a small hurricane of her own making.

Booker looked at Sam, his arms outstretched. Sam came to him, wrapping his arms around his stepfather and they were one. "Sam, what's going on with you?"

"I got in with John. It's my fault for trusting him. I thought it was cool. You know, that we could get back at you for the sex toy thing." Sam raised his head and tossing the hair from his eyes, he searched his stepdad's. "I was mad but I didn't get it till now that John is really pissed. He's messed up, Booker."

Booker saw the sheen of guilt marking his young face and girded himself against judgment.

"Sam, if you know something, now's the time to spill. We're talking about your mom."

"It's was the bones. The ones in the yard. John buried them. He got them from that guy who's living in the grist mill. The dude's some kind of anthropologist. But he's homeless and, and, … pitiful."

"He's living in the grist mill?"

"That's why we went there the day you and Mom were in Cambridge. I didn't know a storm was coming and the fastest way to get there was the skiff. On the way over, John told me he planted the bones 'cause he had a plan. He made it sound like it was just him and me, like we were gonna hassle you a little and no one would find out because he had back up. I thought he meant the guy at the grist mill. I didn't think anybody else knew. I would've told you all this but Grams died and nobody was talking to me."

"Sam, you weren't talking to us."

"I know and things have just gotten way worse. John's not talking to me anymore and I know he's trying to manipulate the guy at the grist mill. He's a harmless old dude, really. Just likes his box of bones and wants to be left alone."

"You don't know if he's harmless."

"I do Booker. When I talked to him, he came out of his shell because I respected his work. He has these shiny animal bones all articulated into skeletons. He said he'd teach me how to assemble them. John just wants to use him to get you in trouble."

"That's because some of them are human bones, Sam."

Sam blinked and his eyebrows came together. "So what's that got to do with Mom?"

"Don't know, do we? But it's time to find out."

A police car sat in the farmhouse driveway, its lights alternating. Booker pulled up behind it and looked at Sam, red and blue flashing on his tender face.

"Go inside and wait for me, Sam," said Booker.

"No. I want to know."

"It's too much, Sam. Go inside, now." Booker removed his suit jacket and placed it in the back seat inside out. He watched the trooper get out and face the truck, waiting at a respectful distance. He looked innocent enough. Sam pleaded one more time but Booker was a steel door. "I'm not going to tell you again." They got out and Booker hugged him before pushing him toward the kitchen door. Sam put his key in the lock and walked in reluctantly, glancing over his shoulder at Booker. *Tell me.*

The state trooper strode over, a clipboard in his hand. "Mr. Solomon? Officer Murray, Delaware State Police." His hand was outstretched.

"Yeah, that's me." Booker had grown weary of introductions and he was ready for the worst. He nodded his head and said, "Okay, man. Get on with it. What do you know?"

The officer nodded and said, "We were notified a couple hours ago by Maryland State Police that a car registered to your wife, a late model silver 450 Mercedes, was found in Assawoman Bay about 5 p.m. today. No one was in it and they were looking for a body but pulled it out empty. There was a pole fixed from the seat cushion to the accelerator." He waited and then asked, "Do you know where Ms. Solomon is, sir?"

"I do not. I've been calling her all afternoon and she's not answering. There was some question that she was driving up to Wilmington or she went up to Lewes to the hospital but obviously none of that happened. Are you actively looking for her?"

"Maryland State indicated this could be foul play, sir. Have you filed a missing persons yet?"

"I am now."

"Yes, sir. Do you have any suspicions about Ms. Solomon's whereabouts?

"In the last six hours, yes. Anything and everything, officer. I've talked to everyone but her boss."

"We can do that as part of our investigation. Maryland will be involved because of the car. Do you want to go inside?"

"No, not with our son there. It's better if we talk here. What did they find in her car?"

Officer Murray flipped the page on his clipboard and read, "A Coach bag with her wallet and credit cards, a briefcase and a box—looks like it says a poor box for homeless people, says Saint Labre on it. Would you know anything about that?"

"Yeah, it's from a client of hers, from her storage unit. It's probably pretty insignificant in the big picture." Booker put his hand on the grill of his truck to steady himself, "Was—was there any evidence of foul play?"

"No sir, not visible," he said, his voice full of earnestness. "The car was towed to the Maryland impound lot in Ocean City. The detective on duty isn't going to release it though, pending their locating Ms. Solomon."

"Where'd they find it? I mean, broad daylight, man. It was found in broad daylight, like somebody wanted us to see it."

"Yes, sir. That could be. It was found down a footpath on St. Martins Neck, nose in the water. They said it was covered in brush but the rear license plate was visible."

"That's not the appearance of foul play. That's foul play. You all better get busy."

The questions began, Booker answering, the trooper running through them as if he'd done it a million times, his pencil scribbling across his clipboard. As he finished, he smiled his encouragement and asked, "Do you want the printout from Maryland? This is your copy."

"Damn right. At least I can look at this and feel like some headway is being made."

"Yes sir. They said they'd be calling you."

"And you, Trooper? Will you be calling me or is my wife getting lost in the serial killings?"

"The lead detective from Delaware didn't come over tonight because he wanted to discuss your wife's disappearance with the FBI. She's missing across state lines, sir."

Booker felt his eyes squint up, wondering if he could believe these words. "And who might tonight's lead detective be?"

"Detective Showell, sir. He's very good. New at the Georgetown barracks. He's from around here originally but he transferred a couple of months ago from Wilmington. He remembered your father who used to treat the animals on his parent's farm. We're lucky to have him, sir."

"Yeah, we've met. Tell him to talk to Brent Fowler from the FBI. He'll have information."

*****

24 CLAIRE

My mouth felt like cotton balls. I could smell something sharp, familiar, like a grille had just been lit. I moved a little and my feet fell onto something soft. My legs were numb, seemingly no longer attached to the rest of me. My captor was pouring water into a small stainless pot on a propane burner.

"Are you feeling more comfortable?"

I took stock of my situation. My bloody clothes were gone and instead I was clothed in a man's clean white button down shirt. The tourniquet had been removed and the fresh bandages on my knee looked professionally wrapped. Reaching up to touch my head, I could feel padding and real gauze, the type a doctor's office would use. The mattress was freshly made with a clean pad, sheets, and my head rested on a pillow. All this and I was still tied to the hook in the wall.

"Yes. Thank you." I was creeped out, wondering how it had all transpired but I didn't want to give it too much thought: his hands, my body, the baby. I wondered again if I would live.

"Do you like cinnamon raisin or maple?" he asked holding up paper envelopes of instant oatmeal. He smiled at me and I shivered in the heat.

"Both," I answered.

He ripped them open and poured them in the pot, stirring a little as he smiled. Taking care of me was domesticating him. But someone had to be providing all this. The linens, the food, the first aid. It wasn't like I'd ever seen him in the grocery store across from Fairhaven. No, he was purposefully off the grid and someone was enabling his ass. I rubbed my eyes and fingered a cold ice pack under the gauze. No wonder I could see. The swelling had gone down.

"What time is it?" I asked.

"Nighttime," he responded as if this made perfect sense. He wore no watch and I looked around for a clue.

For the first time, I really *saw* my surroundings. The ruins of the mill looked large from the outside but I realized this was an optical illusion. The stone foundation was intact all around the perimeter rising a good four feet inside with rough, planked walls above. Gazing up, I wasn't looking into rafters but stars that glowed in the night sky. A full moon was visible and if I calculated my position on the mattress correctly, I thought I was facing an eastern sky. *Of course*, I reasoned, the roof nearest the ocean side would be battered away by years of storms. Earlier, I had lain facing the roadside of the mill, the side with the closet he had opened so I craned my neck behind me to see if I was right. It was double-doored, and spanned the end wall of the mill, shut with a bar jammed through the handles.

The mattress on which I lay was creekside, next to the exterior waterwheel and opposite me was the doorway that led to the forest, framed by two windows. The door was long gone as were the windowpanes. Inside, the grindstones were missing and a round of wood that was a different color and age than the rest had replaced the hole in the floor where they had once turned.

He was watching me with that myopic stare. He held a bowl out, steaming and smelling of cinnamon. I was hungry. I pulled myself up to a sitting position and my head pounded. I grew dizzy and heard the *awhang, awhang, awhang* that would end in a faint. I tried to tuck my head down, but the baby was in the way. I leaned on my elbow.

He knelt beside me, and held a ball of green leaves under my nose. Mint and bergamot came to me, clearing my head. "Better?" he asked.

"Yes."

"Can you lean against the stone to eat?"

I crawled onto my good knee and dragged myself across the mattress, being careful not to show off too much skin. The stone was cold against my back and felt good in the nighttime heat. There was one light on the far wall beneath a window and looking across the room, I realized it wasn't a candle but a hurricane lamp that glowed. Bugs fluttered around it in an arc. I reached for the bowl of oatmeal.

He watched me eat. "Do you want more?" he asked.

"No, I'm good for the time being. Do you have a toothbrush?" I asked putting the empty bowl down. The oatmeal coated my teeth and I couldn't help but repeatedly run my tongue over them.

"No, but I have sassafras." He produced a mason jar that held five or six green twigs, freshly cut. He plucked one and stuck it in his mouth, chewing on it.

I looked at him quizzically. The guy was so far off the grid, he had become some kind of herbalist. I wondered if he tanned his own hides and smoked his own meats. A small laugh escaped as it occurred to me that I could be next to add to his store. Hearing my laugh, he looked hurt.

"I wasn't laughing at you," I said quickly. "I'm amazed at your resourcefulness. How does this sassafras thing work?"

"Soften the end of the stick by chewing on it. Then brush your teeth with its broom. Tastes good. Like root beer."

I tucked one in my mouth and marveled, chewing on it like it was a cigar. I braved the question, "So have you been living off the land for long? I mean you might have instant oatmeal and bottled water but you obviously know how to do without."

"Mankind is too commercial. It would be better if we went back to our roots. Healthier eating. I did more with less when I was locked up."

"You didn't eat in the cafeteria?"

"I did. I learned to eat the vegetables everyone left behind."

"Oh, you don't eat meat?"

"Why? Food sustains us, it's not intended to gratify."

The guy had a vocabulary and a unique way of expressing himself, I'd give him that. "You must have learned a lot in prison?"

"I prayed with the sick and wounded in the infirmary. Eventually, I was allowed to go on work release, part of the highway crew. But I missed the infirmary so they brought me back because they needed an attendant. I was allowed to help with wound care."

"What were you in for?" I asked, calling on my braver soul. I was afraid of the answer.

"Murder. It was my father's doing years ago, not mine. Your Solomon found the bones in the basement of my father's hardware store. He pinned it on me. I wasn't even alive back then."

"Really. How long ago was that?"

"I don't remember. I was more than a child but less than an adult."

"You know, Booker was in the army before he became a detective. He didn't join Maryland State until just after the turn of the early 2000s when he was around thirty." I said.

"I don't know what you mean. I don't count time any longer. I only know seasons and sometimes years."

"All I'm saying is that if you went to prison in Delaware it couldn't have been Booker who put you there. He never worked in this state."

There was a long silence and his eyelids batted hard as if he was trying to see the truth. He reached for the bowl and his hand missed it by inches and he grabbed at it again. I thought maybe his near sight was bad.

"You're wrong of course. Lowery met me at the prison gates on my release and told me it was Solomon."

I nodded my head as if to acquiesce. Lowery again. I didn't want to anger him. "Maybe, but all I can say is that Booker is 40. By your count, he'd have been about 15 years old when he put you in prison. He wasn't even out of high school then."

"It was him. It was him," he said and rose from his chair to pace the room. I watched him at first, passing back and forth in front of the light from the hurricane lamp and fearing he would fall upon me in anger or frustration. He had moments when he was lucid and then this compulsive behavior would kick in. What had he said? It was the others we needed to watch out for. We? Did he mean the two of us? Maybe I was safe because of the baby. The three of us.

"You know, this coming week I have an appointment for an ultrasound." He stopped as if an unknown hand had grabbed him from behind. "That's a picture a technician takes of the baby while it's still inside the mother."

He patted his chest and said, "Ghya, ghya" again before he seated himself on the rickety chair. "A picture? Of the baby?"

"Yes."

"It's softness recorded? The bones not formed. The Caucasian baby is more intelligent because the skull is larger. A human in its purest form before the world spoils it. I want to see this," he said.

"Well, you have to let me go then," I retorted. If he couldn't see the desperation on my face, he could hear it.

"Let me show you how God makes us different."

With that, he opened one closet door and dragged two

large plastic boxes across the floor. He opened one and lifted the complete skeleton of what appeared to be a medium sized dog, fully assembled and articulated, each one of the bones yellowed but shiny and numbered. It moved as if its heart and soul were still intact like those plastic skeletons people decorated with for Halloween. Incredulous, I asked, "Davis, did you assemble this?"

"It's one of many," he said. "This is God's small creature that gives us pleasure and devotion." He turned its face toward me. "Its brain is small by comparison to ours but no one can devalue the position of man's best friend in our world. He is obedient to us and dependent. When you speak of humans, you can't guarantee those qualities."

He reached in the second box and withdrew two human skulls. I inhaled and reached for my throat. They were bright white and smelled of bleach. One was smaller than the other, its forehead sloped backward from gaping eyeholes.

He weighed it in one hand. "Take it," he said.

"No, thank you. Just make your point and put them away."

He laughed at my discomfort. "This is the skull of what everyone calls an African American today. Its smaller, the brain cavity a quarter less than the white man's skull." He raised the other above in the air.

He believed his science and knowing how demented he was, I didn't argue.

"Where did you get them, Davis?"

He looked away from me. Putting them back in their boxes, he acted as if he was ashamed, hanging his bowling ball of a head.

"Davis, where did you get them?" I asked again.

"People have been giving me bones for years because they know I can assemble any type of skeleton. People like my finished product. No one else has this skill. Look," he said. He opened the other box and I saw it was a jumble of spare bones, all clean but yellowed with black scribble on them, as if he had stockpiled them for years.

I didn't know what to say except, "God help you Davis, if you have taken the bones of a murdered person to satisfy your little projects. God help you. The fifth commandment is, 'Thou shalt not kill.' "

"I would never kill anything. It's someone else's choice, not mine."

"You can't hate everyone who isn't like you. That's one degree away from the murderer."

He leaned forward. "You can't trick me. I am part of a bigger picture that's been ordained by God. It doesn't matter if I'm wrong about Solomon. He's still a black devil and must be tried for his sins and removed. All of them must be removed, like I remove the invasive weeds in the creek that are choking the land." He raised his head and sang out, "All must be removed."

The crazies had come between us and I had lost his rational side. Frustrated, I pleaded, "No, no. You're right of course. I believe you. I can help, can't I?"

"Help? What do you mean?"

"I'm a lawyer. I'll try him for his sins. I was brought up in a church. I know the laws of God."

"What church?" he asked. "There is only one holy and apostolic church."

I knew from his words. "Your church. The Catholic Church."

He sighed and closed his eyes, relieved. There was no reasoning with him, no way to predict his response. He was using his faith as a torch to weed out everything bad he saw in the world: an evil that was defined by skin color. Suddenly, I wondered if he was the cause of all the serial killings. It had to be him.

He opened his eyes and walked over to the hurricane lamp. Raising the globe, he moved his thumb in the flame until it must have burned, but he put the globe back neatly. He came to me and leaned in close across the mattress. Involuntarily, I pressed against the stone wall and as his thumb traced the sign of the cross on my forehead, he said, "You are forgiven, In nomine Patris, et Filii, et Spriitus Sancti. Amen."

My shoulders slumped and I let go of my held breath. I asked, "Did you give absolution in the infirmary?"

"When they asked, I gave. No one should go to hell carrying a sin they are sorry for committing. God forgives us all. He forgives the poor man first, but he also forgives the wealthy."

I assumed he meant me.

*****

25 BOOKER

Trixie stood on her front porch, waiting as Sam walked forlornly under the streetlights, past the Gronski's to her house. Booker had lied to the boy, telling him that the trooper showed up to discuss the bones found on the driveway. Sam was insistent, questioning what else they had found and whether they knew about the man at the grist mill. *Did you tell him, Booker? Are you keeping a secret about Mom?*

He told him not to worry, that the trooper said the DNA proved the bones were old and mismatched, knowledge he had not shared with Sam earlier. Sam was restless and Booker called Trixie to ask her if he could spend the night. *Why? Why do you want to get rid of me?* Booker told him he had filed a Missing Persons and was going to drive around looking for Claire's car. If he found it, if he found her, they would come get him no matter how late.

Sam loaded his backpack and looked at Booker with recrimination, but at last, he cooperated. Booker stood on the kitchen steps and watched as Trixie closed the door behind them and the porch light went off. He guessed she wasn't going to make it real welcoming for John if he returned home in the night. Booker looked at his watch. 9:45 and still no word from Claire. He carried his rifle inside.

He tore to the bedroom, and changed into black, tactical pants, kicking off his dress shoes for waterproof boots. Gauging the usefulness of the indiscriminate AR-15, he decided to trade it for his army sniper. Preparing took time and Booker glanced at his watch in frustration as step by step he finally opened the last door of the gun safe revealing his four foot semi automatic M110 with a quadrant sight. It was new, a replacement for his first army issued sniper. A month had passed since he had gone target shooting at Synepuxent when his old army cohort came for a visit. Afterward, he had cleaned and oiled it, not telling Claire where he had been. She became irritated whenever she saw its massiveness and so he never taunted her, only accused her of getting the heebie-jeebies. Once, her hands on her hips, she retorted that she wasn't going to be married to someone who contributed to American gun culture and he laughed and said, *Woman, I'm the one who protects you from it.*

In the kitchen, under the harsh overhead light, he reassembled his tactical gear from the truck, laying everything across the kitchen table. He pursed his lips, deciding the only other thing to add was a switchblade in his pocket. Raising his hands in the air, he closed his eyes and said, "Ma, this is for your family. Make it good."

As he locked the farmhouse, he remembered the

Delaware ducker, a sneak boat his dad had used in the marshes for bird hunting. It was covered in weeds and cobwebs and rested next to the notorious generator. He drove up the path, through the beech trees and parked the truck on the side of the house. He had a plan and by the look of things, he needed to be quick.

He had called Ross and left him a message with Brent Fowler's private number and the FBI's direct line on Delmarva. He also read off Detective Showell's number from the card the trooper gave him. He knew they would be working the serial killings on the peninsula and likely the FBI tip line was busy 24/7.

He needed to mobilize someone with experience on the shore and that man was Fowler. The media was openly calling the murders a string of hate crimes and he was sure with each passing moment no one would have time to look for Claire. He put his phone on buzz hoping for a return call. Until then, he couldn't trust anyone.

Booker carried the 100-pound boat over his head and walked to the grass, upending it. It was filthy inside. Dragging it down to the pier, he dumped it in the water, tying it to the grommets on the back of his Grady White. He walked back to get his truck. Without turning on the engine, he rolled it downhill to the pier. He studied the creek. It gleamed like black glass under the stars, quiet and serene. A blue heron, disturbed by the truck's presence, squawked and rose from the grasses, folding its neck as it gained height.

Booker first removed a Maglite from under the truck's seat, his M110 and then the first aid kit, fixing them securely under the washboards and plank seat of the ducker. The night was quiet, only the occasional hum of a late night party boat passed as families returned from the restaurants, their green and red lights visible above the water, voices carrying in laughter. It was too early for boating drunks to wind their way home from the bars and hours away from serious fisherman leaving on early morning jaunts.

The Grady White's engine burbled and caught. Booker steered her out into the broad creek and cased the distance around the corner to the grist mill by the bridge. He estimated it was a little more than a mile of irregular shoreline dense with reed grasses, much of it phragmites that hid the state duck blinds. Hunters entered by lottery to win a coveted blind for a day during season but it was before the official start. Tonight, there was no acceptable reason for gunshots on the creek, unless it was target shooting or a life was threatened.

For a brief second, Booker entertained the idea that it could be a trap he was entering but in the end, he resigned himself to his plan. He was alone and would make every action count. He only hoped he was wrong, that his colleagues in Maryland State were going to find Claire at most the victim of a summer robbery, alive and wandering the woods in St. Martins Neck.

He slammed his fist against the dash and cursed at the vision in his head, his young wife, pregnant, and lost. Leaning back in the captain's seat, he swore to Almighty God that if he could bring Claire home safely, he would never leave her side again. Never.

He didn't flip on the boat's running lights and hummed

slowly on the water until he saw the outline of a duck blind. He hopped off the front of his fishing boat, carrying the bow rope and two oars. He tied it with two half hitches to the duck blind's cleat and hooked the rope on the ducker pulling it into the marsh grass. Throwing the oars in, he returned to his fishing boat and lifted the sniper rifle out. He stepped midsection, his arms raised to keep his balance. Digging the pole into the muck, he pushed off from the marsh, sat down, placed the rifle onto his lap and oared along the shore toward the grist mill. As he drew close, he heard a woman's scream, *No, No!* and she was muffled into silence. It was Claire.

*****

26 CLAIRE

"Boon, come on out here." I heard voices outside the door and I knew it was the men who had helped Davis. I sat on the mattress, my ankles freed, sobbing softly.

Only an hour before I had to pee again. Davis swung one of the closet doors wide on an angle, anchoring it with a stone as my privacy screen. He carried the cooler behind the door and untied me.

"You need to walk. It's not good to lie around for hours."

"You aren't afraid I'll run?" I asked.

"And beat me to the door?" he smiled, nearly breaking out in a laugh, the first time something had struck him funny.

"Oh, just watch me."

He drew me to my feet but I couldn't straighten my knee. I limped to the closet door, and disappeared behind it. Once I finished, I had some trouble standing up on one leg but I grabbed a closet shelf and pulled myself to my feet. I peeked around the door to see where Davis was. He stood by the doorway, watching me.

"Walk," he said. "Come over here." His boney forehead shone in the ghostly light of the lamp, but his eyes were in shadow and I couldn't read his intention. I was afraid he was going to hand me off to someone else. My time at the grist mill, no matter how frightening, had a measure of security, but I feared it was over now. I walked haltingly, searching his face. As I neared him, he took me by the shoulders and said, "Look."

He pointed to a clearing in the woods, lit by the moon reflecting silver on a freshwater pond. I could hear a bullfrog in the distance, governing his waters. The cicadas's song rose and fell as fireflies pulsed yellow against the dark. My car was gone.

"Look," he said again and I watched as a doe entered the clearing, a spotted fawn following. If they smelled us, they gave no sign, for they both leaned into the water and lapped at its calm surface.

"I named her Claire," he said.

I looked at him amazed and he stared down at me, close enough that he could clearly see me. He admired me, held me on a pedestal. I had never told him my name.

"Yeah, well she can get away. I can't."

He frowned and turned. "Walk to the mattress, over to the closet and back to me. Then repeat."

"What's this?" I asked looking at a broomstick attached to a long, curved blade. It gleamed in the light from the lamp.

"I cut the phragmites with it. It's called a scythe."

"Oh, like a human weedeater."

"The mattress," he said and picked up the scythe, setting it outside the door. I obeyed. When I reached the mattress I looked at him watching me and realized he was somewhere else. His head was cocked like a dog that hears a whistle humans can't hear. I kept walking. When I returned to him, he put his hand on my shoulder. It was hot and so large it covered my collarbone. "Go sit down."

I had gained a sense of balance from this little exercise and was able to raise my eyes from my every step. My gaze was drawn to the open closet where a framework of boards and wire resembling a cross sat. It was big enough to hold a human and a hangman's noose dangled from the top. It dawned on me slowly that this was an instrument of death or torture.

"No, no," I screamed. "What is that? What are you going to do? Please, please, don't kill me. My baby should have a chance at life!"

He rushed over to me and clapped a broad hand across my mouth. "Hush," he whispered and I looked up at his Adams apple that surged in opposite directions as he swallowed. He put his other hand behind my head and dragged me to the mattress like a lion transferring a cub by the neck to its nest. I leaned against the stone, choking back sobs, unable to take my eyes off the hangman's cross.

I had been crying for what seemed like hours, unable to quiet myself. After my outburst, he had gone outside and I heard him talking to someone. He returned, stepping over the threshold, and I watched him slip a phone into his pocket. He wasn't that far off the grid. This was his contact, his enabler.

Shortly, there were tires rolling onto the gravel drive. A man's voice called him Boon.

They stood outside arguing but I didn't hear Davis answer them. I listened intently, waiting. An older voice, with a heavy twang, argued about my car, saying it had been found already and they would have to move me now to the Reliance Wood. The younger man, said, "The Cannon shed is perfect but you have to go too."

I thought they meant Davis and I grabbed up the pillow to shield me. Reliance? I had never heard of it but instinctively knew it was far away, someplace Booker would never find me. Their plan to have me lure him in was breaking apart. One of them stood within view and I could see he was very tall. They stepped away from the door, out of my view.

I got up and slithered toward the doorway, huddling under the windowsill, away from the hurricane lamp. There was no way I could escape but at least I could hear what they said. I peeked over the sill and saw that an old Lincoln town car sat facing the road. The angle of the wide doorjamb prevented me from getting a good look at the older man but the younger one's profile was captured in the lamplight. It was Beavens, the state trooper who had accompanied Lowery at Odessa's house. The other's twang was all Lowery's.

Suddenly, I heard the doof, doof, of a silenced bullet and watched, incredulous, as the car sank low on one side. Lowery and Beavens stopped yammering at each other and looked about, not moving. Davis walked calmly into the grist mill, took his scythe from the door and seeing me huddled on the floor, grabbed me by the arm and dragged me to the mattress.

"He's come," he said.

I yelled, "Booker," and he nodded and smiled.

"He is your sin, Mother."

*****

27 BOOKER

Carrying his rifle, Booker hunched low as he walked the edge of the burned phrags, the mud sucking at his boots. Nearing the mill, he took to the forest and scoped out the entrance. In darkness, he watched as an old sedan backed in from the road, lights off, and came to stop near the door. Beavens exited the driver's side and stretched long, revealing his body armor. He left the car door open. In the glow of interior light, Booker could see Lowery's profile. The fat man rolled out of the car and trudged up the rest of the hill. They were in a hurry, not paying attention.

Booker circled the pond, keeping to the dark and he stopped behind a tree as Lowery called, "Boon, come on out here." In the darkened opening of the grist mill, a tall figure appeared, waiting, as if he was measuring the situation. It was the runner, still in his cut out jeans shirt, ragged shorts, and what appeared to be new steel toed boots. Booker couldn't see his face shadowed by the lintel, but there was no questioning the size of his arms. No, this was the homeless guy, the one who saved Sam and the one who collected bones. Human bones.

The gun's suppressor wouldn't silence the shot completely but in the cushion of night air by the water, it would confuse their ability to locate its origin.

He waited and soon the grist mill's squatter slipped into the gauzy light of the moon. His face shone white and the mound of his rattail fell down his back between his shoulders. His body was rippled with muscle, long and lean, his head large and skeletal.

The men stood outside, two cops batting at mosquitoes while the third stood sentry, his head cocked side to side, alert and listening. Booker thought, *this is the one*. As he receded further into the woods, he heard Lowery say, "they found the car already." Raising the butt of the rifle, he shot out the tires on one side of the car and paused to watch the response.

Beavens and Lowery halted their discussion and looked around. The man they called Boon drew back, and walked into the mill, holding some kind of farm implement.

A hush fell across the woods. Beavens raised his gun and hearing the sound of an errant night creature he fired haphazardly into the forest, four shots, as if he thought he could spook the shooter. *Artless*, thought Booker. If the man kept shooting like that he'd have to change the magazine and he wasn't wearing a duty belt. Booker walked to a young tree, nestled the barrel in a notch of perfect height and tracked Lowery through the gun sight as he scurried inside. The fat man took cover below a gaping window.

Booker pursed his lips and picked up a stone, throwing it

further into the trees. Beavens aimed where the stone hit with a thud and Booker fired on him, knocking the gun from the trooper's hand. Quickly, he fired on the body armor's plate that covered Beavens' heart. Thrown backward six feet into the dirt, the trooper couldn't recover. He clutched his chest, gasping for air. Booker looked through the sight, aimed just above his knee and shot a single bullet into soft tissue. Beveans groaned and rolled to his side.

Lowery fired his gun aimlessly into the night and Booker didn't respond. He walked around the pond to the ruined side the grist mill and crouched beside the stone foundation, keeping low to the ground. The siding had deteriorated from weather and a soft light streamed in horizontal lines between the wood planks from inside. Booker propped his rifle against the stone and drew his 357 from its holster. He pressed his eye against an opening and saw Lowery huddled and signaling, a furious movement of desperation. Claire was nowhere to be seen. Suddenly the light was extinguished, plunging the mill's interior into blackness. He yelled, "Claire, stay where you are!" Resting the pistol against the wood, he took aim from memory and pulled the trigger. He heard Lowery scream as he hit the floor.

Booker shook his head and leaned against the wall. He didn't want a body count; he didn't even want justice, for that would come later. No, he wanted it to be over, he wanted his Ma, his property and his wife back. If this homeless dude who had saved Sam had some ax to grind, it wasn't apparent. He was a pawn and if Lowery was out of the way, maybe he could reason with him.

He walked low to the door's edge and stood to its side. Hearing a strange noise, like someone strangling, he thought he must have hit something vital on Lowery. But if this guy Boon had a gun, Booker wasn't going to give him an opportunity. It was time to evaluate the next step. He quieted his instinct to continue shooting and called out, "Claire, are you in there?"

She didn't answer. Instead the man, Boon, replied, "Come in Solomon. She's here."

Huddled, Booker walked to the corner of the grist mill and peered around it, keeping low. If Lowery were able, he would take a shot at him the minute he entered. If he was out of the running, Claire's captor could kill him at the door or—maybe he would hand her over. But was Claire alive?

Then he heard the man say, "Go ahead, speak to him and let him know you're fine."

*****

28 CLAIRE

"Booker?" I said, my voice shaking, "Lowery's down. I think dead. Davis doesn't have a gun. You're going to let me go, aren't you Davis?"

We stood against the back wall, his one arm holding me lightly across my chest, his other hand gripping the scythe. The moon was high in the sky, streaming in the roof's gaping hole with a ghostly light that illuminated the floor like a theatre spot ready for an actor's soliloquy. Only this was real. I thought I knew where Booker stood as I could see a shadow move across the line of moonlight that seeped through the wood siding. Davis said nothing but had cocked his head in a motion I knew meant he heard something long before me. He couldn't see in the dark of night but he could hear everything. Distracted, he let his hold on me slip.

He had finally pulled his stinking bandanna from my mouth and the taste of his sweat filled me with anger. Even the sight of Lowery's lumpy form seeping blood, balled up beneath the window, didn't derail me. No one ever took away my ability to speak my mind and I'd had enough. I'd allowed myself to grow hopeless. We have a chance, Booker and me. My family, my life was not going to end here in the dank ruins of my prison.

I twisted in his arm and he tightened his grip so I shoved, rounding on him as I tried to grab the scythe from his hand. It was then that I heard a whisper outside and the sound of tires at a distance, the low rumble of engines. Was someone coming to our aide? I lunged toward the door and seeing Booker flash by me, I reached for scythe one more time as Davis' long arm swept upward and his hand made contact with my chin. My head jerked backward and I fell on the mattress.

Suddenly, a man's voice over a bullhorn blared, "Detective Lowery, this is the FBI. Put your hands in the air and exit the building now."

Booker's gun was drawn but as I looked up seeing the flash of his eyes, I knew he wouldn't shoot an unarmed man. He wanted to spare me from seeing something he didn't want me to know—the death of another, no matter how evil.

I screamed for him to shoot.

He didn't fire right away perhaps knowing that Davis and Lowery, if he was alive, were finished. But his delay gave Davis a chance to swing the scythe over his head and like the reincarnation of Zeus, he brought it down on Booker's arm. It sliced through his shoulder like a knife through butter and the gun slid from his grip, scattering to the floor. My man leaned into the pain but he recovered, raising his head as Davis kicked his middle and pushed him to the floor.

I crawled across the mattress and dragged the scythe toward me, watching as Davis kicked Booker again and again. Booker curled up in a fetal position trying to protect his ribs and organs but Davis was relentless and strong. Through the flurry I saw Booker's fingers stretch for his gun. I stood and raising the scythe with all my strength, I brought it down across Davis' back. It cut through his rattail and sliced through his thin flesh, as I dragged its edge the length of his spine. He turned on me, and in the light from the moon streaming through the roof, his eyes were filled with hurt, and question. I shook my head and whispered, "He's my husband, the father of my baby."

Booker took one shot that traveled upward through Davis' rib cage, into his heart and exited his back at the shoulder. The bullet cut a wide swath, as everything I hate about guns tore through him, and I watched as Davis lay dying on the grist mill floor, Velma's child, the reincarnation of all her hate. Booker pushed himself up and I hobbled to him, slipping my arms under his and he rose, wrapping his around me. We stumbled outside into the night. Maglites shown into our eyes and we raised our arms trying to shield them from the glare. Booker said, "It's about time you showed up. Just couldn't make it a little sooner, could ya?"

I had no idea who was there and squinting, my hand over my forehead, I saw Booker's blood gushing over Davis' clean, white, button down shirt. It stuck to my bare skin and I wanted it off.

My eyes adjusted as Brent Fowler came to me, the bullhorn in his hand. A group of FBI agents, their guns drawn, had Beavens in custody. Fowler nodded to us and said, "We have an ambulance down the lane but somebody shot the tires out on this Lincoln and we can't get it up here. You got to wait for the gurney."

"I'm not layin' down for any officer of the law, Fowler. Not even you," he responded, a grin plastered on his face. Then, in a low voice as if they were two colleagues speaking in an office hallway, he asked, "Do you mind sending somebody over to the side of the mill to pick up my rifle? I have fond feelings for it."

Fowler grinned, "Seriously? Almost as important as your wife?"

"Are you an idiot, bro? You never admit that in front of your woman."

"No," I said as I began to quiver all over. It was shock coming on, a feeling I'd had once before but I didn't have Booker then, or my baby. "Especially one with a weedeater." They looked at me like I was crazy but I couldn't explain.

I hopped downhill holding the scythe, hanging on Booker who propped me up with his one good arm, the other hanging by his side. The stone path hurt my feet but oddly, it felt good and I knew I was alive. I realized the shaking in my bones was gone.

Passing a string of Delaware State troopers dressed in blues, one reached out to me and said, "Let me help, ma'am." I took my hand from Booker who stopped and hunched over, he said, "I got to rest for a minute. You go on."

With that, he keeled over backward just as an EMT caught him in his arms. Another met us with a gurney and

The Grist Mill Bone

they loaded him onto it, dizzy but still conscious. He fought with them, and the one by his head said, "Sir, you're safe with us. You can relax now."

"Claire," he shouted. "Get my rifle before somebody steals it." And with that, he passed out. They wheeled him down the slow rise to the rescue squad. The emergency lights whirled, blinding me and I nearly tripped over a tree root.

The trooper and I followed the gurney and when I reached the ambulance someone wrapped an emergency blanket around me. I was lifted onto a stretcher and I leaned back on one elbow looking around for my man. They wheeled him next to me and he was awake. He rolled onto his good arm and looked into my eyes.

"We got this, Woman," he said. I nodded and breathed deeply.

"It's deep, sir," said an EMT who had bandaged his wound. "We're going to need to transport you to the hospital."

"Double that," said the young woman at my side. "She has a head wound that needs attention. Probably an X-ray of her knee."

Booker answered, "We don't need to be transported. Take us to the house and I'll drive us over."

Fowler appeared behind us. "Oh, drop the superhero shit. We have two ambulances. Not taking a chance on you having an accident. We need your testimony for the trial."

Out of the crowd I heard a woman yell, "There they are! I got Sam here. Claire, honey, Sam's here."

And then he stood beside me, his face stricken with worry

and as he fell into my arms, he said, "It's all my fault. I should've told you."

"What's there to tell? It's nobody's fault, Sam," I said, my arms around him. "We're all together."

Booker tried to reach his bandaged arm to Sam, but the EMT put his hand out to stop him. Sam turned to his father, buried his face on his chest and said, "Booker, I'm so sorry." In a constricted voice, he said, "I love you."

*****

HOME

Two months later, On September, 7th, 2012 on a gorgeous fall day, Abigail Odessa Solomon came screaming into the world. Our little family unit is one bigger, not much more at six pounds nine ounces, but she packs a wallop. For a week, we didn't leave the house as we adjusted to the rhythm of our new inhabitant, making mental lists of her noises and perfection. She has hazel eyes, rusty brown fuzz on her head and warm brown skin. She is soft and glorious. Booker is absolutely dazzled. He carries her everywhere in his two good arms, barely giving her up to be nursed. He handles pooh, spit up and baby gas like a general handles the vagaries of war.

It had been a tough pregnancy. My kneecap was chipped from the fall at the mill and I developed a blood clot in my leg, causing it to swell. Booker watched me for a day and then called a vascular specialist in Philadelphia. Since I couldn't fly with an embolism, he rented an ambulance. Over five days, they filled me with heparin until my blood turned the color of rose water. I spent the rest of the pregnancy at home in bed. I say that, and I did mostly, unless Booker or Sam decided to put on a show with Compass and his ball outside my window. I had a steady stream of visitors.

Dean and Ross came from D.C. and briefly discussed the growth of Tosh and the maintenance of the McIntosh family home in Oxford. Booker seemed vaguely interested but when I asked if he wanted to go back, he only laughed, saying, "Ma wouldn't approve."

Pembroke came, his hair cut short to his head, a yarmulke on his crown. It must have been a Jewish High Holy Day. He asked me to return to work when I was ready. His new attorney graduated fresh from law school was "too green; not working out." I thanked him but demurred and he nodded as if he already knew the answer. He brought a silver teething ring. The Gronskis came with their new Maltese and the old man patted my hand saying he would bring her over to sit in bed with me anytime I wanted. An ambassador from the fire hall's ladies auxiliary came with a lemon meringue pie, the best I'd ever eaten. Lydia, Odessa's best friend visited, accompanied by a quartet of chorus ladies from the church. They sang some of Odessa's favorites and we cried together. They said they were throwing me a baby shower when I was ready.

I even had a visit from Nurse Seward at Fairhaven and little Tyneice. Velma had passed away while I was in the hospital in Philly, but in her last moments, she asked for them to tell that Solomon woman to keep up with the African violets. She sent me her favorite cameo clip.

Lowery lived, although part of his shoulder was blown away by Booker's gun. Booker attended the trials that were held in late August and by then the FBI had amassed the evidence on Lowery, Beavens, and Glory Bender along with their extended army of white supremacists. They were tried as domestic terrorists. Beavens was first and Booker said he entered the courtroom in Dover limping badly. He told me privately that it was a shame to see a young man so hateful and beaten.

The crossburning Velma attended out in Reliance had been secretly taped by an embedded FBI agent. After the crowd dispersed that evening, Lowery's little triumvirate passed judgment on a poor, homeless Hispanic man whom they hung in the dark of night, dumping him beside a road. Patty Cannon would have been proud.

The state's attorney combined Odessa's murder with the rest and at first I thought it a mistake, wanting Odessa's memory to have her single day in court. I came to see that was wrong, as Messick was anxious to give her ironclad testimony, calling Booker late at night to tell him details about the casting of the shoe. When he asked about his mother's hair she had found in the laundry room, she said nothing. It turned out that in an FBI raid of Glory Bender's home near Annapolis, they had found the shoe, coated in the sandy soil of Sussex County.

At the trial, she claimed the single strand of Odessa's hair was found buried in Lowery's old Lincoln Town Car along with various bones, smelling of bleach and hidden in the trunk's quarter panels. She identified the bones as belonging to the homeless men who apparently died at Lowery's hand, his DNA found on each one. Booker didn't argue with her testimony but he debated with me the veracity of Messick finding his mother's hair in the laundry room but later in Lowery's car. It was the clincher for the jury. He got the death penalty, although I ponder if lethal injection will be a choice by the time his Delaware appeals are up. Bender and Beavens got life. I don't care. I wash my hands as long as they stay away from me and my family.

Booker moped about the house for weeks after the trial. I could only call him to bed with me and wrap my arms around him, smothering him with kisses for so long. He brooded as he prepared our old farmhouse for the coming nor'easters, caulking the old windowpanes and having the tin roof painted and sealed. One day, five dump trucks rumbled in depositing their loads across our backyard between the house and the water. A frontend loader appeared and with a small army of construction workers, Booker set about building a sea wall. Give a man a piece of heavy equipment and it can occupy him for weeks. I wasn't happy about the project, thinking my view of the water would be ruined at the kitchen window. But I can't have everything. Horizons or floods? It's not even a question. I didn't say anything and when we had a visitor, Booker stopped to chat and seemed to appreciate the presence of a guest as much as I.

Boredom became my worst enemy before the baby came. I took up quilting but was terrible at it. Instead, I festooned our bedspread with gaily-colored squares of material and that made me happy as I waited for a baby girl. Still, thoughts nagged at me.

I worried that Booker wasn't in a good place until one day Trixie called me to say Little John was sitting at her kitchen table and wanted to see Booker. I was stunned remembering the last time I had seen John he lied to me in our yard, setting the whole debacle in motion. I asked Booker not to go to Trixie's, fearing that he would lose his composure and do something awful. That kid always brought out the worst in him.

I was wrong. Later, he trudged up the stairs that afternoon and appeared in the bedroom doorway, studying me, his big whale in the bed. He looked bemused, a slight smile playing about his face and shook his head laughing. "As long as I live Woman, I will never figure this one out," he said.

"What Booker, what?" I asked, ready to smile in return, if only he would give me good news about John.

"John's moved in with Tyneice Armstrong, the little black girl who used to be one of Velma's aides at Fairhaven. He said you knew her."

"No, shit," I said and clapped my hand over my mouth. I had taken a vow to clean up my language before our new baby came and I wasn't being very successful lying around in bed all day.

"Yes, shit," he responded, chortling. "And you'll never believe what he's doing with himself."

"Tell me? He's a grave digger, right?"

"No, he's going to DelTech studying applied science. He wants to major in forensics and work for the FBI."

"I can't believe it."

"Well, get this. He and Tyneice are getting married next spring and he told me he'd be honored if I would be his best man."

After that, Booker was a happy man, except when Sam left his dishes in the sink for Rosa to wash.

We postponed the decision to move to D.C. and were content to stay in the farmhouse for the time being. Sam entered high school, excited to play fall soccer. When the baby came, he dangled shiny keys over the crib, or made cooing noises but was scared to pick her up. He and Booker went fishing on the weekends and every afternoon when Sam didn't have a game, they took Compass out for a swim in the creek. I would watch from the screened porch and yearn for the time when Abigail and I could go with them.

One day in late October after Abigail's arrival, Booker sat on the edge of the bed opening mail as I nursed the baby. The weather had cooled and the incessant rumble of the window unit air conditioners was gone. He said he would remove them to store in his Ma's garage for the winter and asked me if I wanted to move to her home. I smiled and said I loved our old farmhouse and all its wintertime foibles. The truth was I couldn't see us living amongst Odessa's tchotchkes without it burdening our memories even more. Booker nodded but said nothing returning to the mail.

We had received notice from the impound lot that they were going to sell my water logged Mercedes if we didn't pick it up. The bill had ballooned to a few thousand dollars and I didn't want the car anymore. I told Booker to let it go but the letter reminded us that there were still items in the car's front seat. Maryland State had delivered my purse and we conveniently forgot the rest.

Booker had it towed to the house, saying he could sell it for parts online. I didn't argue although the last thing I wanted to see him do was start a hobby of collecting derelict cars that sit on the lawn like broken dinosaurs. I think maybe he needs to get back to work but he swears he won't leave me. When I said I was fine, he laughed, calling me a Pollyanna. I was insulted and he said that's what he loves about me. That conversation ended in a long kiss and more, until we heard little Abby rustle awake.

Later that day, I bumbled around the kitchen, the windows open and a breeze streaming inside. The cicadas' wail had died and in the distance, I could hear the sound of ocean waves. Attempting to cook a roast with all the trimmings for dinner without Rosa's help, I was startled when Booker came in the kitchen door, his everloyal Compass at his heels. He laid a rusted metal box on the table. In his hand, he held a screwdriver.

I ran my fingers over its blackened surface and felt the raised letters on its exterior: *Saint* and *homeless*.

"It's from Velma's storage shed," I said looking at Booker. "Boy, she really didn't want to have anything to do with it. She said it reminded her of Davis' father."

"Huh. It's got a rattle to it."

"Really?" I said. "Let's open it. Maybe there's a good luck piece inside."

Booker put it in his lap, settled the screwdriver into the slots and took out four screws, lifting the bottom plate off. He turned it over onto the table and three tiny white shells bounced out, scattering across the surface. Booker picked one up and rolled it back and forth in his palm. "Looks like a fingertip bone to me."

"That's gross," I said. "I think they're good luck shells."

"Uh-huh. And you want I should ask Messick to take a look?"

I stared at him in disbelief. "What are you crazy, my love?" I asked.

Booker tossed the shells in the trash and put the poor box on top of Odessa's googly-eyed grain pot that sat guarding the corner cupboard and all its contents.

"We're keeping it?" I asked.

"Sure, we might as well use if for loose change," he said. "When we fill it up, we'll donate it."

I grinned. I know how loose change goes. Somebody always raids the box before it gets to the good cause.

And what of me these days? People ask what I need. I look into their eyes as I sit with Abby in my arms and gauge if they mean a glass of water or a fresh diaper, but sometimes I think they're testing to see if I'll say something more. I don't. I have everything I could possibly want. I do yearn for the change of seasons and time, for longer nights with my family around the dinner table and the day we can read Abby good night stories, but I don't want to rush her growing up.

Davis Vickers found his final home in a potters' field near Georgetown. He had no family. Booker and I paid for a marker on his grave and a priest to say a few words but neither of us had the will to go to his burial. As I drive the back roads in my new car, I am content with Abigail cooing in the back seat. She is a healing aloe plant on my soul. But once, as I neared the old grist mill in the buttery autumn sunlight, my heart grew heavy and I thought I saw a ghost in the trees and I wondered if it was the flash of a deer or someone looking for home.